Praise for *The Fallen*

"*The Fallen* feels broad and ambitious—but never overarchingly so, which is why it works so well. Finucan, who has previously published two story collections, has done his homework on a compelling period in history, but he wisely resists any temptation to flaunt it ... This is a war novel in which warfare has effectively ended, yet there is no sense of real respite or freedom ... Finucan does a subtle but formidable job of expressing the desperate confinement of it all."—*Toronto Star*

"Finucan has recreated 1944 Naples with an historian's fidelity; but Finucan is foremost a gifted storyteller, and it is his depiction of a moral man's plight in an immoral world that makes this novel such a compelling and rewarding experience."—Ron Rash, *New York Times* bestselling author of *Serena*

"Finucan evokes this anarchic moment [of those first weeks after the Allies reached Naples] with tight, evocative writing that makes *The Fallen* a compelling and instructive read ... Best of all, and worth the novel's price, is Finucan's depiction of the uneasiness that infects people when they don't know who is in control or what will happen next ... The deeper message—that fighting begets only more fighting and more death—is powerful and inescapable. *The Fallen* is resonant and immediate. For all that it resides in history, it speaks a lesson that we do not seem able to remember."—*The Globe and Mail*

"Finucan captures with impressive clarity the guilt that comes with survival. Especially excellent is his ability to conjure the essence of characters in a few strokes ... These subtle portraits establish personalities with an exactitude it takes other writers whole pages to express ... Subtle, patient, and stately in its revelations ... the novel serves as a powerful reminder that the horrors of war do not end after the guns have been set down."—*Literary Review of Canada*

"A wonderful tale, a story that could only be set in a city that is an open secret, and that city is Naples. Best of all, it is a novel that knows the difference between putting too much faith in people, or too little." —Peter Oliva, author of *The City of Yes* and *Drowning in Darkness*

"A complex tale of naivety, bravery, and the attempt to wrest order from chaos ... Finucan has written a rare thing in Canadian literature: a novel in which the tension arises from a deep moral core. As the novel builds toward its climax, it takes on a near-Shakespearean quality: the reader wonders which characters will survive to the final page and which will perish because of the poor choices they've made. Finucan's style is nearly flawless, and his research into 1944 Naples impeccable. There are no rough edges here: every meticulously gathered detail is integrated seamlessly into his excellent prose. *The Fallen* will stay with the reader and reward repeated readings."—*Quill & Quire* (starred review)

Praise for *Foreigners*

"Just as in life, when we strip away our dreams and misperceptions, Finucan's stories leave us with a sense of compassion, wistfulness, and a hovering, but strangely gratifying uncertainty."—*The Globe and Mail*

"Finucan displays a brilliant skill for detailing the slow passing of an afternoon, of a transatlantic flight, of a walk toward home, ordinary events that suddenly turn weighty and ominous."—*Toronto Star*

"Finucan's writing is superb and assured. His characters live for us in their brief lines of text, and he has the ability to establish an emotional tone in the view of a distant city from the autobahn or in the description of an old widower brushing his teeth … *Foreigners* is a wonderful collection."—*Edmonton Journal*

"Expertly told … [Finucan's] spare, seemingly effortless prose and his willingness to take risks results in a collection of chronicles both haunting and riveting."—*The London Free Press*

PENGUIN CANADA

THE FALLEN

STEPHEN FINUCAN is the author of two collections of short stories, *Happy Pilgrims* and *Foreigners*. He lives in Toronto.

THE
FALLEN

STEPHEN FINUCAN

PENGUIN
CANADA

PENGUIN CANADA

Published by the Penguin Group

Penguin Group (Canada), 90 Eglinton Avenue East, Suite 700, Toronto, Ontario, Canada M4P 2Y3
(a division of Pearson Canada Inc.)

Penguin Group (USA) Inc., 375 Hudson Street, New York, New York 10014, U.S.A.
Penguin Books Ltd, 80 Strand, London WC2R 0RL, England
Penguin Ireland, 25 St Stephen's Green, Dublin 2, Ireland (a division of Penguin Books Ltd)
Penguin Group (Australia), 250 Camberwell Road, Camberwell, Victoria 3124, Australia
(a division of Pearson Australia Group Pty Ltd)
Penguin Books India Pvt Ltd, 11 Community Centre, Panchsheel Park, New Delhi – 110 017, India
Penguin Group (NZ), 67 Apollo Drive, Rosedale, North Shore 0632, New Zealand
(a division of Pearson New Zealand Ltd)
Penguin Books (South Africa) (Pty) Ltd, 24 Sturdee Avenue, Rosebank, Johannesburg 2196, South Africa

Penguin Books Ltd, Registered Offices: 80 Strand, London WC2R 0RL, England

First published in a Viking Canada hardcover by Penguin Group (Canada),
a division of Pearson Canada Inc., 2009
Published in this edition, 2010

1 2 3 4 5 6 7 8 9 10 (WEB)

Copyright © Stephen Finucan, 2009

 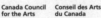

LIBRARY AND ARCHIVES CANADA CATALOGUING IN PUBLICATION

Finucan, Stephen, 1968–
The fallen / Stephen Finucan.

ISBN 978-0-14-301220-7

I. Title.

PS8561.I57F34 2010   C813'.6   C2010-903459-7

Visit the Penguin Group (Canada) website at **www.penguin.ca**

Special and corporate bulk purchase rates available; please see
www.penguin.ca/corporatesales or call 1-800-810-3104, ext. 2477 or 2474

To Alcmene

ONE

The donkey lay on its side in the middle of the road, flesh quivering, tail beating against bloodied haunches, breath steaming in the cold night air. The pavement around it, littered with bits of broken glass, reflected the colours of the fire that licked the walls of the Stazione Marittima.

Huddled in a nearby doorway, Aldo Cioffi watched the dying animal. He knew that before long someone would come to collect the carcass so that it might be sold off to a *macellaio*, and that by morning it would be butchered, cut into slabs—rib steaks and flank steaks and loin filets and sinewy briskets—and laid out on dampened beds of sawdust in a shop window on Via Roma. There would be shank cuts and shoulder clods and cross ribs, too. Nothing would go to waste, not even the offal: the intestines could be boiled, the brain stewed, the tongue sliced cold, the marrow simmered from the bones, and the kidney, heart, and spleen, and whatever else was left, ground up and made into spiced *salsicce*.

The thought of it focused Cioffi's hunger and made him aware again of the nagging pain in his belly. He wished he had some way of taking the beast himself. It would fetch a good price, and he might keep some of the meat—a shoulder cut to stew, the liver for his anemia; it had been a simple, textbook diagnosis: shortness of breath and dizziness, headaches and a mild angina.

The air around him was laced still with the sharp smell of gasoline, and Cioffi could imagine the fire burning for days before the last drop of fuel evaporated. Or maybe it would never go out. Maybe it would become like the eternal flames lit at gravesides, always flickering, a constant reminder of loss.

Though loss was not something of which Cioffi needed reminding. He lived with it every day. More often than not, his life seemed to him an incessant pageant of forfeiture—a relentless dissipation, a never-ending giving up of things.

He had made a list once. And sitting with his friend, Lello Conforti, in the Villa Nazionale, on a bench in the shadow of the Stazione Zoologica, sharing a bottle of honey grappa that he'd stolen from a crate left untended at the back door of a taverna in the Spaccanapoli—how his heart had pounded as he fled the alleyway with the bottle tucked into the lining of his jacket—he'd begun to count off on his fingers all that had been taken from him: "My family, my legacy, my career ..." Lello had stopped him there. "What do you mean, your career?" he'd asked. "I could have opened a practice," Cioffi said. "Or maybe I could have been a surgeon." "You hated the idea of being a doctor," Lello said. "It was your parents who wanted that for you." "I might have changed my mind," said Cioffi. "But you never finished your studies." "That's not the point." Lello shook his head. "It isn't, eh? Then what is the point?" "It is simply," Cioffi said, "that opportunity has been denied me by wretched circumstance." "I see," said Lello. "Tell me, then, this legacy—are you talking about your inheritance? The allowance that your father left to you?" "I am." "But you spent that, Aldo. It wasn't taken from you." "That may be," replied Cioffi, "but who's to say that if I had been able to establish myself in a practice or in a surgery that I wouldn't still have it today?" "You're being ridiculous." At that point a group of German soldiers came towards them along the cinder path. Seeing the honey grappa, they stopped and demanded the bottle from them. Cioffi gave it up without protest, and once they'd gone, he turned back to his friend and said: "Now do you see what I mean?"

He braced himself against the breeze coming in off the bay; it was wintry with the last chill of January. Tonight he could add a few more items to his list of lost things: a decently forged Roman coin bearing the likeness of the siren Parthenope, two twenty-gallon jerry cans of U.S. Army gasoline, and the three hundred lire that Maggio the second-hand dealer had advanced him as payment. But where another man might have cursed his luck, Cioffi had long given up the notion he'd had any to begin with.

When the petrol dump exploded, he had been beneath the portico of San Francesco di Paola, forcing his last twenty lire on the girl he had followed there from the Caffè Gambrinus. She was young: sixteen, maybe younger. He had watched her through the café window while he and Lello drank away the *bancarellaro's* money. She had noticed him, too, and waited in the darkness just beyond the terrace. Lello had tried to warn him away from her, said that it was likely she would take him someplace where others waited to rob him, but by that time Cioffi had drunk enough not to care. Lello reminded him of Maggio and the American military policeman and of all the trouble he had gone through getting the forged coin. A good deal of risk had gone into concocting his little business arrangement, an investment had been made, and not just by himself; it would be foolish to chance it on something so trivial—and besides, he hadn't enough money left to pay a prostitute. But Cioffi would not be discouraged. He left the café and met the girl in the shadows and then followed her across the darkened expanse of Piazza del Plebiscito to where she lived rough in a small alcove outside the basilica. In the shallow niche she had fashioned a bed out of sandbags and cloth sacking, and had collected about her sentimental trinkets: a cracked ceramic vase, an empty wooden picture frame, two small figurines—African heads carved of ebony—and a plaster madonna. She told him she wanted fifty lire and said that there were boys who protected her and she would call to them if he didn't pay. He heard their voices farther along the portico, but when he turned back, she had already lifted her skirts. He stood a moment and stared at her nakedness, then began to fumble with his trousers. He had only just lain down on the sacking when the air-raid sirens began. The girl tried to push him away, but he held her arms. When she cried out, he put a hand over her mouth. She struggled against him, but he was stronger. When her body went limp, he thought that he had smothered her. He looked into her face: her eyes were rolled back, as if she were trying to see something behind her. Then he felt her lips moving against his damp palm. He took his hand away. He realized that she was praying: a whispered appeal to the cheap statuette of the Virgin. He stood up and dressed himself and took the twenty lire from his trouser pocket and held it out to her, but she would not look at him. Then it was as if the gates to the inferno had been thrown open: a great bloom of fire rose from behind the Palazzo Reale, flames curling into the night sky.

It seemed to Cioffi that he was always paying a price for something: a foolish indiscretion, a lapse of judgment. He should have listened to Lello—Lello, his best friend and conscience—and let the girl alone. And he should never have trusted the American MP; he should have given the coin to him after he'd received the gasoline, and not have believed him when he said the canisters would be waiting for him outside the depot fence. He doubted that they had been there at all. And so, once again, he was left empty-handed. It was a familiar refrain.

He looked along the wide boulevard towards the port. The fire brigades had arrived and tanker trucks pumped water. Several warehouses were ablaze, as well as the customs sheds and a number of motor launches moored on the quayside. In the other direction, beyond the Giardini Pubblici and the Marina of Santa Lucia, the searchlights atop the walls of Castel dell'Ovo continued to rummage the night sky.

Then a voice from behind startled him: "Good evening, *dottore*."

He turned round to see Maggio, the second-hand dealer, standing not more than an arm's length away.

"Marcello," Cioffi said. "Where did you come from?"

Maggio grinned. He was a big man, the sort whose body, once muscled, had gone mostly to fat. Heavy jowls that quivered whenever he spoke stretched his round face. His coat was made from stolen U.S. Army blankets that had been sewn together and fixed with large, mismatched buttons. "I've been watching you," he said, and nodded his bulging head in the direction of an alleyway a short distance off. "I thought you had something for me."

"The gasoline," said Cioffi.

"Yes. The gasoline. The gasoline that I *paid* you for."

What Cioffi wanted at that moment, more than anything, was another drink: something to dull his senses. The warm drunkenness from the Gambrinus had drained away and he felt the cold again. "I'm sorry, Marcello, but the bombs … The depot is destroyed."

Maggio stepped closer and Cioffi could smell his breath: cigarette smoke and mint leaves. "And my money?"

Cioffi pointed into the road. "If you help me, we could take the donkey. We could sell it for the meat. I'm sure you must know someone."

Maggio looked over at the animal. It had begun to scrape its hooves across the pavement in a hopeless attempt to raise itself: the forelegs scrabbled, but the hindquarters would not respond—the spine was broken somewhere above the haunches.

Maggio left Cioffi standing in the doorway and went into the street. He found a loose paving stone and picked it up. As he approached, the donkey brayed, its flesh sticky with blood. Maggio looked down at the animal, then he lifted the paving stone above his head.

The sound that Cioffi heard was like the soft thud of something being dropped onto wet earth. The animal trembled once and then was still.

Maggio came back to the doorway. "I didn't come for horsemeat," he said, and slapped Cioffi hard across the face.

The iron taste of blood filled Cioffi's mouth, and his eyes began to water.

"Where is my money?"

When Cioffi did not answer, Maggio slapped him again. When he raised his hand a third time, Cioffi cowered. "Please, Marcello," he said, pressing his palms together. "It's gone."

"You mean you drank it."

Cioffi nodded. "Yes. And a girl …"

Maggio lowered his hand. "A girl?"

"It was only twenty lire," Cioffi said. "We could get it back, I'm sure of it. I know where she is."

"What kind of a *puttana* spreads her legs for twenty lire?"

"It was more. It was fifty. But I lied to her, you see."

Maggio shook his head. He stared at him. Then, after a moment, he reached out and smoothed the lapels of Cioffi's jacket. "I should have known better than to do business with a drunk like you, *dottore*." The title was offered in mockery. Maggio delighted in the reversal of fortunes. There was a time when the Cioffi name was important in the city's garment business, but left in the care of a dissolute only son, its shine had quickly tarnished. "I should never have taken pity on you,"

Maggio said. "You are more trouble than you are worth."

"Yes, Marcello. I am sorry."

"Now I have to tell don Abruzzi that I was wrong about you—and he held out such high hopes, what with your connections."

"What can I do?" Cioffi said.

Maggio smiled. "What can you do?" he said, and patted him gently on the cheek. "You can come and see me tomorrow at the market, that's what you can do. We'll go, the two of us, to see Abruzzi and you can tell him yourself what happened."

"Tomorrow?"

"Yes, tomorrow. What? Have you already got plans, *dottore?* Other business engagements to keep maybe?"

"No, Marcello."

"Good. Tomorrow at eleven o'clock, then. You come and see me. Maybe you can even get my money back."

After Maggio had gone, Cioffi sat down on the pavement. He leaned his back against the cold brick wall of the building. For a time he had difficulty catching his breath and he spat onto the ground beside him. He thought how nice it would be to leave Marcello Maggio with a bloody mouth. The fat *bancarello*—before the war Cioffi wouldn't have noticed him in the street, let alone spoken to him; yet now he grovelled for his favour, let himself be beat for the chance at a few extra lire.

He lifted his head and looked down the street. A young man and a boy had appeared, pushing a low-slung handcart with wooden-rimmed wheels. They came from the direction of the port, like two devils from out of the fires.

It was difficult work loading the donkey; the carcass was uncooperative. Twice the animal, drenched with its own gore, slipped from their grasp and landed, with a wet slap, on the pavement.

Cioffi wondered, if he offered to help them, would they share the profit with him, but the young man, who had noticed him sitting in the doorway, kept an eye. There was something in his look that convinced Cioffi he had no claim on the animal; the young man would fight him for it.

Finally, after rigging a makeshift pulley with bits of rope and using the tilt of the cart as leverage, the young man and the boy were able to shift the donkey into place. Its head hung over the side and the thick pink tongue dangled from between its slack lips.

Cioffi watched them as they started on their way back towards the port and the fire brigades and the flames. Then he lifted himself up and went into the road. He went to where the donkey had lain and looked down at the paving stone that Maggio had used to kill it. He pushed it with the toe of his boot. It was much heavier than he'd imagined.

An American jeep sped into the square. The severed beams of its blacked-out headlamps sliced across the stone lions that stood guard over the Monument of the Martyrs. In the trick of the light it appeared as if the marble beasts had moved, and Thomas Greaves could imagine them lifting themselves from their pedestals and stepping down into the street. Then the jeep was gone and the square was dark again and the lions settled on their plinths.

Greaves stood in the gateway to the courtyard. He'd waited out the raid there rather than go into the cellar with the others, because being locked away in the darkness while the bombs fell all around them seemed too much like the nightmares that already robbed him of his sleep. He preferred to take his chances above ground, under the wide open heavens.

To the south there was a false sunrise: the fires burning in the port bloodying the night sky. The fuel depot that shared the quayside with the ferry docks looked to have taken a direct hit. Twenty minutes earlier, when the terminal exploded, it was as if a great angry fist had slammed into the earth, and the windows in the buildings bordering the square had shuddered and cracked in their frames. And though it was more than a mile away, Greaves had felt the heat of the blast, like the gust from an open furnace, but it was quickly replaced again by the chill of the Mediterranean winter.

He made his way now into the square. He went to the monument and sat down on the plinth of the nearest lion, the one writhing in animated pain from the pike driven deep between its ribs. He took out a cigarette, struck a match, and blew smoke into the cool night air. Then he reached into his pocket and took out the music box he'd purchased the week before from a blind merchant in Piazza Mercato. The lid was inlaid with mother-of-pearl: a likeness of the Sorrentine peninsula—chalky cliffs and fishing boats, white clouds, and the tiny slivers of gulls riding the winds over deep blue waters. He ran his hand over the lid, feeling the smoothness of the lacquer, then glanced back at the palazzo. It looked even shabbier in the pale moonlight—a heap of tumbledown old stones. Even the hand-painted sign on the courtyard gate announcing it as headquarters for 803 Field Security Section had come loose and hung now at a clumsy angle.

Greaves thought it fitting that the place looked as if it were about to fall in on itself. A single detachment of Field Security policemen left to care for military safekeeping of this teeming city: it was a hopeless mission. Before he'd arrived, there had been only one Italian-speaker in the unit, and that was Sergeant Jones, who had such a thick Welsh accent that many of the Neapolitans couldn't understand him. Not that their own clipped dialect was any easier to decipher. It had taken Greaves almost the entire six weeks he'd been in Naples to finally get a handle on it. And now that he had, most of the drudge work came his way: civilian liaison, coordinating the transfer of intelligence with the local police, marriage vetting. He didn't mind so much; he preferred to be on his own. And the other members of the section seemed fine with the arrangement. His secondment hadn't met with much enthusiasm. It was a battlefield transfer, which immediately drew suspicion: a man wasn't moved off the line without good reason. Being Canadian hadn't counted for much, either. King and Country carried little weight with his British colleagues; as far as they were concerned, he was as good as a Yank. The FSO, Major Woodard, had let on as much when he'd arrived, paperwork in hand. It was mid-December and the other members of the section were gathered around a makeshift desk in the foyer, cutting out paper snowflakes to decorate the office for the holidays. The interview was conducted in the large gallery on the main floor of the palazzo that served as the major's office. After he'd gone through Greaves's file and his transfer documents, he set the paperwork aside and leaned back in his chair. He offered up a solemn look, as if he were a headmaster faced with a pupil he was certain would cause him grief. He hesitated a moment before he said: "I've been told by a fellow I know at GHQ that you were found with your revolver in your mouth. Is that right, lieutenant?" When Greaves didn't answer, the major became uncomfortable, and sat forward and flipped again through his file. He cleared his throat. "We don't go in for that sort of melodrama round here," he said. Greaves replied calmly, "No, sir, I don't suppose you do." Officially, he had come to 803 FSS on a training detail; he was listed to assume the Field Security Officer position of a Canadian Section stationed at Campobasso. However, no timetable for the reassignment had been included in his orders. And Greaves understood, as did the major and the others, that his designation to 803 FSS was to be indefinite. Someone at General Headquarters had made up his mind to lose him for a while.

The idea of being lost appealed to Greaves. For the last six months, it was exactly how he'd felt. He had tried to explain as much to the doctors when he was in the field station at Lentini and then later at No. 5 Canadian General Hospital at Catania. "I don't know who I am anymore," he'd told them. "I've completely lost my bearings." At No. 5 CGH they had psychiatrists on staff who wanted to hear more about this sense of disconnection; talking, they told him, would offer clarity. But Greaves hadn't known how to make it any clearer to them. He explained that sometimes, when he looked into the mirror, he didn't recognize the face looking back at him. "I mean, I know it's me," he said. "I can recognize my own features, but at the same time it isn't me. It's a complete stranger." Finally, a course of lithium carbonate was decided upon to calm his nerves. Greaves, though, wasn't convinced that his nerves were the problem. He wasn't like those poor souls from the last war who twitched and jerked and wet their pants when someone dropped a spoon on the floor next to them. His problem was that something had gone missing.

He looked down at the music box in his hand. He gave the key on the side a half turn. Inside, the spiked drum pricked at the stiff metal teeth of the tuning plate. The first slow notes of "Santa Lucia" chimed, and then the mechanism wound down again and the music stopped. Just then the all-clear was sounded, and Greaves could almost sense the stirring beneath the city of all those who had sought shelter in cellars and vaults and sewers, and in the labyrinthine warren of catacombs that ran like veins beneath the skin of Naples. And he thought to himself: it doesn't matter how well you hide yourself.

TWO

Luisa Gennaro pushed the broom over the tiles and swept away shards of broken windowpane. She moved the bits of glass into a pile and pushed the pile towards the corner of the room; then she set the broom aside. She and her cousin Maria had spent a sleepless night in the cellar with the other tenants, shivering in the dark while the building above them shuddered and groaned. Now, with the light of day, the night before was just another unpleasant memory to add to her growing album of unpleasant memories. They had survived the bombardment, and that was enough. She went about her tidying, humming a song she'd heard played the day before on a phonograph in a taverna at the Galleria. Vera Lynn, she had been told by one of the soldiers drinking at a table, a young *inglese* with big teeth and gingery hair who had tried to put a hand on her breast. She'd slapped his face and hurried away, the laughter of the soldiers like a dog snapping at her heels. Still, she had liked the music, even if she loathed the men who listened to it.

She went now to the sideboard and began to straighten the photographs that had been upset during the raid. The frames had been jostled about, and one lay face down. She picked it up and looked at it: a family portrait—the Gennaros, sombre-faced in fading sepia. Luisa studied it closely: her mother, her father, her brother Gianluca, and herself. No one smiling, no one showing any emotion at all, it seemed, except perhaps contempt for the photographer. Her father in a severe dark suit, Gianluca the same, high collars and no cuffs showing. Her mother in a mourning dress, her hair pulled so tight that it strained her face. And Luisa herself, just a girl, in a light-coloured cotton frock, patent shoes, doing her best, she remembered, not to giggle, threats from her father and a hard pinch from her mother to blame for the scowl on her face. And now all of them gone but her: Gianluca on a rain-soaked mountain pass in Albania four years earlier, and her parents the previous winter, typhus taking them only weeks apart.

"What are you doing?"

Luisa turned to see Maria standing in the doorway. "I'm cleaning," she told her.

"Why bother?" her cousin said. "The planes will only come back and mess it up again."

"That doesn't mean we have to live with it like this."

Maria shook her head. "Bombs are falling and you are sweeping the floor. You're young. You should be out there living your life." She pointed at Luisa's clothes. "Why don't you at least put on a dress? You look like a schoolboy."

Luisa turned and looked at herself in the cracked wall mirror. She'd taken to wearing one of her father's favourite wool sweaters, puckered with darning, and a pair of Gianluca's old trousers, the waist cinched tight with a bit of yarn. She had even cut her hair short rather than be bothered to pin it up.

"We're reorganizing the exhibits at the museum," she said. "A dress would be impractical."

"So the old man has you carrying boxes now, does he?" said Maria.

"You're welcome to come and help," Luisa said.

Her cousin laughed. "I am not a pack mule. Besides, I'm meeting someone."

Luisa wondered who it might be this time: a Free French naval officer, perhaps, or one of the Anzacs. Maybe she had found herself another American. The most recent one had been a captain—he liked to hit her for fun. It had taken more than a week for the bruises to go down the last time, and for the first two days they thought her jaw might be broken.

Maria stepped past her and studied her face in the mirror. Her complexion was sallow. She pinched her cheeks until she managed a faint pink blush. "I look old," she said.

"No you don't," said Luisa, and hugged her from behind. "You look beautiful, as always."

It was true. After all the months of hunger and want, when everything around them seemed to fade—even the bright colours of Naples itself—the one thing that seemed not to diminish was Maria's beauty: her straight-backed, full-hipped, patrician beauty. She had always attracted men, as much for her looks, Luisa often thought, as for her strident wilfulness, which her suitors always took as a challenge, like Shakespeare's princes come to Venice to select a casket. Older than Luisa by almost eight years, Maria had married against her parents' wishes: Pietro Bello, a functionary in the Prefettura. He had been chosen to spite them, and then, to spite him, Maria had begun to take lovers before the marriage had reached its first anniversary. When the Americans came, he left her behind and fled north with the other blackshirt loyalists. By then Luisa was the only family she had left in the city, so when the military government confiscated her apartment and belongings, she came to stay with her. It was over five months now that she had lived there, and Luisa could not imagine being without her.

Maria shrugged herself free of Luisa's embrace. She went into the hallway and put on her coat with the moulting rabbit collar. Then she came back and tied a kerchief over her head so that the rain would not ruin her hair. "Do you think Augusto will have more coffee?" she said.

"He might."

"Or those chocolate biscuits? I like those."

"I'll ask," Luisa said.

"You won't forget?"

"I won't. I promise."

Luisa waited until she heard the door close and Maria's footsteps fade down the stairwell, then she picked up the photograph of her family again. Cheerless faces stared back at her. She found it difficult to remember what it had been like with all of them living together in the small apartment. That time seemed now as if it hadn't really existed; it hovered in her thoughts like scenes from a film watched long ago, vague and disconnected. She let the tip of her finger linger on her mother's greying image. Luisa wished that she had smiled for the photographer.

In a street running parallel to Piazza Francese, soldiers dug through the rubble of a collapsed apartment block. The American military police had cordoned off the roadway on either side of the bombed-out building and a striped wooden barrier announced the area temporarily off limits. Two MPs in green rubberized rain ponchos that reached down to their knees stood guard at the barricade. A few yards behind them, on the opposite side of the blockade, a row of bodies was laid out on the rain-slicked pavement, covered haphazardly with grey woollen army blankets.

Standing off to the side, Greaves found himself counting the feet that poked out from beneath the rain-splattered blankets: thirteen dead so far. There would be more. The German bombardments were as indiscriminate as the Allied bombardments had been before them, and those unlucky enough to find themselves living in the vicinity of the shipyards, the warehouse district, or the central rail station often paid the dearest price. And recovery operations like the one now under way could go on for days. First the rubble would be searched by hand, electric torches would be shone into crevices and voids, intermittent calls for quiet would go out so that ears could be turned to the ground to listen for movement, for cries of help. When this search was halted, the engineers would be brought in with their heavy machinery to clear the foundation—or perhaps the engineers wouldn't be called upon, and the site would be left as it was and the stink of the buried corpses would fill the street.

A commotion started at a nearby café, where a small crowd had gathered on the terrace. Women cried and beat their breasts. In the wreckage, another body had been found. There was a glimpse of pale blue through the grime: a nightgown, perhaps, or a housedress. Two soldiers who had been clearing the rubble moved slowly, wary of losing their footing on the slippery debris. They carried the body roughly between them, one with his hands locked around the knees, the other holding tightly to the wrists. The woman's head, the long dark hair damp and matted with plaster dust, sagged loose and lifeless between them. When the soldiers reached the pavement, they placed the body on a stretcher and carried it along the street, where it was added to the blanketed dead.

"What a fucken mess," said the MP nearest to Greaves.

Together they looked back to the café. The crowd had begun to shift. It ventured into the street, milling now between the terrace and the barricade. The sound of their grief, a steady keening, had a peculiar otherworldly quality that unsettled the MP.

Greaves picked out the young man. He stood alone from the crowd, rain-soaked, the singed fabric of his grubby white shirt pasted to his skin.

"Do you think there will be trouble?" Greaves said.

The MP nodded. "I know there will be. Always is when we got something like this."

"What will you do?"

"The usual," the MP said, the resignation in his voice heightened by a Texan drawl. "Crack a few of 'em on the head and hope for the best."

Greaves shrugged. "Can you blame them? For being so angry, I mean."

The American looked at him. He was slimly built, with the wide-open face of a boy fresh from the farm, soft and slightly bemused. "Mister," he said, "I don't blame nobody for nothing. Not anymore. Not after the things I seen."

Greaves turned again to the fallen building. Watching the soldiers pulling away the wreckage, climbing the hills of rain-darkened rubble, passing buckets of debris along a procession of outstretched arms, was like watching an assembly of ants swarm a carcass. Then a shout went up behind him as the young man who had been standing on his own rushed the barricade. He knocked the MP to the ground and then threw himself onto the pavement beside the dead woman in the blue dress. He pulled back the blanket and clutched her body to his chest. From where he stood, Greaves saw the horrible disfigurement of her face: the brow pushed in so that there was a deep hollow in the centre of her forehead, her left cheek smashed, flattened in such a way that it pulled her pale lips into a ghoulish smile, the vacant stare of her bulbous eyes. Then the second MP descended upon the young man, hooking his baton under his chin and crushing it against his windpipe so that his cries strangled in his throat. The first MP got to his feet again and unholstered his pistol and brandished it at the crowd to keep them at bay. Greaves looked on, as if what he was watching was no more than a performance of unfortunate street theatre. Only after the young man had been choked into unconsciousness did he release his grip on the dead woman, who fell back onto the pavement with a soft thud.

"If you steal anything, I will catch you."

The bed of the cart was piled with tins: tins of frankfurters and beans, tins of pork and beans, tins of ham and beans, tins of almost anything imaginable and beans. Aldo Cioffi looked from the tins to the stallkeeper, a tall, thin man with a close-cropped beard that framed his pointed chin; with his tubercular complexion, he did not seem the sort who could run very far or very fast.

"And when I catch you, I will beat you."

Cioffi took stock of himself. Another night spent on the floor of Lello's *salotto* without a pillow or blanket had left him with an ache in his side that might be a cold in the kidneys; and thanks to a crack in the leather of his left shoe, the ulcer on his ankle had opened again; and then there was the fact that he hadn't eaten a proper meal in nearly a week. The results of this cursory examination were not encouraging: it didn't seem likely that he was the sort who could run very far or very fast either.

Cioffi smiled at the merchant. "My friend, I would not think of it," he said, and turned away.

Piazza Garibaldi was teeming. The great square, as well as the surrounding streets that ran between it and the Castel Capuana, home to the law courts, was the heart of the city's black market. Here the spoils of the marketeers were laid out for all to see: sugar and salt, powdered milk, powdered eggs, chocolate bars, and cigarettes; the divested contents of field ration kits—bully beef and hardtack biscuits, haricot and oxtail, treacle cake soaked in molasses; socks and watches, boots and blankets, woollen helmet liners, and undergarments stitched from remnants of parachute silk.

On the far side of the square, near the statue of the great liberator, Marcello Maggio hawked his wares: old clothes and kitchenware, picture frames, lamps, religious figurines, an old commode—items looted from bombed-out apartment houses and deserted villas.

When Cioffi reached his stall, Maggio was arguing with a boy of perhaps fifteen who stood before the heavy-set merchant, his arms piled high with fine china—a serving tray and dish, plates and saucers. Before Cioffi was able to discern the crux of the disagreement, the second-hand dealer swept a weighty hand out at the boy and sent the crockery smashing to the ground. Broken china littered the pavement, and when the boy bent to pick up those few pieces left undamaged, Maggio shoved him hard in the back so that he fell to the ground. Then he looked over at Cioffi.

"*Dottore*," he sneered. "I thought maybe you weren't going to come."

"I told you I would, Marcello," Cioffi replied, and watched the boy pick himself up and begin to gather together the mess of smashed dinner plates.

"Yes, you did. You are a man of your word. Who would have guessed it?" Maggio turned to the boy. "And you," he said, swatting him in the back of the head. "Maybe next time you will listen to me. Now, I have business with the *dottore*, so watch over things until I get back." Maggio came and put his arm around Cioffi's shoulder. He smiled. "Come with me. Don Abruzzi is eager to meet you."

They made their way back across the square towards the central rail station, its expansive edifice pockmarked and scorched, its tall window frames emptied of their leaded glass. The whole while they walked, twisting and turning their way through the crowded piazza, Maggio pinched the thin muscle at the base of Cioffi's neck and told him how he would be thanking him soon. "You see, it is because I like you," he said, "that I'm doing you this good turn. And now maybe things will be even between us, eh?"

Past the rail station, on the south side of the square, they turned down a side street, and partway along the side street they turned again, this time into a narrow alleyway.

There were no windows in the buildings that adjoined the alleyway, and the air was close and smelled faintly of urine. Cioffi grew nervous, and Maggio, as if sensing he might flee, tightened his grip so that his thick fingernails dug into Cioffi's skin. A little farther along, a young man sat on a wooden crate. Until then he had only ever seen Renzo Abruzzi from afar, moving along the crowded pavements of the Spaccanapoli and Pedino with his train of thick-necked cronies. But he had heard the whispers about him and knew enough to be wary. Abruzzi came from the legion of *scugnizzi*, the street boys who haunted Naples's poorer neighbourhoods, castaway children who grew up rough to become burglars and pickpockets. It was said that he was fond of using a knife, and that he liked to cut smiles into the faces of those who crossed him. And now Cioffi saw the knife, a thin-bladed flick knife that, at the moment, Abruzzi was using to peel the skin from an unripened orange. He did not look up at them until he had removed the last bit of green-tinged rind. Then he bit into the orange. Juice ran from the corners of his mouth and down his chin. He wiped it away with the back of his hand. He chewed for a moment, and then spat the mangled pulp onto the ground.

"Tastes like shit," he said. He pointed the tip of the knife blade at Cioffi. "You've kept me waiting."

"I'm sorry," Cioffi said. He stared into the young man's limpid blue eyes. They had all the emotion of the glass beads in a doll's head.

"What time do you call this?" Abruzzi said to Maggio.

"Eleven o'clock."

"It's a quarter past."

"I'm sorry, don Abruzzi."

"Don't call me that. What am I, a fat old man like you?"

The second-hand dealer fidgeted. He didn't appear to know what he should do with his fleshy hands, folding them first in front, then in back, and finally plunging them into the pockets of his trousers.

"Never mind." Abruzzi put the knife away and stood up. He held a hand, still sticky with juice, out to Cioffi. "I know you, *dottore*. Do you know me?"

"Yes, sir. I do."

There was a sharpness about Abruzzi, his features raw-boned: high cheeks and a narrow chin, lips thinly drawn and nose slightly aquiline. There seemed very little to him physically. His slender frame looked lost inside his clothing, as if his dark jacket, his white shirt, his neatly knotted tie were all made for a body two sizes larger than his own. He was smaller than Cioffi, and there was something foolish about the creme in his hair that held the part so carefully in place.

"And are you frightened, *dottore*?" Abruzzi asked.

Cioffi felt a flush of panic. He glanced back along the alleyway and wondered how far he might be able to run before Maggio or the young man caught up with him. Surely both were in much finer fit than the consumptive stallkeeper.

"Yes," he said, his voice uncertain. "I am a little frightened."

"Good," said Abruzzi. "You should be." He held out the peeled orange.

Cioffi, despite his uneasiness, took the fruit from him and greedily bit into it. Juice ran from the corners of his mouth and onto his chin just as it had Abruzzi's, but he did not bother to wipe it away. The flesh was bitter and difficult to chew, and when he swallowed, he felt his throat constrict and for a moment thought he might vomit it up again. He began to cough and tears filled his eyes.

"I told you it tasted like shit," Abruzzi said. "They came in two days ago on a ship from Jaffa, but I think they should have been left longer on the tree." He kicked the crate at his feet. "Maybe I will leave them here for the rats."

Cioffi looked down at the box of unripened fruit. "I could take them for you. If you don't want them, I mean."

"No, *dottore*," Abruzzi said. "You and I have more important business than sour oranges. Tell me about this coin you gave to the American."

"The coin?" said Cioffi.

"Yes. You showed it to Marcello."

Cioffi shrugged. "But it was a fake. Very poor quality. There was sand in the casting."

"Where did you get it?" Abruzzi said.

"Where did I get the coin?"

"Do not play with me, *dottore*. I do not like games." Abruzzi's cold blue eyes scrutinized him.

"From the Museo Archeologico," said Cioffi.

"And how did you get it from there?"

Cioffi ducked his head slightly. "I took it."

Abruzzi glanced at Maggio, and then said: "The museum is off limits to civilians. The grounds are guarded. There are Carabinieri posted at the entrances. You must know someone."

Cioffi nodded. "*Il professore*. He is my uncle."

Abruzzi nodded slowly. "And he doesn't mind that you help yourself to his little treasures?"

"He doesn't know."

"Really? And how is that?"

"I sneak in. When the *carabiniere* goes on his morning break. I know my way around quite well."

"How convenient," Abruzzi said. "For both of us." He put his hand into his pocket. "How long since you have had a proper meal, *dottore*?"

"I can't really remember," answered Cioffi, and let his gaze fall once again onto the crate of unripe oranges.

"And your last drink?"

Cioffi sighed. He looked at Abruzzi. "Last night. A few bottles of cheap Chianti at the Caffè Gambrinus."

The flicker of a grin passed across the young man's face. He withdrew a thick roll of military scrip from his pocket. "Best you should have both food and drink, then," he said. He peeled off several notes and handed them to Cioffi, who counted the money: fifteen hundred lire. It was more than he had seen in months. He glanced sideways at the second-hand dealer.

"Don't worry," Abruzzi said. "Your debt with the fat man is settled. You work for me now."

Augusto Parente, curator of the Archaeological Museum, paused on the middle step. He leaned heavily on his cane: the pace of their walking had aggravated his sciatica. The pain came in electric tremors that coursed along the back of his thigh and on down behind his knee, ending in the knotted muscle of his calf, where it felt as if someone were sticking him with a burning poker. He massaged his throbbing left buttock and looked at Colonel Romney. The man from the Monuments, Fine Arts and Archives Section was still scribbling away in his notebook as he carried on down the staircase. He had a small, womanly build, with the narrow wrists and soft fingers of an accountant. Parente had decided that he was the sort of man who supposed that history could be understood by tallying numbers, as if it were no more than sums on a spreadsheet.

Romney—who before the war had been an assistant curator of the Renaissance collection at the Metropolitan Museum of Art in New York City—had arrived unannounced two hours earlier with an order signed by General Clark himself. It was the general's directive that all sites of historic and cultural import within the city were to be secured and inventoried, so that a proper catalogue of looted artifacts, specifically those taken by retreating German troops, could be compiled. The idea behind the general's order was that, once the items were retrieved, they could be restored to the rightful collections. The general, Colonel Romney explained without hint of irony, intended himself to be the saviour of the national heritage of Italy herself.

Having noticed now that the curator was no longer by his side, Colonel Romney stopped and looked about. For a moment he seemed unsettled by the prospect of the sandbagged statues that lined the shadowy main gallery.

"Are you all right, colonel?" Parente asked.

Romney turned and looked back up the staircase. "Yes, *professore.* I'm fine. Thanks."

"Good," Parente said, smiling his way through his discomfort as he joined the American at the foot of the staircase.

Earlier, when he had been admiring the works of Titian and Caravaggio that crowded the darkened walls of the smaller galleries on the mezzanine, the colonel had boasted about how he'd been in charge of compiling the aerial photographs and surveillance maps that the B-24 pilots had used during the raids prior to the landings at Salerno; he and his staff had worked hard to identify all the sites of historical value that the bombardiers were to avoid. It was, Colonel Romney assured him, an unqualified success. Parente didn't bother to tell him of the three labourers and site manager who were lost when a wayward bomb intended for the shipyards at Torre del Greco destroyed instead the excavation headquarters at Herculaneum. There seemed nothing to be gained in spoiling the colonel's illusions.

As they started off together across the gallery, their progress scrutinized by the eyeless statues, Colonel Romney picked up the thread of the conversation that Parente's sciatic spasm had momentarily cut short.

"Of course," he said, "it is all well and good, and you have done an admirable job of keeping the collection together, which is a testament to your foresight, *professore*—but the truth of the matter is that there are other elements at play of which we need to remain cognizant."

His manner was officious. Parente detected in it the touch of self-importance that comes to a man who, after having resigned himself to being a subordinate, has finally been given a taste of authority.

"This is Napoli, colonel," Parente said. "The list of other elements is quite long. To start with, you have the Fascist holdouts—delusional fanatics who believe Il Duce's Repubblica di Salò is going to rise like a phoenix on the shores of Lake Garda. And then there are the Communists: Marxists, Leninists, Trotskyites, Stalinists, and every combination in between. And let's not forget the anarchists and the monarchists. There are even some who envision Napoli as a reborn city-state. And others, so I have been told, who wish to see Italy become part of the United States itself—a far-off Mediterranean satellite."

"Yes, of course, *professore*," said the colonel, "but I think you know who I'm talking about."

Parente nodded. "Of course," he said. "You mean the Camorra."

In the vacuum left by Badoglio's armistice, the city's old criminal scourge, so long held in check by the Fascists, had resurfaced with a vengeance: potent, like a virus that has lain dormant, or a cancer after a lengthy remission.

"But may I remind you, colonel," said Parente, "that not all of our troubles are native born. The deserter gangs, for instance. Though it is true that they tend to mostly involve themselves in hijacking and small-scale robberies. And, I'm sorry to say, there has even been some profiteering by your own people—within the military government, I mean."

"Yes," said Colonel Romney, his brow furrowed in understanding, "it is an ugly fact, I'm afraid, that there are those who sometimes find it difficult to resist the temptation of power. But really, *professore*, I think we should concern ourselves with a more common sort of criminal. Don't you?"

"Indeed, colonel," said Parente. "But I can assure you the Camorra has not been an issue for us."

What was an issue—what had always been an issue—was the ongoing trade in relics pilfered from the digs. It used to be that it was the labourers that Parente had to worry about, men he'd hired himself and who would return under the cover of dark to sneak off with a drinking jug or shard of mosaic that they could sell to subsidize their income. Now it was more likely to be the soldiers that had been sent by Colonel Romney himself to guard the site who did the pilfering. Regardless of who did the stealing, Parente had long understood that, like a tithe, it was an unfortunate price to be paid. He doubted though that the expenditure could be reckoned in the colonel's accounts, so he did not bother to mention it to him.

They were interrupted by the sound of footsteps. Luisa Gennaro came towards them through the shadows of the main gallery. Parente watched her purposeful stride, and seeing her in her loose blouse and baggy men's trousers, her hair cut short to the line of her jaw with bangs at the front like a boy, he thought how hard she tried to hide her beauty.

He went to meet her.

"I am sorry to bother you, *professore*."

She was always very formal whenever they were in public, even if, as was the case, that public was a single irritating American officer.

"What is it, Luisa?"

"Tenente Greaves is waiting for you in your office."

"Has he been there long?"

"About twenty minutes."

"You were polite to him, I hope."

Parente liked to tease her about the young *canadese* soldier. He suspected the security policeman harboured a fondness for his assistant—like a schoolboy crush, he often joked with Luisa.

"I am always polite, Augusto," she said in a hushed tone.

He noticed now that she was carrying her coat. "You are off somewhere, then?"

"Yes. To the hospital. Only for a couple of hours, and then I'll be back."

"You will tell Benedetto hello for me," he said.

"Of course."

"And don't forget to ask if he needs anything. I can't do much, but I am sure there is some way I can help." Parente turned back to the American. "Now you will have to excuse me, colonel. I have another appointment. If you don't mind, Signora Gennaro will show you out."

The curator's office reminded Greaves of his grandfather's study in the principal's residence of Wycliffe College on the campus of the University of Toronto, with its heavy crown moulding, bas-relief ceiling, and leaded windowpanes that looked out over Queen's Park Circle towards the pink-hued sandstone of the Legislative Building. It was within those darkly panelled walls, hung with portraits of the collared deans who had come before and lined with bookcases overflowing with leather-bound volumes of Cicero and Aquinas and Voltaire, that Greaves had first learned to conjugate verbs—in Italian, but also in Asturian and Aragonese, French and Occitan, Sardinian and Spanish.

Augusto Parente's sanctum, tucked away at the end of a dim corridor in the east wing of the museum, was likewise appointed, and on the sagging bookshelves were some of the very same texts out of which Greaves had first been taught. But more than that, it was a room littered with the scatterings of a historical life. On the wall behind the curator's wide rosewood desk was a collection of photographs: the digs at Pompeii—a narrative of the old man's life. From the square-shouldered, handsome youth, scrabbling about the ruins with pick and shovel in hand, to the man of middle years, directing the workers and standing proudly among the unearthed treasures, and finally the elderly figure bundled in a heavy overcoat, propped awkwardly on his cane.

It was this last photograph that always intrigued Greaves: *il professore* in the amphitheatre, wisps of his snow-white hair curling from beneath the battered brim of his Messina hat; in the distance, low clouds gathering rain, perhaps the storm of things to come brewing on the horizon; and, standing beside him, the familiar uniformed caricature—legs planted wide apart, hands on hips, chin thrust out over an inflated rooster's chest. But of this portrait with Il Duce, Parente would only say that it was like everything else in his life: a scrap of history—worthless, except as a curiosity.

Greaves moved now to the window, where he fingered the piece of newspaper that had been pasted over the crack at the bottom of the pane: it was a page torn from an old edition of *Il Popolo d'Italia*. Then he studied the menagerie of bronze miniatures gathering dust on the window ledge: replicas of the finest pieces from the museum's collection—the Farnese Bull and Hercules, Flora and the Head of Isis.

From behind him, a voice said: "'No man can say with confidence that he will be living tomorrow.'"

Greaves turned to see the old man standing in the doorway, a wide grin on his face. Physically, Augusto Parente was so unlike Greaves's grandfather as to be almost his complete opposite. Where Parente was compact, the Reverend Philip Greaves was willowy, and yet there was a sameness to them, a certain acuity.

"Euripides," Greaves said to the curator. Then he offered in return: "'To himself, every man is immortal. Though he may know that he is going to die, he can never know that he is dead.'"

Parente furrowed his brow. "Is it Epicurus?"

Greaves shook his head. "Samuel Butler."

"Ah, Samuel Butler. A utopian. Very interesting choice." Parente made his way slowly to his desk and sat down heavily in the chair.

"You look tired," said Greaves.

The old man put his cane aside and opened a side drawer, from which he took a short-stemmed pipe. He lifted the bowl of the pipe to his nose and breathed in the faint aroma of the resin.

"You know, if you'd like, *professore*, I could get you more tobacco."

Parente shook his head. "The memory of it is enough." He returned the pipe to the drawer. "I am glad you are here, Thomas. I look forward to our visits."

Of all the tasks assigned to him, it was his biweekly appointments with the curator that Greaves liked best. Officially, he was keeping tabs on Parente. Like all high-ranking fascists who had remained behind after the German withdrawal from the city, Parente was to be kept under surveillance. There was fear of an insurgency. But Greaves had realized early on that there was little to worry about when it came to the curator. Parente had been political not out of fervour but rather of necessity. He was a fascist because the fascists were in power. Before that he had been a liberal, and before that a socialist. Beyond pragmatism, politics did not interest him. Even the importance of his position as head of the Archaeological Museum he made light of, saying that it was not unlike that of the lost luggage clerk at the Stazione Centrale— they both watched over the belongings of others. The only difference, Parente often joked, was that in his case it was very doubtful that any of the owners would be returning to collect their property. The curator preferred to talk about Pompeii and Herculaneum, or bemoan the lack of some delicacy or other that he had enjoyed before the war. Often, it was good coffee, the dark African roasts that accentuated the strong tobacco he liked to smoke.

Parente swivelled in his chair. On a small table behind his desk was a field stove that Greaves had brought him on an earlier visit. He lit the flame beneath a battered tin *caffettiera*. "Luisa has found a foul chicory brew that she insists on calling espresso. Will you join me in a cup?"

"Of course." Greaves came and sat in the chair opposite Parente. "I've got something for you," he said, and took two small brown parcels from his satchel. He set the parcels on the desk. "It's sugar.

I thought you might keep one for yourself and trade the other. You could probably get some meat for it, if there's any about."

Parente picked up the parcels, held them out in front of him—their paper stained with grease marks of whatever they'd held before the sugar—and compared the weight. "This is very good of you, Thomas. Thank you."

"I have something for Signora Gennaro as well."

"For Luisa?"

"Yes," Greaves said. "A peace offering of sorts." He rummaged through the satchel and took out the music box. He reached across the desk and gave it to Parente.

"This is a lovely gift, Thomas." There was a twinkle in the old man's eye. "But I am afraid she is not here for you to give it to her."

"Yes, I know. I thought you might do that for me."

Parente frowned. "If you are going to buy a woman a gift, you should at least give it to her yourself."

"I don't know if she would take it from me. But I do know that she will from you."

Now the old man smiled. "You are learning, Thomas."

This attention he paid to Luisa amused Parente. In the month and a half that Greaves had been coming to the museum, Luisa had shown him little more than scorn, and at times outright hostility, but he had been nothing but polite in return. "Courtesy," Parente had said to him at one point, "can be a most damning quality, because it can be so easily dismissed." More than once Greaves had considered that it was indeed her animosity that stirred his fondness for her. Perhaps it was her censure that he craved? Perhaps it was her contempt?

Parente put the music box to the side. "I will make certain that she gets it." Then he took the boiling coffee from the stove and filled two cups. "Would you like sugar?"

"No, I'm fine," said Greaves, and watched as the old man opened one of the parcels and added three pinches of sugar to his coffee, then closed it up again and put it with the other into the drawer where he kept his pipe. "So you've had a visit from the Americans."

"Yes," said Parente. "A colonel from something called the Monuments, Fine Arts and Archives Section. He and General Clark are going to safeguard our treasures for us."

"And how do you feel about that?"

"I have always been wary of those who come offering help when it has not been asked for." Parente sipped his coffee. "He wants a complete inventory of the museum's holdings."

"That sounds like quite a job."

"It will be. I will have to hire extra staff and they will need to be vetted."

"That shouldn't be a problem. Put together a list and I'll take care of it."

Parente sipped his coffee and made a face. "I could boil water from the gutter and it would taste better than this." He put the cup down on the desk. "I've had enough." He reached for his cane and then struggled out of his chair.

Greaves quickly got up and came around the desk. "Maybe you should rest a bit longer, *professore*."

"Nonsense. I'm too old to rest. Besides, there are some lovely mosaics that we've just brought up from the vaults. I want to show them to you." He held out his arm to Greaves. "And if I get tired, you can help me along."

The smell of the place still got to Luisa: a mixture of lye and human waste—a sewer stink that stayed on the skin. She refused, though, to put her handkerchief to her nose to ward off the stench. She would not do that to those confined to the narrow, iron-framed cots—sometimes two to a bed—that lined the darkened corridor. She would not add to their humiliation.

This was the worst of the wards in Ospedale del Santo Sepolcro. It was the ward that housed the most elderly patients—the ones who, in the face of the disease, had the weakest of natural resistance to fend off the more devastating symptoms. Its atmosphere was further burdened by the smallness of the windows in their thick leaded frames set high up on the wall, which killed the sunlight and left only the candles on the bedside tables to prick the gloom.

The water in the pitcher she carried was still warm from boiling, but she took it to each bed, filled a cup, and held it to parched invalid lips. Luisa knew the course of the affliction all too well: the vivid rash, the worsening fever, the rapid beat of a weakening heart. Twice she had suffered through each stage—first with her mother and then, so soon after, with her father. And sometimes she would get lost looking into the face of a dying old woman or a dying old man, and see one of them looking back, as if for a brief moment they had returned to her.

At that moment, it was her mother gazing up at her through the tired and pleading blue eyes—eyes so frightened and confused at not understanding what was to come. Then she heard her name called and turned to see Benedetto standing at the foot of the bed. Benedetto Serao—what a marvel that at forty-one years old and with all that he had seen, his face was as smooth and handsome as when he was twenty-five. Twenty-five and the fetching young *dottore* who suffered her childish attentions whenever he came to visit his lonely aunt who lived in the flat next door to her family's.

"It is late, Luisa. You should go. Augusto will be worried."

"I have only a few more, and they're so thirsty."

"I will see that they are taken care of."

He came and took the pitcher from her and put it on the side stand. And when he put his arms around her, Luisa felt the strength of his ropy limbs. An embrace so much like her father's—so constricting and so safe—that she hoped he would never let her go.

"Why do you come?" he said. "Why do you put yourself through this?"

She pushed him away. "It helps, Benedetto."

"Does it? To me it seems like you are doing penance. But there is nothing for you to feel guilty about. You must know that."

"I know that being here makes them feel closer. As foolish as that may sound to you."

"You're right," he said. "I'm sorry. But really, it is late." He took her by the elbow and began to lead her back along the row of cots. "Let me get one of the orderlies to walk with you."

"I'll be fine."

"Please, Luisa. It's getting dark. At least part of the way. Augusto would never forgive me if I let you go on your own."

They had reached the end of the corridor. She looked back at the cramped beds. The bodies lying in them looked like heaps of dirty linen. She hated that she could no longer remember in which her mother had died, and in which her father.

"All right, Benedetto," she said. "Part of the way."

Salvatore Varone stayed beneath the portico of the abbey and out of the rain. The uneven ground of the yard began to flood in places and mud bubbled from beneath the paving stones. The man guarding the gate, his nephew Paolo, was swallowed up by the wet night. Only the flare of his cigarette end showed where he stood. For almost an hour he had been waiting for the truck to arrive, though he hadn't uttered a single word of complaint—not like the others, who had slunk back under the tiled roof of the loggia to keep dry.

The abbot, standing beside Varone, fretted that something had happened, that there had been a problem with the Americans. He told Varone that there would be nothing he could do if they came; he would not be able to turn them away. "And this is holy ground," the abbot said. "It is no different than San Francesco di Paola or the Duomo."

Varone looked at the old monk, ridiculous in his dark brown cassock, like a woman dressed for bed. He plucked the crucifix, carved from the hard wood of an almond tree, hanging from a tether around the abbot's waist. He said, "You think maybe you have made a deal with the devil, padre?"

"What will you do if they come to arrest me?"

"Nothing," said Varone.

"Then I think, perhaps, I have."

Varone let go of the crucifix. "You should have more faith, old man."

The abbot pointed an angry finger. "Do not mock the Church."

"I am not mocking the Church, padre," Varone said. "I am mocking you. Now, stop talking."

He hated being out in the rain as much as the rest of them, but he knew it had to be done. He suffered the abbot, and the weather, and the late hour to show the men who worked for him that his business was still his business, and any ideas that might be brewing had best be reconsidered. It was difficult now to know who was looking for opportunity and who was not, which one could be depended on and which might be the one who had decided his turn had come. In the few short months since the Americans had arrived, Naples had been transformed: for those who knew how to work their advantage, the city was like an orchard at harvest, the fruit fat on the tree and ripe for picking. With so much to be had, the temptation was often hard to resist, and Varone understood very well that greater betrayals began with smaller deceits. The men needed to understand that he was watching them—he and Paolo.

A thin whistle sounded through the din of the rain. Paolo signalled with a flash from his electric torch. Varone could hear the truck now, the deep growl of its engine in lowest gear as it climbed through the streets of Montecalvario. This section of Naples, poor as any in the city, was laid out in a network of laneways and alleys and narrow cobbled roads that climbed the hillside towards Castel Sant'Elmo. Varone knew them as well as he knew the faces of his own daughters, and as he listened to the truck approach, he told himself: Now it is coming along Via Matteo, and now along Via D'Engenio.

Across the yard, Paolo lifted the bar from the gate and pulled it open. The stubborn iron hinges screeched in protest. A few moments later the truck appeared, its headlamps extinguished. Paolo shone the torch at the windscreen and the driver shielded his eyes. Then he pointed the beam to a spot on the far side of the yard where he wanted the driver to park.

The truck rocked on the uneven ground and slopped water down from its canvas tilt. When it came to a stop at the far end of the yard, Varone called to the men sitting out of the rain to get to work. They slowly left the shelter of the portico.

"You would think they were going to melt," Varone said to the abbot.

Paolo, standing now at the back of the truck, dropped the tailgate. He climbed inside while the others milled about, their collars turned up against the wet. Paolo's torch cast shadows on the slick canvas. Then the light went out.

He jumped down from the tailgate and told the men to start unloading the truck, then came across the yard. As he spoke, Varone watched the crescent scar that rose from the corner of his mouth and made it look as if he were wearing a crooked grin.

"Some is missing."

"How much?"

"I counted eight crates. We were supposed to get sixteen."

"Do you know the driver?"

"Yes, I know him. He's okay."

"Bring him here."

As Paolo made his way back to the truck, Varone turned to the abbot. "Don't worry, padre. You'll still get what you were promised. I am a man of my word, after all."

The driver was a slight man in his forties with a balding head and eyes that bulged from his hollow face. He wore a padded twill jacket and gloves with the fingers cut out.

"Well?" Varone said.

Paolo nudged the man with his elbow. "Go on. Tell him what you told me."

The driver bowed his head slightly. "I was stopped by some men," he said in an uncertain voice. "In the road behind Ospedale Ascalesi."

"Yes," Varone said. "And?"

"One of them had a knife—"

"Look at me when you're speaking," Varone interrupted.

The driver slowly lifted his gaze.

"Go on," said Varone. "One of them had a knife."

"He …" The driver hesitated. "He put it to my throat." He showed Varone the red mark on his neck, a small nick beside his Adam's apple, where the blade had broken the skin.

Varone nodded. "Did you tell this man who the cargo belonged to?"

"I did, yes. I said: 'This cargo is the property of Signore Salvatore Varone.'"

"And what did this man say?"

The driver spoke softly now: "He said to tell you that it was the cost of doing business."

"And you made no effort to stop this man from stealing from me."

The driver looked worriedly at Paolo, then again to Varone. "He would have cut my throat, *signore*. I am sure of it. I have a wife and three daughters."

Varone shrugged. "And what makes you think that I won't cut your throat?"

A whimper slipped from the driver's lips and his shoulders sank. He began to tremble.

"This man with the knife," Varone went on. "What did he look like?"

The driver described him: small, wore a dark suit coat, creme in his hair, and a face like a *volpe*, sly and narrow.

"Do you know him?" Varone asked Paolo.

"Sounds like Renzo Abruzzi. He runs a small operation in the Pendino and Spaccanapoli. Four or five guys, no more. They shake down the shopkeepers, run some prostitutes out of a *pensione* near to Palazzo Como."

Varone sent the driver back to the truck to help with the unloading. When he was gone, he turned again to Paolo. "Do you believe him?" he said.

"I do."

"That means that somebody talked." Varone looked across at the truck. "Do you think it could be one of this lot?"

"It could be," said Paolo. "It could also be one of the boys we've got working on the docks. Maybe it was one of the port officers."

Varone shook his head. "If it was a port officer making a deal with someone else, we wouldn't have gotten anything. Ask around and let me know what you hear."

"What about Abruzzi?"

"Leave him be for now," said Varone.

He could tell by the look on Paolo's face that he didn't understand. His sister's son had an uncomplicated mind. That was what made him so reliable.

"When the time comes, Paolo, we'll know where to find him. Now, go on and get finished with the truck so we can get out of this rain."

As Paolo loped back across the soggy yard, his torch beam dancing on the puddles, Varone laid an arm over the abbot's shoulder. He drew the old monk close to him. "Do you know, padre, that boy takes his *nonna* every morning to the church of Santa Maria della Concezione to make confession. He was even an altar boy there when he was younger."

"He is a good man, then," said the abbot. "A good man with a good heart."

"Oh, yes. He is a good man with a good heart. And if I told him to, he would come back and break your neck, and he would not even think to ask me why."

The abbot shifted nervously. "Why are you telling me this?"

"I just thought you should know," Varone said.

His family had a summer home on the shores of Lake Rosseau, three hours north of Toronto. It had a sloping, manicured lawn—tended by a local man who also watched over the place in the winter—that descended gently to the water's edge, where a large cedar dock had been built, stretching out from the shoreline and big enough to accommodate a suite of wooden deck furniture. On sunny afternoons his family would take lunch there, the meal prepared and brought down from the house by the two women his mother hired each season to look after the cooking and the cleaning. In the evenings, after the tempestuous summer storms to which the area was prone, he would go down to the dock with his father and grandfather—three generations of Greaves men—to watch the sky clear and reveal its dazzling patchwork of stars, always more brilliant than they were in the city. Their re-emergence overhead had always calmed him, always made him feel secure again after the afternoon's deluge.

But watching from the balcony of his room on the second floor of the palazzo as the stars reappeared through the breaks in the clouds did little now to pacify Greaves. Clear night skies over Naples always meant the possibility of another raid.

He lit a cigarette and felt in his pocket for the letter. Earlier that day, Major Woodard had been to Field Security headquarters at Castellammare for a briefing, after which he had collected the section's post, which he had distributed at evening mess. There was something for everyone: Sergeant Bennington opened a meerschaum pipe from his wife that was meant to have arrived at Christmastime; Sergeant Jones received a letter from his fiancée, Gwendolyn, telling him about an American airman she'd met who also came from a place called Bangor; Corporal Blair got a package from his mother with playing cards, a cribbage board, and a box of stale toffee; Corporal Philbin also got a package, but his came from his younger sister and contained three pairs of knitted socks, one red, one orange, and one mauve; Sergeant Roylance received a membership renewal from a golf course outside Liverpool where he hadn't played a round since late spring 1939; and the major got statements from the Lloyds Bank about the accounts that he didn't trust his wife to manage.

Greaves's letter was from his father—he'd recognized the Massey-Harris Co. livery on the envelope. He had written from his office, and likely, Greaves imagined, had dictated its contents to his secretary. But when he opened the letter and removed the single sheet of company stationery, it was not the crisp Remington typeface he'd expected, but rather his father's thin, spidery hand.

Greaves held the letter up so that it caught the faint yellow glow of the hurricane lamp that leaked through the shuttered doors. He read:

Dear Son,

I am wondering why it is that we have not yet had word from you. I have written several times now, and can only suppose that for some reason my letters have not found their way to you. I hope that this is the case. In the meantime, I have been in contact with Colonel Cosworth, one of Harry Crerar's adjuncts, who assured me that matters have been handled with the utmost delicacy and that you have been placed with a British unit, though its whereabouts he could not say—it was, he told me, a question of security. He went to pains, though, to put me at ease. As far as Colonel Cosworth is concerned, what happened in Sicily was not your fault. Fog of war, as he put it—a man cannot be held responsible for such things. And as for afterwards, he assures me that it will not stand as a mark against you. In such situations, there are great stresses upon a man. But you can and must rise above whatever it is that is troubling you. It will be difficult, I have no doubt, but it is not impossible. Walter Hopkins, you remember him, fought at Passchendaele, and Frederick Barnes was in that horror at the Somme. And yet these men, and others I am acquainted with, have managed quite well despite their experiences. Time heals, Thomas. Soon enough we will all move on and this whole business will be behind us. Have faith, son.

Always,

Your Father

Greaves folded the letter and slipped it back into the envelope. He studied the return address and thought of his father's corner office on the third floor of the Massey-Harris Co. building and all the times he had stood there, staring out at the trains as they rumbled past, the bells ringing as they crossed over King Street, making for some far-off place in the West—for Manitoba, for the Prairies of Saskatchewan and the mountains beyond. All of those places that, as a child, he had so badly wanted to see—all of those places that he now felt he never would.

He reached into his pocket and took out his cigarette lighter. He touched the flame to the corner of the envelope. It caught quickly. He held the letter between his fingers and watched it burn, charred bits fluttering off in the breeze and falling like dying fireflies into the courtyard below.

THREE

A convoy of troop trucks passed, splashing rainwater from the potholes across the pavement. Cioffi stepped back to avoid the spray. He waved a fist at the last truck as it moved off. The soldier standing in the open tailgate grinned and showed him a middle finger.

The water soaked through Cioffi's broken shoes. He looked around him. He had come as far as the university. Across the road from him was the darkened facade of the main building. Seeing it, he thought of another day when soldiers in trucks had crowded the boulevard, though then it had been Germans, not Americans.

On that day the trucks had not driven past. Instead, they had stopped and the soldiers had climbed down and begun to herd the people together. They pushed everyone into the roadway and set up barricades to pen them in as if they were so much livestock brought to market. After that another truck, with a flatbed, arrived; on the back of it was a newsreel camera. A German officer came forward and climbed the steps of the university. He wore a smart grey uniform, freshly brushed and with polished buttons that gleamed in the late summer sun. He spoke to the people through a megaphone, warning that there were traitors among them. On his signal, a man was taken from the front of the crowd. He was led up the steps and bound to a pillar near the entrance. There was a look of bewilderment on his face as the ropes were tied, as if perhaps he thought it was some sort of ruse. On the flatbed truck, the newsreel camera focused on the German officer as he repeated his claim, in stilted but formal Italian, that there were traitors in their midst. There was only one way, the officer told the people, with which these traitors would be dealt. Then he put the megaphone aside and took his pistol from its holster. He placed the barrel of the pistol against the base of the man's neck. The shot sounded like a whip crack, and the bullet, which tore a plum-sized hole in the man's left cheek, erased the expression of bemusement from his face. Slumped against the ropes, his body jerked twice, shuddered, and then was still. Even from where he stood at the back of the crowd, Cioffi could see the spray of blood that sullied the officer's meticulous uniform. After this, the German calmly retrieved his megaphone. He pointed towards the newsreel camera that now panned over the crowd. His amplified voice commanded: "*Adesso applaudite.*" Slowly people began to clap their hands. The officer shouted for them to applaud louder and soldiers moved through the crowd, sticking the butts of their rifles into the ribs of those who did not show enough enthusiasm. Cioffi clapped his hands together as hard as he could; he clapped them until they throbbed. "*Bene,*" the German officer had said. "*Bene.*" Then he had his men set fire to the university.

It was a dangerous time in the days and weeks after Marshal Badoglio agreed to the armistice. The Germans, always cool, had turned from ally to enemy in the blink of an eye. They brought their cruelty to the streets. At best they ridiculed you; at worst they tied you to a post and shot a bullet through your face. But while they were there, Cioffi had managed all right. His training had made him an adept forger, and he had paid his way supplying bogus medical certificates to the prostitutes in the German enlisted men's brothels. A girl couldn't work in any of these establishments without a clean bill of health—

the Wehrmacht didn't want their *Oberschützes* going home syphilitic. But when the Americans arrived, they brought free enterprise with them, and for the brothel business that meant the Camorra, and they didn't bother with paperwork. So with the forgery business dried up, Cioffi went, along with so many others, to offer his services to the liberators of Napoli, confident that his knowledge of English would land him an interpreter's post, perhaps with the Red Cross or maybe even the Rockefeller Institute. That was how he found that his name was on a list. Ten years earlier he had been denounced as a Marxist. The statement against him was still in his police records, and suddenly Cioffi found himself *persona non grata*. There was no room in the new bureaucracy for a Communist.

He looked again at the scrap of paper in his hand. It had been more than a week since he'd met with Abruzzi, but the day before, word had come to him by way of Maggio: he was to get another coin, a real one this time, and bring it to an address on Corso Umberto Primo.

When he found the place, it was a small *ristorante*. Inside, the cramped dining room was busy, most of the tables occupied by soldiers who looked up as he stood in the open doorway. One, sitting at a nearby table, his eyes glassy and his lips stained with wine, shouted at him: "In or out, ginzo. Make up your mind."

Cioffi looked around. He did not see Abruzzi, though Maggio had told him that he would be there. He was about to leave when a heavy-set man came from the back of the room. He had hunched shoulders and a slight limp, and his nose was mashed to the side as if it had been broken many times. He paused a moment and glared at the drunken soldier, then said to Cioffi: "Are you the *dottore*?"

"I am, yes," said Cioffi nervously.

"Follow me."

The man led him past the tables and through a swinging door. They went through a sweating kitchen thick with the stink of sour fish and burnt dough to another door that led into the back alley. Abruzzi was there, sitting at a makeshift table rolling dice with another man, who bore a striking resemblance to the first. He looked up at Cioffi, then he waved a dismissive hand and the other two disappeared back inside without a word.

Abruzzi motioned to the vacant chair. "Have a seat. Would you like a drink?" He reached for the bottle of wine at his elbow. "But of course you would."

Cioffi took the wine. He quickly drank it down and shyly held out the glass for more. Abruzzi pushed the bottle across the table.

"Help yourself," he said, and settled back in his chair. "You have something for me, I hope."

"I do, yes," Cioffi said, and reached into his pocket. He passed the coin to Abruzzi, who turned it over in his hand then ran his thumb along the surface. "It's real," said Cioffi.

"Oh, I have no doubt, *dottore*. You are too smart a man to pass off a fake to me." Abruzzi held the coin up between thumb and forefinger. "Now, tell me, who is this?"

Cioffi swallowed another mouthful of wine. He leaned forward and looked closely at the coin. "It is Vitellius Germanicus," he said.

"Vitellius Germanicus, eh?"

"Yes, that's right," said Cioffi. "He reigned for only a short time. In the Year of the Four Emperors. He was cruel and gluttonous, and it is said that he starved his own mother to death. He was defeated by the Flavians and executed in Rome. They cut off his head."

Abruzzi nodded. "You know your history."

"It is our history. That is what my uncle always told me. The history of Italia is the history of us. He said that we should learn from it, so that when we repeated the same mistakes, we would know why."

Saying the words, Cioffi could hear his uncle's voice in his head, and for a moment he imagined again the endless childhood hours spent in the old man's company, wandering the museum, floor by floor, gallery by gallery, exhibit by exhibit. It had been a convenient arrangement for all involved: It gave his father the freedom to fixate on his business and his mother time to take afternoon lovers. His bachelor uncle took pleasure in having an empty vessel into which he could decant his arcane wisdom. As for Cioffi, who on his own would explore the back corridors and the underground vaults and the other dark places where he was not meant to go, it gave him a taste for theft. The first, he recalled fondly, was a small hair clip made of polished bone that he traded to a boy at school for the chance to watch his sister take a bath.

"And did he tell you?" Abruzzi asked. "Your uncle—did he tell you why it is that we repeat the mistakes of our past?"

Cioffi smiled. "He says that it is in our nature. That we cannot deny our appetites any more than a dog can deny his."

Now Abruzzi smiled too. "He has a point," he said, and slipped the coin into his breast pocket. "Did you have any trouble with the Carabinieri?"

Cioffi had waited until the policeman guarding the front entrance went to the taverna around the corner on Piazza Gagliardi for his morning drink and then slipped into the museum. He made his way quickly through the darkened corridors to the storeroom on the ground floor where the surplus coinage was kept; the museum had far more pieces than could ever be displayed. He went quickly through the shallow-drawered cabinet, selecting a shiny piece that he was sure would impress Abruzzi. When he came out of the front doors again, however, he found that the guard had already returned to his post. "What are you doing?" the policeman demanded of him. A paralysis of fear had gripped Cioffi. He tried to speak, but could only manage an indecipherable stutter. "Who told you to come today?" said the policeman. For a moment Cioffi was convinced that Abruzzi had the man watching him. "Nobody," he said. "Nobody, nobody," parroted the guard. "Nobody tells anybody anything in this city. Well, you can go back to your nobody and tell him that the *professore* is not interviewing for the positions until tomorrow." "The positions?" Cioffi said. "That's why you're here, isn't it? To hire on for the inventory?" Cioffi nodded. "Yes, of course. The inventory." The policeman studied him a moment, then said, "You don't look the sort the *professore* would take on, but then, who knows with that crazy old fool."

"So, he's taking on workers, then," said Abruzzi.

"Yes. The Americans want a complete inventory of the museum's collection."

"That's good. That's very good. You will go and work for him."

Cioffi shook his head. "I don't think he will have me. He doesn't trust me anymore."

Abruzzi picked up the bottle and filled Cioffi's glass again and handed it to him. "You should find a way, *dottore*," he said, "to earn his trust again."

Greaves was tired. He had been on the road since seven that morning and his kidneys ached—a consequence of the long ride on a near-suspensionless Norton motorbike. He had come from the mountain village of Tenerello, where he'd spent the last two days of his week-long security liaison circuit of outlying police garrisons. At Tenerello he stayed with *brigadiere* Francesco Maglietta and his family in their farmhouse on the outskirts of the town. Greaves always made sure to manage his time in Casoria and Aversa and Afragola so that he had a little extra in Tenerello with the Magliettas. The *brigadiere's* wife made lovely meals and his daughters were energetic and curious and would take Greaves for hikes in the mountains, and Francesco himself was always ready to open a bottle of brandy and stay up late into the night talking books and playing endless hands of *tresette*. Being with them was like being in a place outside of time: it was easy for Greaves to forget everything else—even easy for him to forget why he had gone there in the first place.

Now, back in Naples, he waited for Major Woodard, who had left the office some time earlier in search of a tape measure. They had been in the middle of the briefing when the major excused himself. He'd been continually distracted by the conundrum of an empty shipping crate and a floor globe that opened into a drinks table. Finally he'd said: "Look, just give me a minute, will you, lieutenant. I won't be a moment."

Greaves looked at his watch again. He wanted to wash up and have lunch before he got down to typing up his reports. At this rate he might have to forgo one or the other—likely the bathing. He glanced around the major's office. Along with the floor globe, there was a silver coffee service and trolley, and a complete set of Cicero's *Ethical Writings*, bound in red leather.

The door opened and the major came in, a cloth tailor's measure in hand. "Give me a hand with this, will you, lieutenant," he said.

Greaves followed him to the crate.

"Just hold this at the bottom," said Major Woodard.

Greaves took hold of one end of the tape and knelt down while the major pulled it taut. Then they went through the same procedure with the floor globe.

"Just as I thought," the major said. "It's not near bloody big enough." He nodded to his small inventory. "I won't even get the drinks table in, never mind the rest of it. And my fellow at Capodichino tells me I can only send one crate at a time."

At the airfield there had been a crackdown on unofficial cargo being put on flights to England. Even with his security clearances, Major Woodard was finding it more difficult to ship his spoils home.

"I'm sure you'll figure something out, sir," said Greaves.

"Yes, of course, lieutenant. It's more an annoyance than anything else." The major wound the measuring tape around his finger. "Right then, what was it we were talking about?"

"Tenerello, sir."

"Yes, Tenerello. So, what did you find out?"

"Nothing specific," said Greaves. "Rumours, mostly. The *camorristi* in the area are said to be handling heavy machinery: trucks, construction equipment, that sort of thing."

"And does your brigadiere friend— What's his name?"

"Maglietta, sir."

"Right, Maglietta. Does he say how they're getting it?"

"He doesn't. Though my guess would be that the *camorristi* are working with deserter gangs here in Naples. They may even have made inroads into some of the engineering brigades. They are very resourceful, sir. We already know that ties have been established with certain AMGOT personnel, mostly in the civilian liaison department."

"Now, lieutenant, let's not go punching above our weight class," said Major Woodard. "I suppose this *brigadiere* hasn't any solid evidence for us. Nothing we can take to FSHQ."

"Nothing first-hand," Greaves said. "And he's not likely to go looking, either, sir."

The major pursed his lips. "No, I wouldn't think so."

"Well, there is a question of his personal safety, sir."

"And that comes before law and order, does it?"

"In Bandit Country, I'm afraid it does, sir."

Maglietta had made it clear to Greaves early on that in Tenerello he saw to the smaller criminals and let the bigger criminals see to themselves.

"Is he getting any help from the local officials? The mayor and whatnot?"

"They're friendly with the gangs."

"Yes, I'm sure they are." Major Woodard shook his head. "I suppose that was our first mistake, wasn't it? We should have left Mussolini's lot in place to run the show—at least we could have trusted them."

"It's a little late for that now," said Greaves.

"It is a little late for a lot of things, lieutenant," replied the major. "Tell me, what have you got on your plate at the moment?"

"Well, sir, there's a backlog of paperwork I need to get through. And a few proposed brides I'm scheduled to vet. I'm also expecting a list of possible employment candidates from the curator of the Archaeological Museum that I'll need to look up at the Questura."

"So, not much, then."

"No, sir. Not much."

"Good, because I've had a request from FSHQ. They're concerned about stolen medical supplies. Seems that shipments out of the port to 21st General Hospital at Mostra fairgrounds have been routinely arriving light."

"Is that really up to us, sir? Don't the American military police look after the port and the hospital?"

"They aren't having much luck, and Castellammare wants us to help them out." The major shrugged. "I'm not overly inclined to do the Yanks' work for them either, lieutenant. We have enough to worry about as it is. There was a spate of wire cutting while you were away, and the others are busy trying to sort that mess out. But I do as I'm told, and that means that you do as you're told. Just go by the port and have a word with someone there—the same at the hospital. Write up whatever you find out and we'll send it along to Castellammare. That should be enough to keep them happy."

The major took a last look at the globe and the crate, then went back to his desk and made a note on a scrap piece of paper. "Now, do me a favour, will you, lieutenant," he said, holding the paper out to Greaves. "Give these measurements to Corporal Philbin and tell him to show it to the clerk at the supply depot. And do ask him to get it right this time."

Greaves took the piece of paper. "Of course, sir," he said.

By early afternoon, the sun had burnt away the clouds and fulfilled the promise of a warm day. Soon the winter rains would be gone altogether; springtime loomed. And after that there would be the cruel white heat of summer. The war would be gone by then, moved on north to Rome or perhaps even farther; maybe by summer it would have reached the Alps. Either way, Naples would no longer be so important—a southern port, too far away from the fighting. Then, Salvatore Varone knew, it would be dangerous; that would be his time of hunger. So it was better to gorge now, while there was still plenty to feed on.

Leaning over the railing of the wide balcony, Paolo said: "You can't see Montecalvario from here."

Varone went and stood beside him. "That's the point," he said. Below them, the parkland of Villa la Floridiana fell away in a rolling green carpet of umbrella pines and monkey puzzle trees and shifting palms. Then came the terracing rooftops that descended to the sea, to where, in the marina of Santa Lucia, the fishing boats looked like colourful petals cast upon the water, and Castel dell'Ovo, catching the sunlight, resembled a brick of gold floating on the dark waves. Farther along, at the port, even the leaden hulks of the British and American ships at anchor in the basin, motor launches scratching frothy patches in the oily water between them, shone like polished granite islands. It was like a picture postcard; but Varone knew that, like a postcard, the view was a lie that hid the truth of the city—the swarming despair, the sickness and cruelty, the hunger and vice. Naples was like a diseased prostitute who hid her blisters beneath layers of powder and paint.

"When I was a boy," he said, "the man who lived in this apartment would have beaten me if I'd stopped him in the street."

"You knew him?" said Paolo.

Varone looked at him and shook his head. "No, I did not know him."

He returned to the table and sat down, and took a piece of bread from the basket his wife had put out and dipped it into the pot of olive oil. He held the basket out to Paolo. "Here. Eat."

Paolo took a heel of bread. He broke it with his thick fingers and ate it dry. There was still much of the street in his sister's son—the raw hunger, the crude manners, the promise of swift violence. There remained traces of it in Varone as well. He saw it every morning when he stood before the bathroom mirror to shave: the scarred lip that upset the balance of his thin moustache. The man who had given him that scar—he was only fourteen when it happened—was a housebreaker who had beaten him with a sock full of coins to teach him a lesson about moving in on someone else's territory. Varone had found him later in a brothel on Via Toledo and made him beg for mercy before he castrated him, slicing his testicles with a barber's razor. The act had cemented his reputation among the other street boys, and made him known to the local Camorra boss, who took the young Varone under his wing just as he now took Paolo under his own.

"So, tell me," Varone said.

Paolo reached into his jacket pocket and took out a small notebook. He flipped through the grubby pages. "There is a shipment of office supplies in a warehouse on pier twelve. Typewriters, mimeograph, ink, carbon paper. It is going to be moved to American army headquarters at Caserta by the end of the week. It can be arranged for us to pick up tomorrow night, if we want."

"And what did you say?"

"I told them that we would have a truck there at midnight."

"Good. What else?"

"There is timber being moved up from Calabria for a prison camp that the British are building outside of Avellino. They will need drivers."

"No," Varone said. "That's not for us. There are too many toes that could be stepped on. If they brought it through the port, maybe."

"I just thought you should know," said Paolo. "Other than that, we are due to make a sweep of the market."

Varone nodded. "It's time to collect the rent."

"Fifteen thousand a head?" Paolo asked.

"Better to make it ten," Varone said with a shrug. "That way, they will think we are being generous. It's always good to give a man the impression that you feel sorry for him—it makes it easier to pick his pocket."

"And what about the ones that still won't pay?"

"They know the price."

The cost of refusing was an unpleasant confinement in a warehouse on the outskirts of the city, where the dissenter would be bound and beaten until someone showed up with the payment.

"Now, what about this Abruzzi?" Varone said. "Have you heard anything?"

"As far as I can tell," said Paolo, "nobody talked. I think he figured it out on his own. He must have been watching our operation at the docks for a while beforehand."

"He's a clever fellow, then."

"Clever enough," said Paolo.

"He'll know that we will want to find whoever it was that stole from us."

"I think so, yes."

"Can I assume that you've been keeping an eye on him?"

"I have."

"Good." Varone got up from his chair and walked again to the railing. Through the open balcony doors came the sound of his daughters' laughter; their voices were like the melodies of songbirds to him. He looked out once more over the park. In the distance he could see the purple slopes of Vesuvius, a trail of vapour rising from its yawning summit. "It is a terrible shadow to live under," he said.

"What is?" asked Paolo.

Varone turned around. "The mountain," he said, and smiled. "Don't you ever think about how one day it is going to bury us all under a heap of ash?"

Paolo looked at him queerly. "No. I never think that."

"I do," said Varone. "It helps to remind me that nothing matters but today."

Luisa came along the street. Tucked up under her arm she carried a hardened loaf of black bread wrapped in cloth. In her coat pocket she had a tin of bully beef. There hadn't been enough to buy the margarine or the biscuits she wanted, and she couldn't afford the broad beans that the sellers brought in from the countryside. The last of the money that Augusto had given her—the pay packet she brought home from the museum was worth less with each passing day—only bought the bread and canned meat. She had considered trading the music box that Tenente Greaves had given her—a useless trinket, really—but at the last moment had changed her mind.

She tried now to be inconspicuous as she approached the apartment house and saw Signora Ciccione. The old woman lived in the apartment below Luisa's. She was sitting on a straight-backed chair near the courtyard gate, running the beads of a rosary through her stiff fingers. Luisa had been frightened of the elderly widow, who seemed to her to have always been old, always stooped and withered, ever since she was a child. The *signora's* face was pinched and shrivelled like a dried apple, and to Luisa she had always been *la strega*—the witch.

As she lowered her head and made for the gate, the old woman's soft voice stopped her.

"What are you hiding, my child?"

Luisa gave her a sideways glance. "It's nothing," she said.

"No," Signora Ciccione said, the phlegm catching lightly in her throat. "You have food. Let me see it, child. Show it me."

"It's very little. Some stale bread. A tin of meat."

"Please," the widow implored. "I only want to see it."

Luisa took the bundle of cloth from beneath her arm and held it out. When Signora Ciccione grabbed at it, she pulled it back. "I'm sorry, *signora*," she said. "There isn't enough. This will feed only my cousin and me."

The old woman gave her a fierce look. "Why don't you let the *puttana* feed herself?"

"I beg your pardon?" said Luisa.

"I hear her. I hear her through the ceiling. With the soldiers. In the afternoon, when you are gone away. Rutting like a pig." Signora Ciccione's tongue flicked through the wide space in her teeth, licking the soft pinkness of her bare gums. "Maybe you are the same, eh?"

When she laughed, the sound rattled in her throat and she began to cough. Luisa watched her, sickened by the sight, as she leaned to the side and spat a thick wad of rheum onto the ground.

"That's not true," Luisa said.

"Everybody knows," said the old widow, and tipped forward on the chair. "They talk about her. They talk about how you brought a *prostituta* to live under your roof." Signora Ciccione laughed again. "But she will need to be careful, that one. She's not such a peach anymore. Not so juicy. Maybe soon she'll spread her legs for the *negri* in the alleyways, with her back to the wall like the rest of the street sluts."

Before Luisa had even realized what she was doing, she stepped forward and struck the old woman hard across the face. Signora Ciccione cried out and put a bony hand to her jaw. A drop of blood appeared on her thin bottom lip and her cloudy eyes filled with tears.

"I'm so sorry," Luisa said.

"You filthy bitch."

"Please," said Luisa, and held out the stale loaf to her. "Please forgive me, *signora*."

The old woman grabbed the bread and stuffed it under her shawl and struggled to her feet. "You shame your mother's memory. Thank God that she is not here to see what you have become." Then she turned and hobbled through the gate.

The Port Authority office was abustle with clerks rushing about and ships' crew waiting to be debriefed and supply officers shouting across one another in an effort to get their cargo either loaded or unloaded before the next man. It was the chaos of a harassed beehive, and Greaves wondered how anything managed to get done. He had shown his credentials to a red-faced clerk behind the reception counter and been told to take a seat against a far wall and wait to be called.

It was another half-hour before the door to one of the smaller offices opened and a young man stepped out. The clerk went to him and they spoke. The young man looked over towards Greaves and nodded his head. Then he came from behind the counter and held out his hand.

"The name's Michael Mangan," he said. "I'm one of the assistant port officers—one of the many." He spoke with a soft lilt and it was obvious that he purposely shaved the rough edges from a harsher northern Irish accent. "My man here tells me you've got some questions need answering, lieutenant. Is that right?"

"That's right," Greaves said. "My FSO thought I should come by and have a word about—"

"Yes, yes," Mangan interrupted. "Missing medical supplies. I've been told."

The clerk was at the young man's elbow again. "Excuse me, Michael, but we're having some problems with one of the dredgers."

"What is it?"

"The captain is refusing to take her out. Says that yesterday he was almost sunk by a frigate coming across his bow."

"You might mention to him that's why he's to be out there. And if it doesn't set with him, tell him we'll be more than happy to find another man to sail his barge while he cools his heels in the brig."

"You want me to threaten him with charges, Michael?"

"I do, yes."

The assistant port officer turned his attention back to Greaves. "Sorry about that. We're after trying to plough a few more channels so we don't have ships running into one another. This may well be the biggest harbour in the south of Italy, lieutenant, but I'm afraid it's not half as big as we need." He put a hand on Greaves's shoulder. "Why don't we go into my office and get a little peace."

The office of the assistant port officer was as tidily arranged as the port officer himself. The desk was orderly and the logs on the shelves behind were neatly set out and labelled so that they could be quick to hand. A window opened onto the port itself, and through it came a soft breeze that carried the smell of brine and diesel.

"Would you like a drink, lieutenant? A whisky, maybe?" He poured the glasses without waiting for Greaves's reply. "I'd like to say that you caught us on a busy day," he went on, "but pretty much every day is a busy day. I've got fifteen ships at anchor, clogging up the harbour waiting for a resupply of food and water, while four hospital ships are stuck out in the bay because they can't get in until I get these others out."

"A typical day at the office, then," said Greaves.

"Indeed it is, lieutenant."

"You seem to be taking it all in stride."

Mangan smiled. "To tell you the truth," he said, and handed Greaves his drink, "I love it. Best bloody thing ever happened to me." He motioned for Greaves to take a seat and then sat down behind his desk. "Tell me, lieutenant, what is it that you did before all of this?"

"I was at university."

"Really? And what were you studying?"

"Romance languages."

"Did you want to be a teacher, then?"

"Yes. A professor, like my grandfather."

"Ah, a scholar, eh?" Mangan smiled. "My grandfather was a physician. My father, too. I should have been next, but I ran off and left Belfast and all it had to offer behind. Now I'm a good little Paddy working for the British Ministry of War Transport. I'll tell you, the look on my da's face was brilliant when I told him. Though I don't think he was quite as stunned as when I told him I wanted to be a poet."

"A poet?" said Greaves.

"A flight of fancy," Mangan answered. "Sure there's more money in working for the British than turning rhymes."

Greaves couldn't help but like the man, with his ironed-out brogue and easy openness. He was struck too by his youth: Mangan had a clear, pale face, the skin reddened in places as if it was not yet accustomed to being shaved, and there was a sprinkling of freckles across his nose. And yet he seemed so composed amidst the confusion of the place.

"If you don't mind my asking," Greaves said, "how old are you?"

"I'm twenty-one," said Mangan. "How about yourself?"

"Twenty-four."

"Well, there you are, then. We're two old men ready to set the world to rights." Mangan finished off his whisky in one mouthful and set the glass aside. "Now that we've got that sorted, let's talk about these medical supplies."

"Yes, of course," said Greaves. "I've been asked by my FSO to make some inquiries, specifically about supplies that are bound for 21st General Hospital. A significant quantity of that cargo is not making it to its final destination."

Mangan held up his hand. "Lieutenant, this port has over six hundred civilian workers. We land almost two hundred ships a week. The tonnage in cargo that passes through here on a given day would boggle your mind. We have military police that patrol day and night. They have orders to shoot looters. And still, over one-third of everything that reaches dockside disappears without a trace. You're asking after medical supplies. Three weeks ago we lost six four-ton lorries and two Bailey bridges—straight out the front gates and gone." Mangan got to his feet. "I wish I could help you, lieutenant, but your guess is as good as mine. You ask me, your FSO has you chasing your tail on this one." Then he gently ushered Greaves to the door and shook his hand. "Best of luck to you."

Lello Conforti glanced nervously about the café. He held his drink in both hands, as if expecting at any moment it would be snatched away. There was a commotion at the bar: a drunken American soldier who wanted another bottle of whisky. The barman ignored him and continued polishing glasses. When the soldier slapped his hand down on the countertop, Lello flinched.

"I don't know why we always come back here," he said. "There are better places to drink. Cheaper places."

Cioffi looked at his friend and laughed. "But it's the Gambrinus, Lello. There's nowhere as good as the Gambrinus."

"It's not like it used to be, Aldo. It will never be like that again." Lello swallowed a mouthful of wine. "We should leave."

"Never mind," said Cioffi. "It is good here. Good memories."

For Cioffi, the Caffè Gambrinus was like a moment frozen in time: the gilded mirrors, the veined marble floor, the plaster relief on the vaulted ceiling, the frescoed walls. Once, it had been the beating heart of freethinking Naples: art, literature, philosophy, and politics. What stories its walls had heard. Socialists, anarchists, and bohemians of every bent came there to drink and talk. The disgraced Oscar Wilde. Alexandre Dumas, too. And de Maupassant. In the years before the war it was the avant-gardes that crowded the tables, sipping anise and conspiring with anti-fascists, until the authorities closed it down and rounded up the agitators. Lello Conforti had been among them. The six months he spent in Poggio Reale prison had soured him on the merits of the Gambrinus.

"The dark days are over, my friend," Cioffi reminded him as he refilled their glasses. He nodded to the barman to bring another bottle. He knew that, for Lello, drink was the only cure for frayed nerves. He held out his glass. "To forgetting," he said.

Lello, though half-heartedly, returned the salute, for he knew that they both had things to forget. For him, it was a promising law career cut short by political recklessness, because there was no place for subversives in the Castel Capuano. He'd often wondered since if his principles were worth the cost of a bright future. As for Cioffi, who had wasted his future on far less, any sense of regret he felt was tempered by the fact that he'd never really had any desire to become the physician his father always dreamt he would be.

The barman delivered the new bottle. He set it down and waited to be paid. Cioffi handed him a hundred-lire note and told him to keep the rest.

Lello watched him put the thin roll of military scrip back into his pocket. "Do you know what you're doing?"

It was the sort of question his friend had been asking him since their days together at the university, and Cioffi answered him as he always did: "You worry too much."

"You don't know anything about these people you're dealing with."

"And you do?"

"I know them better than you think, Aldo. And trust me, if you let them down, they will make you pay."

Cioffi wished now that he hadn't said anything to Lello about Abruzzi. "Don't fret. I have a plan."

"Listen to yourself," Lello scoffed. "You're like a boy playing a game. If you cross these people, Aldo, they will kill you and not give it a second thought. You're nothing to them—I hope you know that."

Cioffi tried to ignore his friend's concern. He lifted his glass and took a long drink. Then he said, "Tomorrow, I will go and see my uncle's friend in the security police."

"You are a fool," said Lello.

"Perhaps," replied Cioffi. "But I am a fool who is filling your belly with wine. So quit complaining and drink, before you ruin the rest of the night."

FOUR

When the nightmare first came, he would wake screaming. That was before the field hospital, before the young corporal found him with his revolver. Greaves never put the barrel in his mouth like the major had said, it hadn't gotten quite that far, though he had considered it, indeed must have been considering it on that morning when the corporal, getting no response to calls, came into his quarters and saw him staring at the weapon in his lap. It had been the tenth night running that he'd managed no more than a few fitful hours of sleep—the tenth night running that he'd had the dream. And it was always the same. He was on a scorched mountain pass. Across the valley lay the town of Agira, a stony, sun-baked outcrop. His nose filled with the stink of dust and diesel fuel. Then darkness fell and he found himself climbing down into the valley amidst a full company of men who made their way by touch in the starless night. He stayed close to the sergeant and the round-faced wireless operator, a boy of eighteen. Somehow they lost their bearings, got turned off course, and were unable to find their markers. Then the shelling started: the barrage was timed so that they could follow it in. They moved towards the shell bursts and found a ridgeline. He huddled behind some rocks, shouted new coordinates into the wireless handset, and waited for the bombardment—a mixed salvo of high-explosive and incendiary charges that landed short, near the edge of the village. The concussions thumped in their chests and the heat was like the noonday sun on their faces. Afterwards, there was a stretch of quiet—then the screaming started.

Greaves couldn't say who it was that claimed he'd had the gun in his mouth. Perhaps it was the corporal, who, in his shock at having found him in such a state, had imagined the circumstance different than it was; or perhaps it was simply a case of a story that grows in the retelling. Whichever it was, or whether it was something else altogether—a disgruntled soldier, maybe, who thought he should be punished for his incompetence—the tale of his suicidal tendency became the focus of his therapy. The diagnosis was combat exhaustion, but Greaves was sure that he hadn't seen enough combat yet to be exhausted. At any rate, the doctors, both at the field hospital and at No. 5 CGH, were pleased with his response to the lithium carbonate treatment. They pointed to the fact that he no longer awoke screaming in the night. That the dream had ended was the first step to a full recovery, they told him. What he had not told them, however, was that the dream was still there; he had simply taught himself not to scream anymore.

So now, when the nightmare came, as it did that night, he woke soundlessly and threw back the blankets, his chest seized by the familiar panic until he realized where he was: the dim outline of the dressing table and the writing desk, the hurricane lamp extinguished at his bedside—the hiss of the rain against the shutters. He lay down and covered himself again, and waited for the sun to come up. With the dawn he drifted off, and when he woke a few hours later he found that he'd slept through mess and would have to go without breakfast.

He washed in a basin in his room, shaved, put talcum powder under his arms, and then put on a fresh shirt and tie. He wet his comb and ran it through his hair. Then he pulled on his tunic and stood before the dressing table mirror. His cheeks were sunken and he had dark circles under his eyes; he looked as if he were in the grip of some wasting sickness.

In the foyer downstairs, he found Corporal Philbin at his makeshift desk sorting through a file box that had been sent along from FSHQ the week before. He was working with the help of a translation dictionary and entering suspect profiles into a swollen ledger so that they could be checked against records at the central police station. These new profiles would then be added to the section's burgeoning archives, which already amounted to three full-sized metal cabinets in a room on the second floor.

The corporal shook his head. "There are more Espositos in Naples than you could wag a bloody stick at." He had the same uncertain gaze and cheeks flushed with rosacea as the teenaged wireless operator of Greaves's dream. "This came for you," he said, and held out an envelope. "Lady dropped it by about an hour ago."

Greaves opened the envelope and took out the neatly typed list of names. "She didn't want to speak to me?" he said.

"No. Just wanted me to give that to you." Philbin nodded at the page in Greaves's hand. "Will you be checking those names out at the Questura?"

"I will," said Greaves.

"Would you mind looking into a few more while you're there? It would save me having to go myself."

Greaves took a scribbled list from the corporal and put it into his satchel along with the list that Luisa Gennaro had delivered.

He left the palazzo and started across the square. Walking along Via Santa Caterina, he thought about the music box. Maybe it hadn't been such a wise idea after all. Luisa might have taken it the wrong way. Then again, in what way had it been intended? Greaves wasn't certain himself. He had joked to Parente about it being a peace offering, and in a way it was. He had wanted to do something nice for her because she seemed the sort of person in need of a kind gesture. But if she thought there was something more behind it, then that might push her farther away. All of which begged the question: did he want her closer to him? There seemed little sense in beginning something that could not be finished.

Greaves continued to mull this over as he turned into a street leading to the central police station and came upon a delousing operation. It was only one of many that moved like a troupe of travelling players through the poorer quarters of the city.

There was a ragged line of people gathered before a table staffed by two army nurses, who searched their hair for nits. From there they were sent on to one of the three stations, where an orderly waited with a spray canister filled with talc and DDT. A sign posted on a nearby wall showed the figure of a giant louse with a large red X drawn over it and the slogan *Lice=Typhus* written in both English and Italian.

While he watched, two boys were led by one of the nurses to the first delousing station. The younger of them was crying, but the orderly, a sullen private with pale cheeks and a receding chin, took a stick of chewing gum from his pocket and offered it to the child. As the boy unwrapped the foil from the gum, the orderly picked up the spray canister and began to work the plunger. He dusted both of them in a fine white powder that clung to their hair and clothes. The nurse, wearing long surgical gloves, rubbed their heads to make sure the powder reached their scalps. Then the boys, laughing and looking like apparitions of themselves, ran past Greaves. He recoiled slightly as they went by.

"How bad is it?" he asked one of the nurses, who had looked up to see him standing there.

"It's not an epidemic," she said. "Not yet, at least."

At the next station along, an old man had been made to lower his trousers. The skin at the back of his knees was raw and speckled with a rash that roped its way across his naked thighs. The second orderly was shorter than the first, with a thuggish, square-jawed face. He aimed the spray canister at the old man's thin legs, then made him pull out the waistband of his yellowed underpants and sprayed there too.

Greaves watched the old man wipe a tear from his dusty face, then left the street and the delousing stations behind.

At the Questura, he had to pass through a cordon of military police who were keeping an uninterested eye on a small group of men who had come there on the false rumour of work. The records department was on the top floor of the building. It was a wide, open room with a long wooden counter, behind which were ranged row upon row of file cabinets that reached from the floor very nearly to the ceiling. There were stepladders on rollers in each of the aisles so that the uppermost drawers could be more easily reached. The extent of the archive spoke to the thoroughness of the former fascist authorities.

Greaves did not recognize the clerk on duty, who greeted his arrival with an indifferent nod and continued reading the day-old copy of *Risorgimento* spread out on the counter before him.

"*Tu parli inglese?*" he said.

The clerk shook his head. "*Niente inglese.*"

"*Va bene, allora parlo italiano,*" said Greaves, and removed the two lists from his satchel and laid them on the counter. He turned them so that the clerk could see. "I need you to find a few names for me."

"I'm very busy."

Greaves looked down at the newspaper. "Yes, I see," he said, and took out a packet of cigarettes. He offered one to the clerk, who accepted it with a smile and leaned forward for a light. "I really do need to find these names, though," Greaves said, and pointed again to the lists.

The clerk shrugged. "And I told you that I am very busy."

"What are you called?" Greaves asked.

"Giovanni Ianiero."

Greaves repeated the name to himself. "That sounds familiar to me. I think it's the same as a Communist agitator that we have on our books."

"I'm no Communist," the clerk said, his tone flat and undeterred.

"I didn't say that you were. But it would be too bad if someone were to make a mistake. It happens sometimes, you know." Greaves pushed the papers towards him.

For a moment the clerk remained where he was, cigarette smoke curling from the corner of his mouth. Then he nodded, picked up the names, and walked away.

Greaves dropped his cigarette onto the floor and ground it out with the heel of his boot. He had learned early on that sometimes the Naples police needed to be coaxed into doing their job.

Cioffi hadn't given much consideration to his plan not working. In fact, he'd been quite confident. But the doubt Lello had expressed the night before had worked on his thoughts and he wasn't so certain anymore. What if Tenente Greaves did not even recognize him? They had only met on one occasion, and that was more than a month ago now, when his uncle had caught him skulking around the museum. Cioffi had come upon the two of them as they left the gallery on the mezzanine that housed the bust of Seneca. His uncle hadn't bothered to ask him what he was doing there, nor had he inquired as to how he'd gotten in past the *carabiniere* guarding the entrance. He'd just given him a disappointed look and then, even though he could probably smell the wine on his breath, had introduced Cioffi to the *tenente*, because regardless of whatever his nephew had become, Augusto Parente was always a proper gentleman, and proper gentlemen made introductions.

He waited now—and worried—in the shadow of the monument in Piazza dei Martiri. If he could not get the *tenente* on his side, what would he do? He could not go to his uncle himself; he could get past the guard, but he would never get past Luisa.

Across from where he sat was the headquarters of the British security police. It was housed in a palazzo that was made conspicuous not only by its lesser size but also by its pale yellow brickwork and the crumbling state of its top floor, which had been damaged during the naval bombardments of late summer. Strangely, it was the only building on the square that had suffered so.

As he sat there, a sharp pain gripped his bowels. For breakfast that morning he had shared a pot of boiled sea urchins with Lello. They'd come from a fellow that Lello knew who worked in the kitchen of a restaurant on the Lungomare. It was obvious by the pungent, fishy stink that the urchins were spoilt. Not even the last clove of garlic from Lello's bare pantry could mask their rottenness. And their rancid taste filled his mouth again. He needed a drink to wash it away.

Then he saw the *tenente* coming through the square from Via Santa Caterina. He moved with a loose-limbed stride that Cioffi envied. What it must be like, he thought, to have so few cares.

He stood up and checked his coat, brushed a spot of lint from his lapel. He crossed the square towards the courtyard gate. "Tenente Greaves," he called out, and then faltered when the man turned and stared at him, as if taking a quick mental inventory in an effort to place him.

"I am *dottore* Aldo Cioffi, *tenente*. My uncle is Augusto Parente."

"Yes, of course. How are you, *dottore?*"

Cioffi sighed. "Sometimes I am good. Sometimes I am not so good." He smiled weakly. "At the moment, I am afraid, I am not so good."

"I'm sorry to hear that. Is there anything I can do?"

"Yes," Cioffi said, and ran a smoothing hand down the front of his jacket. He did his best to sound solemn. "I must talk with you. It is a delicate matter, *tenente.*"

"Is that right?"

Cioffi nodded, and then glanced about. "We can go somewhere, maybe? Perhaps we will have a drink?"

Greaves watched as the *dottore* finished off his third glass of *limoncello* in a single, swift gulp, then motioned to the barman to pour him another.

From the side, Aldo Cioffi looked a young man. With his high cheekbones and patrician nose, his dark hair and gently sloping forehead, he was very nearly handsome. But the handsomeness quickly faded and he appeared very much older when seen straight on: his cheeks were drawn and sagged into jowls; grey speckled his stubbly beard; and his eyes, jaundiced, were set deep in darkened sockets. His actual age, Greaves recalled from his police file, was only thirty-one, but anyone would be hard pressed to guess it.

Cioffi held up his fresh glass and in a maudlin tone pronounced: "'*Soltanto i morti vedranno la fine della guerra.*'"

"'Only the dead will see the end of war,'" Greaves said. "Plato. I see that you are as fond of quotations as your uncle."

"Yes," said Cioffi. "My grandfather was the same. It is a weakness, I suppose. Always speaking the words of great men, in the hope of sounding great ourselves."

A bout of laughter rose from the far end of the bar and Greaves glanced over his shoulder. There were three men, two old and bent-backed, the third younger, short, and broad-shouldered, with a thick, squarish head, close-cropped hair, and a pale pink scar curving from the corner of his mouth like an extended smile. He had noticed him come in a short while earlier. He'd stood the other two a round of drinks. Greaves caught his eye and nodded and the young man acknowledged the greeting.

"Do you see that, *tenente*?" Cioffi was pointing across the square towards the bay.

"You mean Castel dell'Ovo?" Greaves said.

"Yes, that's right. Castel dell'Ovo. It means the Castle of the Egg. Now of course, *tenente*, you also know the poet Virgil."

"Yes, *dottore*. I know Virgil."

"Ah." Cioffi raised a finger. "But did you know that Virgil was also a sorcerer? He practised *la magia bianca*—the white magic. You see ..." Cioffi held out his hand, cupped like a bowl. "He put a spell upon an egg. And this egg he placed into the foundation of the castle. Now, we are told that if this egg is ever broken"—here Cioffi snapped his hand closed—"then Napoli will be destroyed." He laughed and shook his head. "I think, *tenente*, maybe it is broken already, no?"

The conversation so far had touched not only on Virgil but also on the Caffè Gambrinus, a place that seemed very dear to the *dottore's* heart, as well as the Rinascente, the San Carlo opera house, and the proliferation of brothels in the traditionally middle-class quarters of the city, a sign, Cioffi had remarked with a grin, of a socialist shift in Neapolitan society. Because Greaves found the *dottore* amusing, he didn't mind so much being played for drinks. Judging from the sorry state of the man, Greaves thought he could do with a little charity. But even charity had its limits.

"Perhaps, *dottore*," he said, "we should talk about your situation."

"Yes, of course, *tenente*. I am taking up your valuable time."

"Well, I do have other things to attend to."

Cioffi nodded. "I understand. I will get to my point, then." He took another sip of his drink and set the glass down on the bar. "You must understand, *tenente*," he began, "that for some time now my relationship with my uncle has been not so very good. He does not approve of the way I have chosen to live my life. He believes that I have squandered my talents, and this may be true. And my mother, his sister—I broke her heart, you see. She wanted a son that would make her proud, but instead she ended up with me. I was not even there when she died, and I don't think Augusto has ever forgiven me for that." The *dottore* hesitated.

"Go on," said Greaves.

Cioffi fiddled with his glass. Then he said, "I want you to speak to my uncle for me, *tenente*."

"You want me to talk to the *professore*? About what?"

"I know that he is hiring men to work at the *museo*. You must understand, *tenente*, I know the place better than anyone. I know it almost as well as Augusto does himself."

"You're asking me to help you get a job at the museum?"

"Yes, that is what I am asking."

"Why not just talk to your uncle yourself?" said Greaves.

"You, he trusts," said Cioffi.

"And you, he doesn't?"

The *dottore* shrugged. "I am afraid that I have used up most of the goodwill he had for me."

Looking at him in his ragged coat, his trousers held up with a length of twine, his bare feet in his battered shoes, Greaves didn't doubt that he had used up the goodwill of a great many others too.

"I don't know," said Greaves. "If your uncle feels the way you say he does, I'm really not sure that my talking to him is going to change that."

"Please, *tenente*," Cioffi said, and pressed his hands together. "I am desperate. There is nothing for me. I have no way to make a living."

"But you're a doctor."

"In name only, and hardly that. There are a thousand men like me in Naples—men with titles but no qualifications. And I have been branded by false accusation. I have a police record."

On that account, the *dottore* was telling the truth. Greaves remembered reading the entry in his file.

"I don't think I can help you, *dottore*. That accusation, false or not, is still on record. It's unlikely that you would pass the vetting procedure."

"But you could take care of that for me, couldn't you, *tenente*?"

"You mean I could look the other way?"

Tears began to well up in the *dottore's* eyes. "I have nothing, *tenente*. This is the only hope left to me."

Greaves was uncomfortable. He found the *dottore's* display embarrassing. "I tell you what," he said. "I'll be speaking to your uncle later today. I will mention our conversation to him."

Cioffi's face brightened. He took hold of Greaves's hand and pumped it excitedly. "Oh, thank you, *tenente*. Thank you."

"I am going to leave the decision up to him, *dottore*, so I wouldn't get my hopes up if I were you. If I've learned anything about your uncle, it's that he's stubborn. If he does not want you, I'm not going to push it."

"Of course, *tenente*. I understand."

Greaves stood up. He ordered the *dottore* another drink and then paid the barman.

"And how will I know his decision?" Cioffi asked. "Should I come see you again, perhaps?"

"Why don't you give it a day or two," Greaves said, "then drop by the museum. If the *carabiniere* lets you in, then you'll have your answer."

Aldo Cioffi crossed Piazza dei Martiri towards Via Santa Caterina. His stomach was settled considerably now that his head was swimming with drink. It was like the comfort of a warm blanket on a cold, damp night.

Things had gone well.

He stopped outside the window of a butcher's shop near the Ponte di Chiaia. On the other side of the glass a collection of wooden bowls had been laid out in the display case. He saw intestines and chicken heads, a liver that looked too small to have come from any reasonable sort of livestock, and a mound of sweetbreads that glistened and attracted flies. Cioffi thought of the donkey Maggio had killed—it would have been so much better fare than what was on offer here.

After a moment, he sensed someone standing behind him. He looked up and saw the young man's reflection in the butcher's window. Cioffi recognized him from the taverna. He turned around and smiled. "I haven't any money," he said, "if that's what you're after. It was my friend who bought the drinks. And if you must know, he is with the security police. So, I suggest—"

"What's your name?"

"My name?"

The young man took hold of Cioffi's elbow and squeezed tightly. "I asked you a question."

Cioffi could not keep the grimace from his face. It felt as if the bones in his arm might shatter. His fingers began to tingle. "My name is Aldo Cioffi," he said. "Dottore Aldo Cioffi. Please, sir, you are hurting me."

The young man let go of his elbow. Then he turned and walked away. He crossed over the street and disappeared down a side alley. Cioffi massaged his bruised arm and looked about. No one seemed to have taken any notice. He wasn't even certain himself what had happened, but he knew that no good ever came from strangers approaching you in the street. His sense of fear came in a cold wave of nausea and he shuddered, the *limoncello* churning in his guts, stirring up the foul residue of the urchins. He turned back towards the butcher's shop window and retched a puddle of vomit onto the pavement at his feet. The stink of his sick made him retch again.

There was a banging on the glass, and he looked up to see the *macellaio* standing there in his bloodied apron, waving him away.

Cioffi wiped his mouth with the back of his hand and straightened up. The *macellaio* shook his fist. Cioffi watched him a moment, then looked off again in the direction the young man had gone.

Greaves telephoned the museum from the section office. He suggested to Parente dinner at Zi' Teresa's on the seafront, where they could discuss the list of possible employees. He invited Luisa Gennaro to join them.

He met their car at the causeway that led out to the marina and had the MPs shift the barrier so that they could drive through; a private car left at the curbside on the Lungomare would not last long before it was stolen.

The restaurant was crowded with military personnel—mainly officers from the Free French Naval Forces, who seemed to have commandeered the eatery as their unofficial club.

Parente appointed himself as Greaves's guide to the wonders of the local cuisine. They sampled a number of specialties, beginning with Spaghetti con le Vongole, followed by Frutti di Mare, Pesce all'Acqua Pazza, and Sartù di Riso. To drink, it was two bottles of Lacrima Christi. "The tears of Christ," Parente said, "and as sweet as heaven."

Greaves went through the curator's list as they ate. There were only a few names that had to be struck off—fellows whose desperate situations had seen them run afoul of the law on too many occasions. They whittled the list down to ten men who passed muster. All of them had worked for the *professore* at some time in the past, and Parente felt they could be trusted.

Afterwards, while they were drinking real coffee and sipping honey grappa, Greaves said: "By the way, I spoke to your nephew this afternoon."

"You talked to Aldo?" said Parente.

"Yes. We had drinks at the Bar Vittoria."

"How is he?"

"He's had better days," said Greaves. "He wanted me to speak with you. He knows that you're hiring men. He wants a job."

"And he could not ask me himself?"

"I got the impression that he thought you wouldn't see him."

Parente shook his head and looked out of the window to where the beggars had gathered on the quayside. There was a woman, middle-aged, wearing a dark habit, and gathered around her were a number of children dressed in rags.

"He should have come to me."

Luisa, who had remained quiet all through dinner—aloof, almost, Greaves thought—now put her hand on Parente's forearm. "You do not have to help him, Augusto," she said.

Parente raised his eyebrows and shrugged. Then he nodded towards the window. "Look at them out there, Thomas," he said.

Greaves saw the collection of unfortunate things: some club-footed, others with twisted spines and malformed limbs. One of them, a blind girl of perhaps seven, sat off on her own, feeling the ground for bits of stone that she then put into her mouth.

"When the Americans arrived," Parente said, "there was a banquet held at the Palazzo Reale in honour of General Clark. It was a tribute to the man who had come to save our poor city. When they asked him what it was that he wished to eat, he told them that he would like to eat fish. After all, we are famous for our seafood. But, you see, the harbour was still mined and all the boats had been ordered to stay in port. So, instead, they went to the Stazione Zoologica. Unfortunately, the aquariums had already been emptied. You must remember that the city was starving. The only thing left was a single baby manatee. So it was butchered and cooked with garlic and tomatoes. And the general ate it. He and his staff—his colonels, his majors, his captains—between them they ate the entire manatee. I was there—I watched them with my own eyes." Parente sipped his coffee and sighed. "So, you see, Thomas, this is what you need to know about Napoli: some people get to eat fish, and some people do not." He patted Luisa's hand. "She does not like it when I tell that story, because whenever I do, it means that I am going to do something foolish."

Luisa pulled her hand away from Parente's and stared coldly at Greaves. "Why are you doing this?" The note of accusation in her voice caught him off guard. "What has he done to deserve such generosity? Has he turned someone in to you? Has he agreed to inform on old friends? What?"

"It's not like that at all," said Greaves. "He seemed a little down on his luck. I just thought I might be able to help him out."

"Is that what you do, *tenente*? You are the good Samaritan?"

Her anger seemed all out of proportion to him. He had somehow insulted her, but in what way he did not know.

She stood up from the table. "I have a cousin," she went on, glaring down at him. "She sleeps with soldiers for favours. Her husband has left her and gone north with the Germans. She was thrown out of her home. Would you help her too? Or is it just thieving drunks that you pity?"

"Please, Luisa," Parente said.

She ignored him and began to gather together the scraps of their meal and put them into a folded napkin. "It will be curfew soon," she said to Parente. "I will wait for you outside."

As she left, the old man smiled in apology.

"She really doesn't like me, does she?" Greaves said.

Parente shook his head. "It's Aldo she doesn't like. You she does not trust."

"I don't know why. I haven't given her any reason, have I?"

"It's not your fault, Thomas. You are a soldier, and in Luisa's mind, that means you are the war. And it is the war that has taken everything from her."

They watched her through the window as she approached the woman in the habit. She pressed the napkin of leftovers into her hand. As the woman kissed her cheeks, Greaves was suddenly glad that he had not brought up the music box.

Parente watched out of the passenger-side window. It was growing dark and the curfew was less than an hour away, but still the pavements were crowded. In the streets soldiers moved in packs, like wolves on the prowl. They were loud and drunk, and they commanded the roadsides, pushing others towards the curbs. Women loitered in the mouths of the alleys, old men stood in doorways, and young boys sat on window ledges, all of them watching, all of them waiting. Waiting, Parente supposed, for the cover of dark—to do what, though, he didn't like to imagine.

He turned in his seat and looked at Luisa. She steered the battered Berlina—the car was registered to the museum—with calm precision along the busy street. She had always been a good driver, and Parente had always preferred being a passenger.

She glanced over at him. "What's wrong?" she said.

"You shouldn't be so rude to him," said Parente.

"To who?"

"You know who I'm talking about."

Luisa shrugged. "No, I don't."

"To Thomas. You should not be so rude to Thomas. He is not like the others, you know that."

"And why do you think that? Because he takes us to dinner? Because he brings you sugar and chocolate? Because he's willing to help Aldo, who we both know is a drunk and a thief and who will always disappoint you no matter how much you hope otherwise? He is a security policeman, Augusto. And in the end, you will mean nothing to him. If they tell him to arrest you, he will do it without a second thought."

Parente shook his head and looked out of the window again. As they passed through Piazza Trento e Trieste, he watched as a man picked the pockets of a British naval officer who was occupied by the attentions of a young woman in a floral print dress. While she rubbed her palm against the front of the sailor's trousers, her partner lifted his billfold.

"I think you are wrong about him, Luisa," Parente said. "I think he is different. There is something about him. It's like a sadness."

"A sadness?" said Luisa.

"I don't know. I think there is good in him. And I think if you gave him a chance, you might think the same."

Luisa did not respond. When a soldier stumbled into the roadway, she sounded the horn and yelled out of the window at him. Parente reached out and touched her hand that held white-knuckle tight to the steering wheel.

"Is everything all right?" he asked. "How is Maria?"

He felt the tension release somewhat in the grip. She sighed. "When I got home last night," she said, "I found her with a black eye and a split lip."

"Is she okay?"

"She's fine," said Luisa. Then she looked at him out of the corner of her eye. "It's true what I said, though, Augusto. She is selling herself. She's a *puttana*."

"Are you certain, Luisa?"

"Yes, Augusto, I'm certain."

They continued in silence for a time, and then Parente said: "Perhaps Thomas *will* be able to help."

Luisa laughed quietly to herself. She drove the car through Piazza Francese and passed Teatro Mercandante, then down the narrow street that led to her apartment house. She pulled the car to the curb.

"Will you be okay from here?" she said.

Parente told her that he would. He climbed out of the passenger side and went around the front of the car. Luisa held the door for him. It took him a moment to settle behind the wheel. He knew that working the clutch was going to aggravate his sciatica, but he did not let on.

"Do you know," she said, looking down at him, "sometimes you put too much faith in people." She closed the door.

He lowered the window, reached out, and gently caught her arm. When she turned back, he said, "And sometimes," he said, "you put too little."

FIVE

Another unseasonably warm day brought people to the Villa Comunale, where they strolled the avenues free, for a few hours at least, of the squalor of their unlit, broken homes. There was the sound of birds in the trees, and of gulls floating on the gentle breeze coming in from the bay. On a bench inside the main gates, a storyteller stood waving his arms about, and children gathered on the pavement before him, their mothers watching on. When the storyteller, a man in his mid-fifties with scruffy whiskers and a dark, threadbare suit, drew his arms up above his head, the children leaned forward, as if pulled on a string. And when he thrust his arms out in front of him, fingers wagging, and made the howling sound of a great wind, the children shrank back again, clutching themselves, and shrieked in fearful delight.

Salvatore Varone, sitting on a nearby bench, said to the police clerk at his side: "Do you know this tale he's telling?"

"Of course I do," the clerk said. "We heard it when we were kids in school."

"And what do you think of it?"

"I think it's shit."

"Yes," said Varone. "I thought you would."

He studied the clerk. The man had taken care to brush his dark blue uniform; he had polished his buttons, too. But the epaulettes, and the braiding that ran over the right shoulder, were dingy, the white silk gone grey. It was this lack of thoroughness that told Varone all he needed to know about the clerk: he was inconsistent. Just the sort of policeman that Varone liked.

"Tell me what you know."

"There is still the matter of payment," said the clerk.

Varone glanced over to where Paolo stood near the tall iron fence. He nodded. Paolo came over to the bench and withdrew a soiled envelope from inside his coat. He passed it to the clerk, who opened the envelope and looked inside.

"I should count it, maybe," he said.

"If you like," said Varone. He waited as the man counted the money, feeling each note, before folding the envelope and putting it in his breast pocket.

"He trained as a doctor," the clerk said. "There is no record of him having practised, but that isn't unusual. From a well-to-do family—made their money in the garment industry. Parents died some time ago, no siblings. And no family riches left, either. All spent on the bottle, it would seem. In thirty-eight he served a few days in Poggio Reale for being a red propagandist, but I would guess that was probably just bad luck. He doesn't seem the type that would actually be involved in anything of substance. A few other charges for public drunkenness and causing a disturbance—that sort of thing." He shrugged. "I don't know why you would be interested in this man. He is nothing—a nobody."

Varone watched a small black lizard creep out onto the seat of the bench to warm its belly on the stone. He reached slowly into his pocket and took out a piece of biscotti. He broke off a crumb and placed it on the seat a few inches from the lizard.

"That is your opinion, is it?" he said.

"It is," said the clerk.

"And you are confident in it?"

"I am, yes. Fully confident."

"Then maybe you can tell me why this man—who you say is a nobody—spends his time talking to the security police?"

"Are you sure about this?" the clerk asked.

"If I say it's so," said Varone, "it is so."

The lizard's head twitched. It began to inch itself forward, and when it did, Varone brought his hand quickly down on top of it, cupping it against the stone. Then he pinched his fingers together at the base of the lizard's skull and picked it up.

"How should I know why he is talking to them?" the clerk said, and shifted slightly away. "They don't tell us anything. They think we are a joke."

"And are you?" said Varone. "Are you a joke?"

The clerk straightened his tunic. "No, we are not. Maybe he is telling them stories, like this one here." He motioned towards the storyteller, who was stamping now on the other bench and making noises like a lion.

"Perhaps," Varone said. "Perhaps."

The lizard hissed between his fingers.

"Do you know that some lizards, when they lose their tail, they can grow it back?"

"I've heard that," said the clerk.

Varone looked at the clerk and smiled. "Unfortunately, this isn't one of them."

With the thumb and middle finger of his free hand, he pinched off the lizard's tail. The creature twisted madly and drops of blood fell onto the leg of Varone's trousers.

"Our friend here," he said, "will have to run if he wishes to survive.

If he can run long enough, his wound will heal and he will live. If he cannot, he will be killed and eaten."

Varone set the lizard on the ground and watched it scurry towards a clump of shrubbery, an uneven red stain, like a shaky brush stroke, marking its path. Then he leaned across and took the envelope from the clerk's pocket. He removed a single note from within and called Paolo over again. He gave him the note and said: "Give it to the storyteller." Then he put the envelope into his own pocket.

"Give me your hand," he said to the clerk. He put the severed lizard's tail into the man's palm, where it continued to squirm, like a leech doused with salt. "You will find out what this *dottore* has been saying to the security police."

The clerk stared at the wriggling, bloody stump in his hand. "But how?" he said.

Varone closed the clerk's fingers over the lizard's broken tail. "You seem like a resourceful man to me. I'm sure that you'll find a way."

"And if I can't get you the information?"

Varone let go of the clerk's hand and stood up from the bench. He wiped away the blood on his fingers with a clean white handkerchief.

"How fast can you run?" he said.

After mess was the morning briefing. Sergeants Bennington and Jones brought the major up to speed on their investigations into the wire cutting—not an organized operation, it seemed, but merely coincidence: residents in the Spaccanapoli district were taking advantage of a scale-back in military police patrols to help themselves to the telephone cable that had been laid by the engineers the month before; the copper wiring was sold off to black market scrap traders. A few suspects had been brought in for questioning, but as they were no longer in possession of the stolen wire, they'd been released, though there were still a number of leads to be followed. Sergeant Roylance and Corporal Blair were both scheduled to give testimony at the Castel Capuano courts against suspects who had been denounced by their neighbours. Corporal Philbin reported that there was little of interest in the file boxes collected from FSHQ, and Greaves confirmed that the same was true of the names he'd chased down at the Questura.

When the briefing was finished, every man went his separate way. Major Woodard took the staff car and headed for a meeting at GHQ at Caserta, and Bennington and Jones struck out for the British officers' club to take advantage of the major's absence and to delay what they knew would be another fruitless canvas of the Spaccanapoli. Philbin left on one of the section's two motorbikes for Field Security HQ at Castellammare with the weekly dispatch, leaving Greaves to see to the petitioners.

He collected a box of sharpened pencils, two notebooks, a number of string files, and the ledger and brought them to the table that had been set up in the courtyard. Before he opened the gate, he organized the small crowd waiting there into a queue, giving each person a number written on a sheet of paper torn from one of the notebooks, ignoring the warning *No erasures, No pages to be detached* written on its cover. Then he sat down and called the first person.

Twice a week the section opened its doors to civilians, and Greaves split the duties of liaison officer with Sergeant Jones. In the first weeks after the occupation it was *dottori* and *ingegneri*, *avvocati* and *professori* who presented themselves, credentials in hand, and tendered their services as translators and informants. But in the months since, the traffic to 803 FSS had been almost solely of those seeking retribution—against old enemies and new; against neighbours and business rivals and relatives and strangers; against anyone who, with cause or without, they perceived had done them wrong. And every Tuesday morning Greaves listened to them, made notes, assured each that he would look into their accusation. And when he had taken in all of the numbered pieces of paper he'd distributed, he closed the gate and told those who had arrived in the meantime that they would have to return on Thursday, when they would become Sergeant Jones's headache.

The last petitioner dealt with, Greaves gathered his notes together and put them into his satchel. Then he climbed aboard the section's second motorbike and left for the Questura.

On his way to the central police station, he detoured to the museum. He took Via Roma and weaved his way through the troop transports, jeeps, and dull green sedans with white stars painted on their doors that shared the crowded roadway with the drays and the handcarts. The air reverberated with the sound of horn blasts and gunning engines. When he reached the museum, he parked the motorbike at the curbside.

The *carabiniere* guarding the front entrance nodded as he came up the steps. "Checking up on the *professore* so soon?" he said.

"No," replied Greaves, and reached into his satchel and took out the envelope on which he had neatly printed Luisa's name. He held it out to the policeman. "I was hoping you might give this to Signora Gennaro for me."

The *carabiniere* took the envelope and turned it over in his hands, then looked back at Greaves. "It is a love letter, maybe?"

"Actually," said Greaves, "it's official business."

"Then why don't you deliver it yourself? I'm not an errand boy."

"Look," said Greaves, "I'm in a bit of a hurry. Would you just make sure that she gets it?"

"Have you got a cigarette for me?"

Greaves took one out and gave it to him. "You won't forget?"

The *carabiniere* shrugged. Greaves handed him the rest of the packet. The policeman grinned and said, "The first chance I get."

Cioffi shifted restlessly in his chair. On the table between them was a plate of *sfogliatelle*. Abruzzi picked up one of the pastries and took a bite; he wiped away a spot of cream from the corner of his mouth. Then he said: "Help yourself, *dottore*."

Cioffi grabbed for the plate. He put an entire pastry into his mouth, and then took another.

"You'll find that I am a fair man, *dottore*," Abruzzi said. "If you can deliver what you promise, then I will take care of you."

Cioffi looked up at him, his cheeks full, and waited to hear what might happen if he didn't deliver on his promise; but Abruzzi did not elaborate. Instead, the young man turned his attention to the crowded dining room of the small restaurant. Interspersed among the soldiers were several refugees from the city's middle class, sitting wan-faced at their tables sipping chicory coffee and doing their best not to appear destitute.

"We're getting a better class of beggar in here," he said.

Cioffi glanced around. "Beggars are beggars."

"That's true, *dottore*," Abruzzi said. He laid his hands flat on the table. "When do you see your uncle?"

"I will go tomorrow morning."

Abruzzi grinned. "The fox in the henhouse, eh? Now, tell me again about this man who approached you. He asked only your name?"

"Yes. But he was very threatening. He very nearly broke my arm."

"Stocky, with a big square head like a block of marble?"

"Yes, that's right. His hair was dark and cut very short."

"And he had a scar on his cheek?" Abruzzi said. "You're sure of that?"

"Like a crescent moon. Do you know who he is?"

"Paolo Fortuna. He belongs to Salvatore Varone."

Cioffi stopped chewing. He could feel the colour drain from his face. "Salvatore Varone. But what does he want from me?"

"From you?" said Abruzzi. He laughed and reached across the table and took the half-eaten pastry from Cioffi's hand. "He doesn't want anything from you, *dottore*. It's me that he's after."

SIX

Luisa sat on the arm of the red leather chair and looked down at her cousin perched on the edge of the seat cushion. Maria was nervous and picked at the tips of her nails, searching out flaws in the polish. The anteroom was less than half full now. The interviews had been going on for well over two hours, and before that the hopeful had stood a further hour outside in the street, waiting for the American officer to come out with his clipboard and take down their names.

Luisa had found out about the new officers' club the Americans were opening up in the Banco di Napoli building from the letter that Tenente Greaves had left with the *carabiniere* at the front entrance of the museum four days earlier. There were, the *tenente* wrote, openings for waitresses and cashiers. He'd included in the envelope a reference attesting to the suitability of Maria's qualifications; it was typed out on security police stationery.

There must have been a hundred women applying for the handful of positions. They came with their hair fixed, makeup on their faces, wearing the best dresses in their ever-shrinking wardrobes, doing their utmost to conceal the hunger that rumbled their bellies. It was better not to appear too needy. The soldier, a corporal in a pressed khaki uniform who sat at the desk outside the captain's office, watched them, making no secret of his interest: he had already spoken to many of the women, making sure that the prettier of them went into the office first. If Maria had noticed this, she didn't let on to Luisa. She had spent so much time trying to look her best. She'd changed her dress three times, combed out her hair so that it lay in a wave over her shoulders, put on rouge and lipstick, her good black shoes with the thick heels. She had even unbuttoned herself to show her cleavage.

"There are only ugly girls left."

"Don't talk like that," said Luisa.

Maria let out a sigh. "I don't want to do this."

Luisa ran a gentle hand over her cousin's long dark hair. "You'll see. It will be better this way."

They had argued the night before, and that morning too. Maria had cried, but Luisa would not back down. She told her that she would have to leave the apartment if she did not agree. The other tenants were talking, she'd said, and what Maria was doing was shameful. It had made Luisa feel sick to her stomach to take sides against her cousin; she had done so because she wanted Maria to be safe. She only hoped that her cousin, in time, would understand this. Even now, the faint shadow of bruising showed through the powder below Maria's left eye.

The door to the office opened and a young woman emerged. The captain, who had earlier taken down their names, held her by the arm. With him was the interpreter, a middle-aged man with neatly oiled hair and wearing a dark suit with a pale yellow tie. He fit well with the surroundings: he had the arrogance of a loans clerk. The young woman began to cry, and the captain turned to the interpreter and said: "Will you please tell her that making a scene won't help matters."

The interpreter bowed politely and then, in a harsh voice, told the young woman to get herself back onto the street where she belonged because his American friends weren't in the business of hiring whores.

The young woman wiped away her tears. She gathered herself and strode through the waiting room and out into the corridor.

Pleased with himself, the interpreter cast an eye about the room. He noticed Luisa watching him. "What are you looking at?" he demanded.

In precise but accented English, she answered: "A coward."

This caught the captain's attention. "What did you say?" he asked her.

Luisa felt Maria squeeze her leg, and she let her unfriendly stare linger a moment longer on the interpreter. Then she said: "It is nothing. I wonder only when my cousin will be called."

The captain picked up the clipboard from the corporal's desk. "What's the name?"

"Maria Rosetta Bello."

He ran his finger down the page, and then frowned at the corporal. "I should already have seen this woman."

"Is that right," replied the corporal, unconcerned. "My mistake, I guess."

"Well, I'll see her now, then." He dropped the clipboard onto the desk. "If you'll follow me, Signora Bello."

He turned back into his office. The interpreter stood holding the door as Maria got to her feet and smoothed the hem of her dress. She touched her hand to her hair and then looked anxiously at Luisa.

"Don't forget this," Luisa said, and handed her the *tenente's* letter. "Just give it to them. And if they ask what it was that you were doing before, you tell them that you were an assistant at the Museo Archeologico and you lost your job because of cutbacks. Mention Augusto's name. They can contact him if they wish. He will speak on your behalf."

Maria hugged her and Luisa felt the flutter of her heart and smelled the delicate tang of her perspiration.

"I'm frightened," Maria said.

"You'll be fine," said Luisa. "I will be right here waiting for you."

Maria let go of her embrace and took a deep breath. Then she turned and walked into the office, ignoring the fawning welcome of the interpreter, who glanced once more at Luisa before closing the door.

Quonset huts stretched the length of the Mostra fairgrounds, at the far end of which stood the whitewashed exhibition hall, looking like a shrunken Moorish palace complete with minarets and palm-shaded gardens. Mussolini had built the complex to house the world's fair, but the war had scuttled his plans. Looking about, Greaves thought they could be in Oran or Mers el-Kébir rather than on the outskirts of Naples.

"I liked North Africa better," said the chief clerk. He was glad to be out of his office and wandering the compound with Greaves. "We were at Bou Hanifia then. Great place. It was a resort hotel. You could lie on the beach, go for a swim—sip drinks and dance with French ladies."

"It must have been nice," Greaves said.

"There wasn't much action then. We were just pretty much sitting around waiting. But here ..." He shook his head. "Here, we've got them coming in from Cassino and the Liri valley, and now Anzio too. Not to mention all the ones getting themselves stabbed or shot down in the city, fighting over women and booze. And that's part of the problem, lieutenant. The more we've got coming in, the more supplies we're going to need to fix them. That means bigger shipments, and when you've got bigger shipments ... I mean, Christ Almighty, lieutenant, this is Naples. If it isn't nailed down, then someone's gonna steal it. You should know that."

They passed by two white-coated army surgeons who stood smoking cigarettes beside an empty oil drum.

"Mostly it's the morphine they're after."

"Any idea who it is that we're talking about?" asked Greaves.

The chief clerk shrugged. "Could be anybody. There are some small-time operators who steal from the storerooms or the wards—orderlies, nurses, even some of the doctors probably. They off-load it to guys in Piazza Garibaldi, I suppose. But that's to be expected. Happens in any hospital, even stateside. The stuff you're talking about, though, that's different. Diverting entire shipments, hijacking loads—that's organized, that's Al Capone stuff. That's the ginzoes."

They stepped into one of the Quonset huts. The smell of the place was immediate: the sour pong of infection mingled with the sharp scent of liniments and salves and the earthy fragrance of the human waste collecting in bedpans and catheter basins.

A woman in her mid-forties, with ruddy cheeks and a heavy bosom that strained the fabric of her pale blue uniform, looked up from a desk in the corner. While the chief clerk chatted with her, Greaves looked through the split in the curtain that divided the small nursing station from the rest of the ward. On the other side of the curtain, where the smell was much stronger, there were three rows of canvas cots, perhaps forty-five in all. Several faces turned towards him, staring blankly, and he was struck by an odd thought: it was of a photograph he had seen in a copy of *Life* magazine that showed an American Red Cross worker handing out candy and cigarettes to bedridden soldiers; there were smiles on the soldiers' faces, as if the small gifts were enough to ease the pain of their wounds. But by the look of the men in these beds, limbs encased in plaster, bandages wrapped about their heads, tubes draining their bodies, it didn't seem likely that any amount of chocolate or tobacco would bring them relief.

The nurse came from behind her desk and pulled the curtain closed. "We're not running a sideshow here," she said.

Greaves apologized, then followed the chief clerk back out into the sunshine.

"I really don't know what else to tell you, lieutenant," he said. He nodded at the surrounding Quonset huts. "In the end, all that matters is that these boys here get what they need. And so far, that hasn't been a problem. Until it is, I don't think you're gonna have much luck finding anything out."

Greaves held out his hand. "Thanks for your time. You've been very helpful."

"Not at all," said the chief clerk. He shook Greaves's hand and then wandered back off towards his office.

It had been three days since Cioffi had taken a drink, and they'd felt like the hardest three days of his life. It was worst at night, when he shivered and sweated himself to sleep on the floor in Lello's salotto. He had bad dreams, too. Horrifying visions of being chased down darkened alleyways. He never saw who it was that pursued him, only heard their footfalls—heavy and ringing, as if they wore iron-soled boots. And always, just when he thought he had gotten free of them, Renzo Abruzzi stepped from the shadows, the blade of his knife catching a glint of light before he plunged it home, driving it deep and twisting, cutting through entrails and scraping against bone. The night before when he'd had the dream, he felt the warmth of his blood as it pooled beneath him, only to wake up a moment later to find that he had wet himself.

Being sober was a misery to him—but a misery, for the time being, he was willing to suffer. He needed Augusto to believe that he had changed. It was the only way he could get the old man to trust him enough to leave him alone. Since he'd been working at the museum, his uncle had hardly left his side. He hovered over him while he struggled alongside the others, hauling crates up from the cellar vaults and dragging them through the galleries. It seemed to Cioffi as if everything were made of stone. Even the packing straw was heavy to him. The day before, he'd grown faint while unloading a trundle cart of crated mosaics and dropped one of the boxes. It split open, but nothing, in the end, got broken.

Now, as he waited in his uncle's office, he felt a slight dizziness again at the prospect of another day of slogging and another day without drink. He went to the desk and opened the drawer where he remembered Augusto had always hidden a bottle of sweet amaretto. Perhaps just a sip, he thought—a taste to see him through. Then he heard his uncle's voice behind him.

"I know what you're looking for, Aldo. I don't keep it there anymore."

Cioffi closed the drawer and turned around. He smiled. "Maybe some coffee, then."

"I have some brewed," said his uncle. "Sit down. I will bring it to you."

Cioffi did as he was told. He watched as the old man went to the field stove and poured out a single cup. He noticed that Augusto moved more slowly today. His back was bothering him again. Cioffi had never imagined that the day could come when his uncle would not be able to take care of himself. He had always been so strong, so vibrant. An ox of a man, who scrabbled his way over the ruins long after other men the same age had retired to café terraces to bore people with stories of their younger selves. Now his hand shook as he passed Cioffi the cup.

"You know, Aldo, I'm proud of you." Augusto hobbled around his desk to sit down. "I didn't think you would be such a hard worker."

"I always knew I could be good at something, uncle."

"Oh, you aren't good at it," Augusto said. "You're a hard worker, yes—but not good." He started to laugh. "In fact, you are very nearly hopeless."

Cioffi set his cup down. "But, uncle—"

"Come, now, don't look so surprised. Face it, Aldo: you weren't built for hard labour. It's just not in you."

"What am I to do, then?"

Augusto got up from behind his desk and went to a high bookcase in the corner of the room. From a middle shelf he collected several ledgers bound in black leather. He brought them back to the desk.

"You will help me to inventory the collections. The heaviest thing you will have to lift," he said, holding up a ledger, "is one of these. Do you think you can manage that?"

Cioffi came to the desk. He picked up one of the ledgers. It felt light in his hand. This, he thought to himself, must be the weight of luck.

Luisa waited outside the courtyard gate. The *tenente*, she'd been told by one of the *inglese* soldiers inside, was expected back soon. He had offered her a seat in the foyer, but she politely declined, preferring, though of course she did not say so, the street to his company.

When she heard the rumble of the motorbike coming across the square, she looked up. Tenente Greaves was not wearing his cap and his dark hair was mussed, and there was colour in his cheeks from the wind of the ride. All of which made him look much younger to her. He brought the motorbike to a stop before her and turned the engine off.

"Signora Gennaro," he said. "Is everything all right?"

"I came to thank you, *tenente*. For what you did."

"Your cousin," he said. "The new American officers' club. Did she get a position?"

"Yes. She will start working next week. She will be a cashier."

"That's great. I'm glad to hear it." He looked past her towards the courtyard, and then said: "I haven't got anything pressing to do right at the moment. Maybe you'd like to get a drink. A coffee, perhaps."

"I have to get back to the museum."

"Please." He climbed off the motorbike and began to push it through the courtyard gate. "Just let me park this and I'll be right with you."

He did not give her the chance to protest, and so she waited for him.

A train rumbled past the warehouse, picking up speed as it moved along the newly repaired rail lines towards Stabia and Torre Annunziata. Salvatore Varone watched it from an open doorway. The carriages were crowded; faces filled the windows—soldiers and their women, old men, families with children. People had begun to travel again, day trips to the towns along the coast. An opportunity to escape the city, if only for a few hours, for those who could afford it, was worth the inflated price of the tickets. Varone had even thought about a trip himself; perhaps he would take his wife and daughters to Positano for a few days. There was a villa there, on the hillside above the town, pink stone with a red roof, and a pool on the terrace. From the balcony off the main bedroom you could see Capri. There was a ferry in the harbour that made hourly crossings to the island. He could take the girls and their mother to lunch in the Piazzetta in Capri Town, at the café near the Chiesa Santo Stefano, and then later to the shops along Via Camerelle. And afterwards, a taxi ride up the mountain to Anacapri and the gelateria in the small street off Piazza San Nicola. But then the train was gone and his thoughts of Capri and Positano faded. For now, his business remained in Naples.

The smell of fresh paint filled the warehouse. In a far corner, behind a low wall of emptied packing crates, a group of men worked with stencils, changing the serial numbers on the three American two-and-a-half-ton trucks that Varone's men had stolen in those first chaotic weeks after the Allies had reached the city, when there was almost too much to take.

Varone looked over at Paolo. He was sitting on an overturned crate, absently picking at the dirt beneath his fingernails with a splinter of wood.

"And our friend from the Questura—what did he have to say?"

Paolo shrugged. "Nothing much. I don't think he tried very hard."

"No," said Varone. "I didn't expect him to. He is as frightened of the security police as he is of us. If he asks too many questions, he might find himself in Poggio Reale."

"They would show him a fine time there," said Paolo.

"How did you leave him?"

"With bruises."

"Just bruises?"

"And I gave him the money, like you told me."

"Did he count it again?"

Paolo nodded.

"Good," said Varone. "It is always best to leave a man with some sense of dignity. If you do that, then you can own him and he will not even realize it."

"You don't think he will do anything?"

"Like what? Try and have us arrested?" Varone chuckled. "No, he won't do that. He will always be a greedy man. A few bruises is not going to change that. He'll think of it as the price of doing business— and he'll think it is a price he can afford."

"But we know better."

"We always know better, Paolo." He glanced back towards the empty train tracks. "Perhaps it's time we had a visit with Abruzzi."

"Do you think he will agree to it?"

"I expect," said Varone, "he's just been waiting for an invitation."

High above, the sun shone through the empty girders of the vaulted ceiling. The glass roof of the Galleria Umberto Primo had succumbed months earlier to the bombardments: navy ships lying off the coast had laid siege to the city through the early weeks of September. Whenever it rained, the long marble arcades of the shopping precinct were as slick as ice rinks—but today they gathered the heat of another springlike afternoon, and Greaves could feel the warmth radiate from the pale stone floor.

The waiter came across the arcade from the taverna, carrying his tray with both hands. He seemed impossibly tall to Greaves, and thin, like a wraith, with pale skin the colour of his apron and his hair a dusty grey. The slight hump in his back from years of having to bend from his great height made him appear all the more a figure from the other side. He set the tray on the table and removed the glasses of vermouth. His long, trembling fingers threatened to spill the drinks. Greaves paid him twice the cost and watched as he shambled back towards the bar.

"You do know that it is an act," said Luisa. "Only a play for sympathy."

"I do, yes," Greaves said. "But he's quite convincing, don't you think?"

He looked at her. Her short dark hair framed her face, softening it, drawing attention to the paleness of her skin. And there was a gentle V-shaped crease in the middle of her brow that deepened when she sipped her drink.

She set the glass down and made a face. "It tastes horrible."

Greaves tried his vermouth. It was foul and bitter, the herbs overpowering the wine, and it left a sour film on the tongue.

"Would you like something else?" he asked her.

Luisa shook her head.

On the walk from the section office, because he could think of nothing else to say, he had told her about his visit to 21st General Hospital and about what the chief clerk had said. He'd told her, too, about his visit with the assistant port officer. She'd walked beside him with her arms folded across her chest, and though she nodded on occasion, he couldn't be sure that she was listening.

"I was wondering," he said now, "about the music box. Did you like it?"

She glanced away and her cheeks coloured slightly. "Yes. It is very lovely. But you shouldn't have done that."

"I wanted to."

She smiled.

"I think that's the first time I've seen you do that," he said. "Smile, I mean."

"Well, there is not so much to smile about."

"No, I suppose not."

He saw that he was making her uncomfortable and so changed the subject. "How is Dottore Cioffi making out at the museum?"

"Aldo," she said plainly. "Aldo is a thief."

"What do you mean?"

"Ever since he was a boy, he has stolen from the museum."

"But why wouldn't the *professore* have said anything to me?"

"Aldo is his nephew," Luisa said. "He isn't going to say anything against him to you. You are the security police. Besides, Augusto thinks he will change."

"But you don't," said Greaves.

"His sort cannot change."

"And what sort is that?"

Luisa stared down at her glass. "The sort that thinks only about himself."

"I see."

At a table behind theirs, an argument started between two young women who had been sitting with an English soldier. As they yelled at one another, the soldier stood up and started to walk away. The bickering stopped and the women went after him, each taking an arm, and the three of them went off together.

"People sell themselves cheaply in Naples," Luisa said. She took another drink of her foul vermouth, and then looked intently at Greaves. "What will you do when you find them?"

"What will I do when I find whom?" asked Greaves.

"The ones who are stealing the medicine."

"Oh, I won't find them."

"What do you mean?"

"My inquiries are just for show. So we can put something in our report that will keep the commanders happy up at Field Security HQ."

"But what if you do? What if you are able to catch them?"

Greaves shrugged. "I'll arrest them, I suppose."

"And what would happen after that?"

"They would go on trial at Castel Capuano, likely be found guilty, and then be sent to Poggio Reale or to the prison on Porcida. That's the way these things usually play themselves out."

"And the medicines?"

"They would be confiscated. Returned, I assume, to the supply depot or to 21st General Hospital, or sent along to the evacuation hospitals and field stations up north."

"Shouldn't it go to the people who need it?"

"It would," said Greaves.

"You mean the soldiers."

"Yes, of course."

Luisa considered this for a moment, then she stood up from the table. "Thank you very much for the drink, *tenente*."

"Do you have to leave so soon?"

She nodded. "Yes, I must get back to the museum."

"Perhaps we could do this again?" said Greaves.

"Perhaps," she said, and turned and began to walk away. Greaves watched her, hoping that she might glance back, but she did not.

SEVEN

The private boxes at the San Carlo rose like the tiers of a pink
wedding cake, the carved balcony fronts like seams of pale icing
between the layers. The house lights were dim; the lamps in the
sconces, four tall on each pillar, shone low, as if they'd been starved
of their brightness. In the pit the orchestra tuned its instruments,
an atonal accompaniment to the chaotic scene of patrons finding
their seats. The effect was a dissonant murmur that put Varone
in mind of a herd of goats clambering through a rocky laneway.
A shout came from the next box over, and an American soldier
leaned out over the railing and waved his arms to get the attention
of another soldier in a box on the opposite side of the theatre. He
put two fingers into his mouth and let loose a piercing whistle.
Varone's younger daughter, Giulia, put her hands to her ears.
When the American whistled again, Varone's wife leaned forward
and loudly shushed him.

The soldier frowned at her. "What's it to you, lady?" Then he looked
at Varone. "Hey, ginzo, what you starin' at?"

"Nu' sputa' 'ncielo, ca 'nfaccia te torna."

"What was that?" the soldier said. Varone's stare did not waver and
the soldier gave a nervous laugh. "Crazy fucken wop," he said, and
retreated into his box.

The house lights went down. The hum of the audience swelled momentarily, then settled into a respectful silence. The curtain lifted to reveal a bare stage, the boards lit by a single light. The cloth backdrop was painted in dreary greys: a monochrome of colonnades and a lacklustre countryside beyond. There were no set pieces, no props, and it made Varone sad to see the magnificent San Carlo humbled so.

But as the opening aria began, his mind wandered from the performance. Other matters occupied his thoughts, foremost among them Renzo Abruzzi. The night before, dreams of the young man had disturbed Varone's sleep: visions of Abruzzi sipping cappuccino on the balcony of his apartment and playing with his daughters. It wasn't so much the young man's boldness that worried him; hijacking the shipment from the port had been a calculated move to get his attention, and he had to give him credit for that. Rather, what bothered Varone, what nagged at him, was Abruzzi's relationship with the *dottore* and the security policeman. If Abruzzi had managed to make a connection within the security police, it could spell trouble for Varone. If this were, in fact, the case, his own friends in the American military police would be of little help to him.

He looked out over the darkened theatre. The lead tenor was midway through his solo and the audience was enthralled. Giulia, at his side, had slipped her arm through his. Varone leaned over and kissed his daughter gently on the top of her head.

"Are you enjoying yourself?" he whispered.

"Yes, Papa," she said, and nuzzled against him.

Varone turned his eyes to the stage and to the singer illumined in the weak glow of the spotlight. He would have to be careful with Abruzzi, he decided, until he knew for certain the extent of his connections.

The torch beam splashed a puddle of light across the marble floor. Cioffi quickly shielded the lamp with his hand. His knee hurt. He had banged it against a packing crate in the corridor. A nail, or a loose sliver of wood, had torn a hole in his trouser leg and pierced his flesh. He could feel the warm trickle of blood run down his shin; it itched.

From the street outside, he could hear shouting: drunken GIs causing a commotion in the square. There came the noise of smashing glass; someone had thrown a bottle. Every sound was amplified in the dark emptiness of the museum—even his own breathing, which rasped loudly, as if he were panting into his own ear. He kept his hand over the torch as he passed through the main gallery, the statues' shadowy faces staring down at him from behind their sandbag bulwarks.

In the side corridor he stopped and took out his handkerchief. He wiped away the sheen of sweat from his face, then he carried on.

When he reached the narrow gallery at the end of the corridor, he switched off the torch. From here he would work in the dark. The display case he wanted was just inside the doorway. He found it easily and opened the glass door. The cabinet was crowded with statuettes. He felt for the one he was after: a smoothly carved quartzite dog that he had failed to make note of that afternoon when he was entering the pieces into the ledger. He took it from the shelf and put it into his pocket, and carefully rearranged the surrounding statuettes so as not to leave a conspicuous void in the exhibit. Then he closed the cabinet and hurried back into the corridor.

He turned the torch on but again shielded the lamp, using only the weak light that leaked between his fingers to guide his way back across the main gallery. He could hear the soldiers in the square again, shouting now. They would keep the *carabiniere* at the front entrance occupied, but Cioffi was sure that the American MPs would soon come to break up the argument. He did not want to be there when they arrived, so he went quickly along the next corridor to the service entrance on the north side of the building. He found the door and removed the shim he'd used to wedge it open. He put the piece of wood into his pocket with the statuette and went out into the alleyway.

"Turn off that light, you fool!"

Lello stepped from the shadows, a panicked look on his face.

Cioffi switched off the torch. "Sorry."

"You'll be sorrier if anyone saw you," Lello hissed back at him.

Cioffi smiled calmly at his friend, though his heart continued to pound. "You worry like an old woman," he said, and patted his pocket. "Come on, let's go get a drink."

EIGHT

A truck was stopped in the square and a crowd had begun to gather round. They milled about it in a loose circle, weighing the resolve of the Kiwi rifleman standing at the tailgate. He held his carbine out before him like a cudgel. The cargo lay uncovered in the bed: a load of crated field ration kits bound for the divisional camp on the flood plain below Monte Cassino. In the cab, the driver turned the ignition, while the second rifleman, only half visible under the open hood, fiddled with cylinder wires. The engine sputtered but did not catch. Then a small boy scrambled forward. He climbed the rear tire and reached over the side. But before he had a chance to grab anything, the rifleman leapt over the crates and brought the butt of his carbine down on the boy's hand. The child fell to the ground and held his broken fingers out in front of him; they were at odd angles, pointing off in different directions. His screams masked the starting of the engine. The second rifleman dropped the hood and hurried around the tailgate. He clambered up and fetched his carbine from where he'd left it lying in the cargo bed and pointed it at the crowd. He almost fell over when the truck lurched forward and started across the square towards Via Santa Caterina.

Major Woodard turned away from the window. "I hate this place," he said to Greaves, who stood on the far side of the desk. In the major's hand was the official request for a prisoner transfer that had been delivered by a courier from the Questura during morning briefing. "And now we have this nonsense to deal with—again. The third time inside of a month. It really is ridiculous. I mean, how are we to do our work—our proper work?" The major ran a hand through his thin, sandy hair. His face had begun to redden. "It's Biblical, is what it is. All this eye-for-an-eye foolishness."

"Yes, sir. It is." As much as he disliked the major—Greaves found him for the most part petty and narrow-minded, and was always reminded of those dull-witted boys he'd gone to school with whose view of the future ran no farther than their next rugby match—he couldn't help but feel sorry for him. He'd been dealt a bad hand with 803 FSS. In the last week his staff of six had been whittled down to four. Sergeant Roylance had been sent to Sorrento to take over the detachment there after the intelligence officer in charge, a young captain, had been co-opted for administrative duties at Castellammare. And two days earlier Sergeant Jones, while driving one of the Nortons on the Lungomare, had taken a spill and ended up with several stitches to go along with the badly wrenched knee that had him hobbling about the section office on crutches. While the manpower available had always been stretched thin, now it was alarmingly so.

"I understand that a vendetta is a serious thing," Major Woodard continued, as if explaining himself to Greaves. "It can be a destabilizing factor. If people start taking sides, the whole district could split. And if we don't step in, then the Camorra will. But honestly, lieutenant, sometimes I just don't understand these people."

The major dropped the request onto his desk and rummaged through his pockets for his cigarettes. He lit one for himself and then passed the packet to Greaves.

"You know this fellow," he said. "You don't suppose he just wants to fob off his prisoner on us so he can go about his business, do you?"

"No, sir," Greaves said, leaning across the desk to light his cigarette off the burning match the major held out to him. "If Brigadiere Maglietta is asking for help, sir, then I would say that it's very likely that he needs it." In the back of his mind, though, Greaves didn't doubt that Francesco Maglietta also saw the prisoner transfer as an opportunity to share some plum brandy and a few games of *tresette*.

"I thought as much," said Major Woodard. "Well, I'm afraid it's going to have to be you that goes, lieutenant. You're familiar with the area, and if it's bad, I'm sure the *brigadiere* would like to see a face that he recognizes. Besides, the fact of the matter is that I haven't anyone else I can send."

"I understand," said Greaves.

"You'll have to take the staff car. There's no way you'll get a prisoner on the back of a motorbike."

"When do I go?"

"Unfortunately, I've had to send Corporal Philbin on an errand down to Ravello. He won't be back until late this evening. So, your friend will have to wait until tomorrow."

"Then I'll leave first thing in the morning."

"Yes, lieutenant. That would be best."

Greaves watched as Major Woodard wandered back to the window and looked out again at the square. The crowd that had gathered to try to steal rations from the truck continued to loiter, but there was no sign of the boy with the broken fingers.

"I wish I were home," the major said quietly, as if to himself. "I wish I were anywhere but here."

For a time, after her parents died, whenever Luisa looked at Parente, she imagined him in their place. For more than half a dozen years already he had been a surrogate. Her own father, who'd worked his whole life in an accountancy firm, had neither the time nor the inclination to nurture his only daughter's boundless curiosity. And her mother had wanted for her only what she'd had herself: a steadfast, if listless, husband and a family. They had been against her taking the job at the museum, and only a visit from Augusto himself—who saw in the schoolgirl, whom he'd interviewed alongside young men just graduated from the university, a longing for knowledge—had finally convinced them.

More than his assistant, she became his pupil. At his side she learned of ancient things: disappeared civilizations, dead beliefs in dead languages. It was as if he had opened up his mind for her, pushed the doors wide to the vault of his knowledge; and wandering through all that he knew was as enlivening as wandering through the ruins themselves. It was an adventure for her. So much so that, when her mother got sick, and then her father too, she felt as if she really didn't know them anymore, and that brought with it a terrible remorse. And then, when they were gone, her first thought was to replace them. She almost convinced herself that she could. She wouldn't go home to the empty apartment—that small set of rooms, tucked up under the eaves of the building, which still smelled of them. Instead, she envisioned herself going home to Augusto's apartment on Riviera di Chiaia overlooking the seafront, where the noise of the water would drift in through the open windows while she made their dinner, and then, afterwards, she would rub his stiff joints with liniment before she pulled back the blankets on his bed and got him settled, turning out the light as she left to go to her own, smaller room at the far end of the corridor, with its high, narrow bed with the lace-trimmed canopy. She knew it was all empty fancy, a whimsy born of grief and guilt: a dream into which she fled to hide from the ache of being left on her own.

"Are you all right?"

She looked up from the ledger in her lap. Parente had come from behind his desk and stood now next to the sofa.

"Yes," she said. "I'm fine."

"Are we making progress?"

She shrugged, and then reached for the other ledgers on the low table in front of her. She flipped through the pages. "It will take another week, perhaps two. There are the vaults still to go through, and we haven't yet begun with the bronzes or the Farnese collection."

"Any concerns I should know about?"

Luisa frowned. "There are some discrepancies, some mosaics that cannot be accounted for. Small pieces, mostly, but they may have been missing for some time."

"I see."

"We should have been more careful, Augusto," she said, recalling the chaos of trying to secure the collections during the attacks that had preceded the arrival of the Allied armies. Then Augusto had been so concerned with protecting the larger pieces—the statues in the main-floor galleries and the paintings on the mezzanine, the priceless glassware and Pompeian frescoes—that the storage of more minor pieces went unsupervised. It had been an error in judgment, but at the time neither of them expected that the museum would survive the violence of the bombardments.

"We did what we could," he said. "Nobody can ask more than that." He took the ledgers from her and laid them on the table. Then he sat down beside her on the sofa. "Luisa," he said, taking her by the hand, "I'm worried about you."

"What do you mean?"

He smiled. "You take very good care of me. You always have. I wouldn't know what to do without you."

"Augusto," she said, looking him straight in the eye, "why are you talking like this? Are you not feeling well?"

Now he laughed. "I am a seventy-two-year-old man, Luisa. My back hurts, sometimes I get dizzy, and after I climb a flight of stairs I have to stop and catch my breath. Every time I cough, I think I am going to have a heart attack."

She pulled her hand away. "Stop that. It isn't funny."

"Yes, I know, I know. But this is what I'm talking about. You spend all of your time worrying about me, when the person you should be worrying about is yourself. All of this"—he swept his hand through the air—"all of this means nothing. It doesn't matter. It is you that matters— you and the world that goes on outside these walls. But you shut yourself off from that world. You always have. And that's my fault."

"You're talking foolish," she said to him, and stood up from the sofa. "Now please, Augusto, we have a lot of work still to do. The men will be back from their lunch soon, and I want to be through with the ceramics on the third floor before we leave for the day." She walked to the door. When she turned back, he was still sitting on the sofa. "Well? Are you coming or not?"

Augusto shook his head and sighed. "You're very stubborn, my darling," He pushed himself to his feet. "Maybe too stubborn for your own good."

Roviale's *Scenes of the Last Judgment* took precedence on the wall behind the magistrate's bench. In the gallery, a commotion had started: there were shouts, a slap, then two women fell to the floor in a scuffle. The sweet-faced boy of eighteen being led from the prisoner's box wept openly while the MPs who guarded the courtroom moved to separate the two women.

Abruzzi leaned towards him and said: "What do you think?"

"I think it is ironic," replied Cioffi, looking up at the mural. "I would not want to face the judge with that over my head."

"I'm not talking about the painting, *dottore*," said Abruzzi. "I'm talking about the boy."

He shrugged. "Loving two women can only get a man in trouble."

Abruzzi laughed. "Loving *one* will do that."

Cioffi looked at him, at his sharp-edged face, and wondered if he could actually know such a thing. He could not imagine Abruzzi loving anyone. He had the cold eyes of one to whom affection, even simple fondness, is a foreign concept. He'd come up from the streets, been a small boy who had to fight his way out of the gutter. How could he have known anything but the intricacies of fear?

The women were escorted out, and the young prisoner was taken through a side door to await transfer back to Poggio Reale prison. The magistrate, an American colonel with grey, brush-cut hair and a wearied expression, was busy shuffling paperwork, while the consuls, also army officers, chatted to one another and waited for the next case to be called.

"These Americans," Abruzzi said, nodding towards the court officers, "they like to go on about Justice being blind. What do you think about that?"

"I think Justice doesn't exist," said Cioffi. "At least not in Naples."

Abruzzi smiled. "And you would be right, *dottore*. Now, what have you brought me?"

Cioffi reached into the pocket of his shabby coat and removed a small bundle. He glanced around before he unwrapped the stained handkerchief.

"What is it?" Abruzzi asked, unimpressed.

"It is Egyptian. A statuette." Cioffi lifted it closer. "A dog."

"I don't see a dog. All I see is a rock. A rock that I could find on any beach in Naples."

"No, no. Look closer." Cioffi touched his dirty fingernail to the carving. "Here is its snout. You can see the ears too. The piece is corroded, I warrant, but that shows its age. It is made from quartzite and comes from the time of the pharaoh Akhenaten."

"Akhenaten, eh?"

"Yes, that's right."

"Is it valuable?"

"To the right people," Cioffi said, "it is very valuable. There are collectors who would pay a great deal to have something like this. I used to know a man in Rome. He knew others, in Switzerland. But perhaps you already know of someone."

Abruzzi nodded. "Yes, *dottore*. Don't you worry, I have someone in mind."

A side door to the courtroom opened and there was a buzz in the gallery as the next defendant was led in. Abruzzi slipped the carving into his pocket, then he said to Cioffi: "This is the one I'm interested in. I think you might be interested too."

The man in the dock was a sad-eyed fellow with sparse, grey-flecked hair and pronounced jowls. The magistrate had the charges read into the record. The main telephone line in Piazza Mercato had been cut, and the defendant stood accused of possessing the copper wire with the intention of selling it on the black market. The indictment included a charge of sabotage.

"Do you know him?" Abruzzi asked.

Cioffi shook his head. "Should I?"

"Well, he is a *dottore* too. An abortionist. He takes care of the girls in our brothels. Protects our investments, you might say."

"Then you've come to help him?"

"Help him?" Abruzzi laughed. "No, I have not come to help him. I'm the reason he's here."

The defence counsel entered a plea of not guilty. "I have depositions, sir," he said. "Sworn statements attesting to the defendant's character. He is a respected physician. He's been assisting the Red Cross at the typhoid clinic in the Ottacalli district, sir."

The magistrate impatiently held out his hand. "Give them to me."

The counsel began to search the papers spread over his table. He opened one string file then another. "If I could have just a moment, sir," he said. He rummaged in his attaché case, began to empty its contents onto the seat of his chair.

Cioffi noticed now that the prisoner stared at Abruzzi and that Abruzzi stared back.

"It is interesting, isn't it, *dottore*, how a man will cling to his pride when he has nothing left."

The magistrate said, "I'm waiting, counsellor."

"Yes, sir. It's just that ..." The officer sighed and shook his head. "I can't seem to find the documents, sir. I'm afraid they've been misplaced."

The prisoner's cheek twitched slightly. His stare faltered.

In a hushed voice Abruzzi said: "I don't think that the papers are going to be found."

"Begging the court's indulgence," the counsel said. "Perhaps I could have a continuance until I can locate the affidavits."

"There's no room on the docket for a continuance. Let's hear the case. If the documents turn up, we'll revisit it then."

There was a murmur in the gallery and someone shouted. The magistrate called for the heckler to be removed. As the MPs began to make their way towards the man, whom Cioffi recognized from the *ristorante* on Corso Umberto Primo, another disturbance broke out on the other side of the courtroom. The magistrate motioned the court interpreter to the bench and told him to advise the spectators that he would clear the room if order was not restored. Half-heartedly, the interpreter relayed the message. No one paid him any mind. Then, over counsel's protests, the magistrate ruled summarily against the defendant: a sentence of three years and a fine of three hundred thousand lire were imposed.

The prisoner shuffled, head down, out of the dock. Abruzzi waited until he had been removed from the courtroom, then he took an envelope from his pocket and handed it to Cioffi.

"You see, *dottore*," he said, "it is best not to disappoint me."

Cioffi folded the envelope and slipped it into the lining of his coat, then looked towards the door through which the prisoner had been taken. "What did he do?" he asked.

"Something I suggest you avoid," said Abruzzi. "He developed a conscience."

Parente steadied himself against the low railing and gazed down on the cork and clay city—Pompeii, rendered in painstakingly precise miniature. His eyes roved, from the Temple of Apollo to the Temple of Jupiter, from the Grand Teatro to the Gladiators' Barracks. In his thoughts he wandered through the Forum to the Law Courts and on again to the Macellum, the market where meat and fish were sold and where the money-changers plied their trade. He roamed the city in his mind: along Via dell'Abbondanza, past the House of the Tragic Poet and the House of the Moralist, until he reached the Stabian Baths, and from there on to the Amphitheatre, where the beasts were slaughtered for the entertainment of the masses—tigers and lions and giraffes and elephants, brought across the sea from Africa.

It nearly broke his heart to see it there, lying at his feet as if he were a god—a tired, old god fallen from grace, a god corrupted and corporeal. His wars in heaven had become wars of the flesh. His body had become his greatest enemy. It had been months now since he'd last gone to the ruins. Any overseeing that was to be done he now left to Luisa, because it was almost too much for him even to climb the stone roadway to the Porta Marina: he would find himself out of breath and tormented by his searing nerve before he managed even to reach the gates of the ancient city. And with each passing day he grew more convinced that standing there at that railing was as close as he would ever come to setting foot again in that place he loved so much. His Pompeii was this now: a glorified diorama.

"I thought I might find you here."

Parente looked up to see Greaves standing in the doorway to the exhibit.

"Thomas," he said. His joints had stiffened and it took him a moment to straighten himself. "Is it time already for another of our visits?"

"No, *professore*," Greaves said, coming into the room. "This isn't an official call. I just thought I'd drop by and see how things were with you. When you weren't in your office, I took a chance that you'd be here."

"You know me too well, Thomas." Parente motioned him to the railing. "Come, join me."

Greaves came and stood beside him.

"Do you know," Parente said, "that many of the frescoes that are depicted in the model no longer exist? They have been lost forever. The only example of them is here, on these tiny walls, and they are near-perfect replicas. It's amazing, don't you think?"

"You miss it, don't you, *professore*," said Greaves.

"Yes, very much, Thomas." Parente stared longingly at the duplicate city. "I spent most of my life in the ruins. I began when I was just a young man, younger even than you. With my own hands I dug out Pompeii. I paid in blood and blisters and broken bones to see what was buried there." Parente sighed and shook his head. "And you, Thomas," he said, his tone brightening, "you have not even been there yet, have you?"

"Not yet, *professore*."

"How can that be?"

"I suppose that I just haven't gotten around to it."

"That is not an excuse that I will accept."

"Perhaps you would take me?"

"Oh, no," Parente said, and shook his head vigorously. "Not me, Thomas. I don't think I will go back."

"You mean you won't go back ever?"

"Why would I do that to myself? Every step I took there would remind me that I am one more step farther away from the person I used to be. No, Thomas, I would not do that—not even for you."

They were interrupted then by Luisa, who came into the exhibit room carrying in her arms several inventory ledgers. She acknowledged Greaves with a half smile, then said to Parente, "I've been looking all over for you." She held out the ledgers to him. "You left these behind in the Salone dell'Atlante. One of the workers found them."

Parente took the books from her. He flipped through the pages of the topmost, then shook his head. "I did not leave them there. Perhaps it was Aldo."

"Aldo?" Luisa said. "Please don't tell me that you have him cataloguing pieces, Augusto."

Parente shrugged. "What was I to do? He couldn't carry packing straw. Besides, he knows this place almost as well as you and I. We'll finish sooner with his help."

"Some help—I haven't seen him all day."

"He hasn't come in?" Parente said, unable to hide his concern.

Luisa scoffed. "He's probably drunk somewhere."

"Please don't talk like that."

"I'm sorry, Augusto." She took the ledgers back from him and then said with a frown, "I just wish you had told me."

He had always enjoyed the fieriness of her temper: it was quick to spark, and almost as quick to burn itself out again. Like a child's tantrum, he thought. He gently touched her elbow, a conciliatory gesture to show her that he had been in the wrong.

"I was just looking at *il modello* with Thomas," he said. "Do you know that he has not yet been to the ruins?" Now, with his other hand, he brought Greaves, who had been standing to the side during their brief disagreement, back into the sphere of their conversation. "I thought that since I'm no longer capable, either physically or mentally, perhaps you might take him."

Luisa hesitated, and a slight flush came into her cheeks. "But there is still so much work that needs to be done here," she said.

"After we are finished with the inventory, of course," said Parente.

"Actually," Greaves said, sounding almost apologetic, as if he were interrupting, "I came here to ask if I could take you somewhere, Signora Gennaro. To the Caffè Gambrinus, for a drink, or maybe for something to eat."

Luisa's face was now in full flush.

"Well, there you are," said Parente, enjoying the moment of awkwardness between the two of them. "You can discuss your trip to Pompeii over a glass of wine and a plate of *struffoli*."

"I can't," said Luisa.

"Why not?" Parente asked.

"I have to go to the *ospedale*."

"You can miss one night."

"It's important, Augusto. You know that."

"Luisa, really. One night is not going to make a difference."

"No," she said, and the note her voice struck was final.

"I'm sorry," said Greaves, "but I don't understand. What hospital?"

"The Ospedale del Santo Sepolcro," Luisa said.

"Is there something wrong? Are you sick?"

"No, Thomas," said Parente. "Luisa goes to the *ospedale* to help."

"Really?" Greaves said. "What exactly do you do?"

Luisa took a breath and let it out slowly. "I help with the patients," she said, her gaze turned slightly to the side. "The older ones. I try to make them comfortable. I change their bedding, give them water. Sometimes I clean them when they mess themselves."

For a moment Greaves did not speak. He seemed to be considering what Luisa had told him. Then he nodded his head slowly. "May I come with you?" he said.

"I beg your pardon?" said Luisa, looking straight at him now.

"If it's all right, I would like to go with you to the hospital. I would like to see what you do there. And then, afterwards, if you feel like it, we can go to the Gambrinus. And if you don't feel like it, that's fine too."

She turned to Parente, her expression slightly panicked, and at that moment she seemed so very young to him.

"I think it might be good for Thomas to join you," Parente said.

"Yes, then," said Luisa. "All right."

"How much did you pay the interpreter to lose the paperwork?"

"That's the beauty of it," said Abruzzi. "It didn't cost me a thing. It's funny sometimes what one man will do for another, what he will risk, out of respect."

"Is that what you call it?"

Cioffi stood off to the side, unable to take his eyes from the thin pink line of the scar that rose like the sliver of a crescent moon from the left corner of the man's mouth. When they'd come out onto the steps of Castel Capuano, he had recognized at once the face he'd seen reflected in the window of the butcher's shop near the Ponte di Chiaia. This was Salvatore Varone's man.

He seemed to Cioffi the sort of fellow who enjoyed intimidation and violence—the sort who, when he beat a man, or cut him, or shot a bullet into his knee or his heart or his head, took pleasure in a job well done.

Now Varone's man looked at him. "It is good to see you again, *dottore*."

Cioffi felt his knees weaken and his bowels loosen.

The man smiled, and then turned back to Abruzzi. "My boss wants to speak with you. He extends an invitation."

"Really? An invitation?" Abruzzi glanced at Cioffi. "What do you say, *dottore*? Would you like to meet the infamous Salvatore Varone?"

"Not him," said Varone's man. "Just you."

Abruzzi brushed the front of his jacket then plucked an invisible piece of lint from his lapel. "When did he have in mind for this meeting?"

"What's wrong with right now?"

Abruzzi nodded. "Right now will be fine."

In the nearest bed was an old woman. She lay on her side, her thin grey hair damp from fever and matted to her scalp. She moaned softly as the doctor pulled the blanket away. The stink came like a wave of heat from an opened oven.

"You see, she is shitting herself to death." Benedetto Serao pointed then to her naked thigh, to the purple inflammation that clouded her skin like an awful birthmark. "After the rash, the fever worsens, the heart rate is weak and rapid. Then comes the diarrhea. Sometimes there is blood. We give her fluids, as best we can, but the reality is that the dehydration will likely kill her."

The shock of what he had said registered on Greaves's face.

"Don't worry, *tenente*. She can't hear me. She is delirious. She spends her days in fluctuating states of consciousness. This morning she had brief moments of lucidity, but right now she is not with us."

Greaves moved the candle on the side table to see the woman better. Then he bent down and put his hand to her cheek. "She's so hot."

"There have been cases," Serao said, "where the fever has not broken for six weeks."

Greaves glanced up at him. "What does she need? What will help her?"

Serao let the blanket down. He smoothed it over the edge of the mattress. "She needs what we do not have. Antibiotics. Saline. A steady supply of fresh water. But we cannot even give her that. Our water supply is wholly unreliable, and what we are able to get is hardly potable. It must all be boiled."

"But what about the Red Cross?" Greaves asked.

"They give us what they can. But it is not enough."

"And the army? The Medical Corps?"

"They came once," Serao said, and laughed disdainfully. "Doctors in gowns and masks. They wore caps on their heads. The wards were sprayed for lice and then they took pictures with the children. They have not been back since."

"I don't understand."

Serao looked across the bed at Luisa. "What have you brought me here? *L'ultimo uomo innocente?*" He turned back to Greaves. "There is little to understand. The old are of no matter to anyone. It is easier to take pictures with smiling children. Something nice to put into the newspaper so the people at home can feel better about what goes on here."

Greaves stood up and followed him to the bed where an elderly man shivered uncontrollably beneath his thin blanket. Serao inspected the sores that covered his lips.

As they'd made their way through the wards of Ospedale del Santo Sepolcro, Greaves had felt as if they were descending through Dante's circles: each brought a horror worse than the last. But this was by far the worst of them. It was like a dying room—for those who were brought here, there seemed little hope of ever leaving.

"Is there nothing that can be done?" he asked.

Serao shrugged. "Without the proper medicines, the best we can do is to try and make them comfortable and hope that they are strong enough to recover on their own."

"And if they're not?" said Greaves.

Serao glanced again at Luisa, who remained standing off to the side. Then he said matter-of-factly: "If they are not, then they will die. For some it comes quickly, for others they linger. That is the way it is. If I could do something more for them, I would. But I am a realist, *tenente*."

"It just isn't right."

"Nothing ever is," said Serao.

A nurse came rushing along the corridor and Serao went to speak to her. They huddled together out of earshot. Then he turned back to Greaves. "You must excuse me, *tenente*, but I am needed for triage."

"What is it?" asked Greaves.

"There has been an incident at the American naval depot. The cooks set fire to the rubbish heap to keep away the foragers. I have several patients coming in with burns. I do not know how many."

"Can I help?"

"Thank you, but we'll manage."

Serao came and shook Greaves's hand, then he rushed away with the nurse. There was something in the way Luisa watched him as he hurried down the ward that caused a spark of jealousy in Greaves.

"He's a good man," he said.

"He is more than good," said Luisa.

"You're fond of him."

"I admire him very much, yes."

Greaves nodded, and then glanced about at the crowded cots. What he saw sickened him. He thought of the wards at 21st General Hospital, such clean, antiseptic spaces in comparison. Ospedale del Santo Sepolcro seemed like a place where diseases were born rather than cured.

"I wish there was something I could do," he said.

"Do you really?" said Luisa.

He noted the doubt in her voice. "Yes, of course I do."

She walked past him and went to the empty nurses' station. There she dipped a cloth into a basin of water and brought it back to the bed where the old man lay. She held it to his blistered lips and he sucked, like a baby at his mother's breast, and all at once Greaves felt like an interloper, an unwanted witness to an intimate act.

She looked back at him over her shoulder. "These people need more than sentiment. If you can give them nothing else, then there is no point in your being here."

"I heard that you killed a priest when you were sixteen years old. Cut his throat and let him bleed to death on the altar."

Varone continued to watch the young man as he admired the two-and-a-half-ton supply trucks with their drab paint and stencilled markings that were parked at the back of the warehouse. Somehow he had expected that Abruzzi would be bigger. He had expected a physical presence. He had expected a wolf. What stood before him was a rabbit. He was small, his movements somewhat jumpy, almost nervous. He imagined that he might start easily and that he could no doubt move quite quickly should the situation call for it. He didn't wonder that he preferred to use a knife.

"Sometimes," Varone said, "things get exaggerated."

"Really?" said Abruzzi, and already there was a hint of disappointment in his voice. "What happened, then?"

"I beat him with a pipe for buggering altar boys."

Varone recalled how he had cornered the priest in his rectory and how the man begged to be let alone. But Varone dragged him into the middle of the floor and hit him about the arms and chest, swung hard into his stomach so that he lost his wind, levelled blows at his thighs and buttocks—struck all those parts of his body that would be covered by his cassock—and then left him tear-stained, with snot bubbling from his nose and painting his lips, muttering prayers of forgiveness.

"If it was me," Abruzzi said, "I would have killed him."

"Is that right?" said Varone.

"I would have cut his throat like a pig. And I'd have done it right on the front steps of the church, for everyone to see."

"You don't like priests, then?"

Abruzzi shook his head. "I don't like showing mercy. It makes people think that you are weak."

The young man, Varone realized, lacked all sense of proportion; neither could he comprehend the tangible effects of shame. He was unable to appreciate that the punishment Varone exacted was more fitting, because from then on, whenever that priest walked through his parish, everyone would know why it was that he limped, and they would know the truth about what he was, and that would forever rob him of the esteem and reverence that killing him would not. But the subtlety of this was wasted on Abruzzi, whose train of thought had drifted and who was now admiring the trucks once more.

"You could do a lot with one of these," he said.

Varone ignored the comment. "So tell me again why I should agree to this."

Abruzzi smiled. "Because you are a shrewd businessman."

"You seem shrewd enough yourself."

"That may be. But I am also a small fish. A small fish that would, one day, like to be a bigger fish—maybe big like you. But I can't do that without being on your side, and without you being on mine. Big fish eat small fish, and I don't want to be eaten. And besides, you have the sort of connections to handle this type of thing. I do not."

Varone nodded. "Like I said, you're shrewd yourself." He turned and walked back towards the table at the far end of the warehouse where Paolo sat waiting. "You do know," he said over his shoulder to Abruzzi, "that Aldo Cioffi is a worthless drunk."

"I don't concern myself with the character of the people I deal with," Abruzzi said. "Just so long as they can do what they say they can do."

"That's where we differ, then," said Varone. When he reached the table, he picked up the lump of white stone. "To me, character is the most important thing. It goes without saying that if you understand a man's character, then you understand the man. If he is of poor character, then it doesn't matter if he brings me a brick of gold. In the end, he'll be more trouble than he is worth."

"And what if he brings you ten bricks of gold?" Abruzzi said. "Or twenty? Or thirty?"

Varone looked at him and smiled. "If that's the case, then he might just be worth the trouble." He held up the carving. "I'll keep this as repayment for what you stole from me. And I want to meet the *dottore* myself. Bring him to the Villa Comunale tomorrow morning at six. I will wait for you at the Cassa Armonica."

"We'll be there," said Abruzzi.

"It just didn't seem right to me, working on wheat and beef and pork quotas when so many others were going overseas. I didn't think I could live with myself if I'd done it. If I had the choice again, though ..."

Luisa was only half listening to him—something about his father and friends he had in government, a position in the Ministry of Agriculture that would have kept him out of the army and that he had turned down. But her attention was divided. She couldn't stop herself from gazing around. The Caffè Gambrinus—it was not as she remembered it. Her memory was of a shining place: gilt and polish. She had only ever been a few times, with Augusto before the war. Her parents had disapproved—her brother, too. But Luisa, on those few occasions, had revelled in the freedom of it, like an oasis of sorts, a place of liberation, where people did not have to guard themselves, where, for a time, they could speak their minds without fear. It was much shabbier now.

The tables around them were crowded with soldiers and their tarted-up Neapolitan mistresses: wan-faced men trying to impress women who needed no impressing. Sitting there, even in her trousers and shorn hair, she thought how much she must look like one of them.

Then she realized that he had stopped talking. He was looking intently at her.

"Are you all right?" he asked.

"Can we leave?"

"Yes," he said. "If that's what you'd like."

She went outside and waited just beyond the terrace while he paid the bill. Then they walked across the expanse of Piazza del Plebiscito towards the waterfront, and passed the Palazzo Reale. There was a warm glow to the evening. The moon shone high over the bay and the breeze coming in off the water carried the soft scent of the sea. Luisa was glad that for once Naples did not smell like something unwashed.

They walked the Lungomare and stopped on the pavement outside the Hotel Vesuvio and looked out at the shadowy bulk of the Castel dell'Ovo. He recounted the story that Aldo had told him and asked her what she thought of it.

"Some people believe it is true," she said.

"And you?"

"There is nothing magical about human misery. It isn't a sorcerer's trick. Cruelty is our most banal attribute."

Then she showed him the place near the Giardini Pubblici where the Germans had shot people in the street and left their bodies to rot.

"So many have died already," she said. "And so many more are waiting to die. And when it's all done, they will just be numbers. Someone will tally them up, someone will do the math, and try to tell us who won and who lost." She tipped her head back and looked up, the constellations like a swirl of pinpricks in the night sky. "But it will be like trying to count the stars."

She turned to him. He was standing a short distance away, his hands pushed deep into his pockets. "Have you ever tried to count the stars, *tenente*?"

"I wish you would call me Thomas."

"All right, Thomas," she said, and liked the feel of his name on her tongue. "So tell me, Thomas, have you ever tried to count the stars?"

"When I was a boy, yes, I tried a few times."

"And?"

He shook his head.

"My family," she said. "My brother, my mother, my father. I am the only one left. There is only myself and Maria. It isn't going to matter who won and who lost. Do you understand what I am saying?"

"I think so, yes."

"I go to Ospedale del Santo Sepolcro because that is where my parents died. It is the only place anymore that I can feel close to them. This is what it has come to for me: the only place that I can feel solace is among the sick and the dying."

He did not seem to know how to take this. For a moment she thought he might try to comfort her. He shifted his feet and glanced, almost shyly, at her. Took his hands from his pockets but then plunged them in again. Then he turned and peered into the street, his stare so intent it was as if he were looking at something in particular, perhaps imagining there the corpses that the Germans had left behind.

"I think, Thomas," she said, "I would like to go home now."

Aldo Cioffi's father had given him the medical bag as a gift upon his graduation from the university. It had come with great expectations, all of which had been disappointed. It was the only thing left to him, his sole possession, aside from a few changes of clothing: a pair of knee-worn trousers, two shirts, a stained vest, three pairs of yellowed underpants. Everything else that he had once owned had been either sold or traded away, sometimes for food, sometimes for shelter, mostly for drink. But he'd always held on to the sturdy leather case with the brass clasps, feeling somehow that one day he would have need of it.

He had kept it tucked away on the top shelf in Lello's bare pantry. Now he took it down and opened it and was greeted with the smell of the tanned cowhide. He took it into the *salotto* and began to pack his clothes.

Lello came from the other room carrying a handful of pamphlets. He stopped in the doorway. "What are you doing?" he said.

"I am leaving."

"What do you mean you are leaving?"

"Just what I said. I am leaving Naples."

"For where? And with what?"

"I don't know," Cioffi said. "I will go south. To Salerno, or maybe to Cosenza. I have some money left. Enough for a train ticket."

"What's happened, Aldo?"

Cioffi looked up at him. "You were right. I didn't know what I was doing. I am in over my head."

"What are you talking about?"

"Not what," Cioffi said. "Who."

"You're not making any sense."

"Salvatore Varone."

"For God's sake. What have you done?"

"Nothing yet. But his man came today for Abruzzi. And he knows who I am."

"And your answer is to run away?"

"Yes, as fast as I can."

Lello came into the room. He dropped the pamphlets and grabbed the bag from Cioffi's hands and began to unpack his clothes.

"Stop that," Cioffi shouted.

"I'm not letting you go."

They began to struggle with one another, pulling the bag between them until it was upset and the clothes spilled onto the floor. Cioffi got down on his hands and knees and began to gather them again.

Lello stood over him. "You can't leave," he said.

"Why not?"

Lello grabbed hold of his shoulder and spun him around. "If Salvatore Varone knows about you, that means he also knows that Augusto is your uncle. And if you're not here, then he will go after him. That's the way these people work, Aldo."

Cioffi pushed him away. "Augusto can take care of himself."

"Whatever you've done has nothing to do with him. He's a helpless old man."

As he stood up, Lello pushed him to the wall. Cioffi struggled to get free.

"I would like to be an old man too, someday," he said.

"Listen to yourself, Aldo. This is your uncle you're talking about. You've got to go to him. You've got to tell him what's happened, what you've done."

"It's out of the question," Cioffi said. "If I tell Augusto, then he'll tell the security police. I'm not going to Poggio Reale."

Lello slapped him across the face. "I won't let you go."

Cioffi put his hand to his mouth. When he took it away, there was blood on his fingertips. He swung the bag hard and caught Lello in the softness of his belly, knocking the wind from him. Lello gasped and sank to the floor. Cioffi raised the bag over his head, but when he did, he caught sight of something out of the corner of his eye, movement in the doorway to the *salotto*. He looked over and saw Renzo Abruzzi standing there with a smile on his face.

"You really should keep your door locked. You never know who's just going to come strolling in." Abruzzi came into the room. He bent down and picked up one of the pamphlets from the floor. "*L'Associazione Comunista Napoletana*," he read, and shook his head. "Really, *dottore*, you do keep some questionable company." He looked around at the clothes strewn across the floor. "I hope you weren't thinking of going anywhere."

Cioffi lowered the bag. He felt slightly faint.

Then Abruzzi called to someone in the hall, and there appeared behind him the thick-browed thug from the *ristorante* on Corso Umberto Primo.

"I think it's better," Abruzzi said, "that you come with us, *dottore*. We have an early appointment tomorrow."

NINE

Salvatore Varone liked the Villa Nazionale best in the early morning, when the cinder paths were empty and the only sound was the wash of the sea against the stony shore and the soft hum of a gentle breeze passing through the ironwork of the Cassa Armonica.

"Your father owned a garment factory," he said.

"Yes, that's right. Women's underclothes and nightdresses."

"But you decided to become a doctor. Why is that?"

"My parents wanted me to do something that they could be proud of. They wanted me to become a professional man. A man with a title. Respectable."

"A professional man with a title, eh? And that's what makes a person respectable, is it? I've met many men with titles, but I don't remember any of them being respectable. Are you respectable?"

The *dottore* shook his head.

"And your parents, did you make them proud?"

Another shake of the head.

"You know, when I was younger," Varone went on, "I worked for a man that made part of his living hijacking shipments from warehouses. All sorts of things: building supplies, machine parts, and clothing too—boots, stockings, suits, dresses. We probably hijacked your father's goods."

Beside him, Aldo Cioffi shuffled his feet. "I suppose that is the risk of doing business in Napoli."

Varone laughed. "No, *dottore*. Not the risk. It is the business. Your father would have known that. In his factory he would have made stock to be sold and stock to be stolen. Who knows, he may even have been in on it. Took a cut out of what was taken from him. Some did that, you know. It was a tidy little arrangement in those days, back before that fool Mussolini stuck his nose into things. Now look at the mess we're in."

Across the walking path, near the fence that separated the park from Via Riviera di Chiaia, Paolo stood waiting with Abruzzi. Varone had sent them away so that he could talk to Cioffi alone.

"Do you understand what I'm telling you, *dottore*?"

Varone studied him. Cioffi stood gripping one of the iron pillars as if he were afraid the kiosk might start to spin about like a carousel and throw him off. The glass roof of the gazebo cast him in shades of green and yellow. There was the sour smell of fear on him, and he appeared to have slept in his jacket and trousers. And Varone recognized the look on his face: it was that of a man who has come to realize that he is no longer a player in his own fate; whatever happened to him now was for others to decide.

"I want to know about this security policeman who Paolo saw you with," Varone said. "Who is he?"

"A friend," said Cioffi.

"Have you told Abruzzi about him?"

"I didn't think he needed to know."

"That's good. You made the right decision. He really isn't the type that would appreciate that sort of thing. He would probably think that you were setting him up somehow."

"But I wouldn't do that," Cioffi protested.

"Oh, I know, *dottore*. I can tell that you are a man to be trusted."

A small convoy of military supply trucks came down the roadway that ran along the seafront. Varone watched them through the trees as they passed. When the trucks had gone, he put his hand on the *dottore's* shoulder and gave it a gentle squeeze. He could feel Cioffi tremble under his touch. "What kind of man is he?"

"Who? The *tenente*?"

"Yes. The *tenente*."

"An honest man."

Varone smiled. "We are all honest men, *dottore*. In our own way." He looked back to where Paolo and Abruzzi stood. Then he said to Cioffi: "There is a small café on Piazza Amedeo called the Diplomatico. Do you know it?"

"I have seen it, yes."

"It belongs to me," said Varone. "I like to go there in the afternoon to have my espresso. In two days you will come to see me there. And you will bring me something. Something pretty that I can give to my wife." He saw Cioffi glance over towards the fence. "You're worried about Abruzzi?"

"Yes," said the *dottore*.

"Don't be," Varone said. "He's not going to be a problem for anyone anymore."

Greaves left Naples at dawn, by mid-morning he had passed Nola and started into the mountains, and an hour and a half after that he rounded the bend on the narrow, winding road that brought him to the wide plateau, across which lay the village of Tenerello, a gathering of low-slung, flat-roofed buildings the colour of wheat that clung like a rocky outcrop to the mountainside. His heart lifted. It wasn't unlike the feeling he had experienced as a boy whenever he arrived at the summer home on Lake Rosseau: a sense of having returned to a place of welcome familiarity.

When he entered the village, though, he found the streets empty. Everywhere windows were shuttered. It was as if the population had left en masse, as if a hasty exodus had taken place. But Greaves knew better. The people hadn't gone; they were just keeping themselves out of sight. It was worse, then, than he had expected. The village was afraid.

He turned the car into a narrow side street that led off the main square. Partway along, a painted sign overhanging a doorway on the left announced the Carabinieri station. Greaves pulled to the side of the street and sounded the horn. The station door slowly opened and a nervous face peaked out. It was a young policeman; aside from the *brigadiere*, he was the garrison's sole officer. He looked the length of the empty street, and then along the vacant rooftops of the buildings opposite, before he stepped out onto the pavement, making sure that the pistol he held in his right hand was plain for Greaves to see. He came towards the car.

Greaves opened the driver's-side door and stepped out, and when he did, the young policeman tensed, his right hand rising slightly from his side, until he realized it was Greaves and he relaxed again.

"We didn't think you would come," he said.

"Well, I have," said Greaves.

The policeman stood and regarded Greaves a minute longer, and then he turned his head and shouted back towards the open doorway behind him.

After a moment, Francesco Maglietta emerged, a wide grin stretching out his thick moustache. He had a napkin that was darkened by a spot of grease tucked into his shirt front. He removed it and wiped his hands. "Our saviour has arrived," he said, and came over to Greaves and kissed him on the cheeks. "It is good to see you again so soon."

"It's good to see you too, Francesco," said Greaves. "Though I'd rather the circumstances were different."

"You and me both. You'll stay the night, of course."

"Of course."

"Good." Maglietta clapped him on the shoulder. "Now come inside and let me show you this terrible villain we have captured."

The Carabinieri station was a simple room, large, with a stone floor and bare walls that had small, boxy windows cut out at eye level. The only furniture was a desk pushed back into the corner and a plain table with two straight-backed chairs. On the table were a basket of bread and cold chicken and a bottle of wine.

Maglietta went to the desk and opened a drawer. He took out another glass and filled it for Greaves, then replenished his own. "*Salute,*" he said.

They drank a toast, and then Greaves said: "So, where is this prisoner you're so desperate to get rid of?"

Maglietta nodded to the far side of the room, where the door to a cramped storage closet stood open. Inside, shackled to a chair, was a boy of perhaps sixteen. He sat with his shoulders hunched.

"That's him?" Greaves said, noting his ungainly adolescent frame, all knees and elbows, and the liberal scattering of acne across his cheeks.

"Doesn't look like much, does he? But that didn't stop him from killing a man. Isn't that right, you little shit?"

The boy lifted his gaze. The uneasy expression on his face made him seem even younger to Greaves, and he didn't like to think of how he was going to get on in the communal cells at Poggio Reale prison.

"It's his prick that got us into this mess," Maglietta said. He went to the closet and ran a hand over the boy's head, ruffling his hair. "Or was it love, my friend? Because you know that is what gets us into the worst trouble." He glanced back at Greaves. "The neighbour's daughter, only twelve years old, but a fetching little thing. Someday she will be a beautiful woman. Not that this one will ever know it." He tugged gently on the boy's forelock. "He went to her house in the middle of the night, drunk on Strega. Made such a fuss—throwing stones at the shutters, calling her name out, saying things to make a grown man blush. He woke the whole family. When the brother came outside to clear him off, our little man here takes a swing. Only he forgets that he still has the bottle in his hand. He hits the brother square on the temple. The poor bugger was dead straight away, before he even hit the ground."

Greaves looked at the prisoner again. He had such thin arms: the shackles seemed as though they might slip over his wrists. There was very little of the man he might one day become in his face; he had the eyes of a frightened child.

"What do you think?" Maglietta said. "A story fit for the San Carlo?"

"Might be too much even for the opera," Greaves said.

"Yes, you may be right."

Maglietta came back to the table and poured another glass of wine. He drank it off in one swallow and wiped his mouth with the back of his hand. "I feel bad for the little bastard," he said.

Greaves felt sorry for him too. An accident was all it was, and yet it would end up costing him his entire future.

"But enough of that," Maglietta said. "Let's get you to the house. Cordelia and the girls are waiting. You've brought them gifts, I hope."

"Of course I have."

"Good," Maglietta said with a laugh, "because I told them that you would."

Cioffi stood by the wash basin cleaning sick from the front of his shirt with a damp cloth. The smell of sour lemon and the acrid tang of spoiled wine filled the air. He stopped what he was doing and leaned over the toilet bowl and retched again, but there was nothing left in his stomach to bring up. The *limoncello*, the bottle of Chianti, the stale biscotti that he'd forced down after leaving the Villa Comunale, had already been spilled across the porcelain, as well as over his shoes and on his pants leg. He wiped the bits of vomit from his shoe tops. When he stood up again, a wave of dizziness struck him and he had to grab hold of the basin to steady himself. He was sweating and there was a sharp pain in his bowels. He desperately wanted to be sick again, desperately wanted to spew the rottenness from his guts. He breathed quick, shallow breaths.

He could hear Lello moving about the apartment, from the *salotto* and into the kitchen, then along the corridor to the lavatory.

"Aldo?" he called. "Are you in there?" He opened the door.

Cioffi dipped the cloth into the basin again and wiped at the stain on his shirt front. "What do you want?"

Lello looked at the mess he'd made. He hesitated, and then said: "I've come to tell you that I want you to leave. I want you to find someplace else to live."

Cioffi watched his friend's reflection in the mirror, but Lello would not meet his gaze.

"And where do you propose that I should go?" he said.

"I don't know. I just know that you can't be here anymore. Not after what happened yesterday. I don't know what you've become, Aldo.

I will always love you, I will always be your friend, but I cannot be around you."

Cioffi's head sank. "When?"

"I will give you until next week to find something, but after that I want you gone."

Lello closed the door and shuffled back down the hallway. After he'd gone, another spasm stabbed Cioffi in the belly and he doubled over. For a brief instant he considered that it might be his appendix; perhaps it had swollen and was ready to burst. And then he thought how that useless little organ could explode and fill his abdominal cavity with its poison, choking the life out of more vital organs: his kidneys, his pancreas, his hardened liver.

Then the spasm passed, and with it some of the dread he'd been feeling since that morning. He wet his hands and ran them through his hair, then looked at himself in the mirror—his eyes jaundiced, his skin papery.

He thought: *I have nothing left.*

The soldiers had grey, washed-out faces, scruffy beards, and hollow eyes. They stood about in shirt sleeves, staring vacantly, exhausted. One, with the smooth features of a man who keeps himself indoors, tried to goad them into a cheer, but fatigue, and perhaps something else, stifled their enthusiasm. The headline flashed on the screen: MARINES REST AFTER SEIZING STRONGHOLDS IN THE MARSHALLS. The next caption, which followed a scene of stretcher-bearers carrying wounded along the gangplank of a hospital ship, proclaimed low casualties, but Luisa expected half-truths; she had lived too many years in a propaganda state to believe what was said in newsreels.

She looked at the others sitting beneath the marquee, their faces tilted so they could see the projector screen that had been set up against the garden wall. She hadn't wanted to come, but Augusto had heard that the Red Cross would be handing out blankets and coupons for paraffin. Luisa told him both would soon be pointless now that the days were growing warmer, but he wanted a blanket so he could take it to a tailor to be cut into a pair of waistcoats. She agreed to go only after he threatened to go himself. She had been angry with him, said he was a stubborn fool, but now she felt relief at being out of the museum for a spell. Sorting the collections, everything to be checked and catalogued and organized in the galleries according to Augusto's precise instructions, was draining work. And Augusto himself had become draining—hovering over everything, his temper snappish. It was a strain on him, she knew, having Aldo there. Each day spent waiting for his nephew to disappoint him again.

A murmur passed through the rows as the screen filled with familiar images: narrow, cobbled streets; squat, thick-stoned houses; the crying faces of women, their heads covered by dark scarves; Germans lying dead in the rubble or being led away with their hands in the air. The legend read: FIFTH ARMY PRESSES ON AT CASSINO. There were more wounded soldiers, bandaged and lying on litters on the ground, smoking cigarettes and smiling. Luisa found herself wondering about Thomas. He had said, the day before, that he wanted to help. She wanted so badly to believe him.

Generals filled the screen next, gathered about a table map in the great hall of the palace at Caserta. The title proclaimed: CLARK AND HIS STAFF CONFIDENT OF BREAKING NAZI LINES. Then the images flickered and the screen went dark while the reel was changed.

Laughter and applause greeted the arrival on the white screen of a cartoon mouse dressed in coveralls and a peaked cap and whistling

as he twirled the wheel of a steamboat. Luisa stood up. She excused
herself as she moved along the crowded row to the aisle.

A Red Cross nurse, seeing her, came over. She put her hand on
Luisa's elbow and, in a slow, saccharine voice, said: "You can't leave,
ma'am. We won't be giving out the packages until after the pictures
are finished."

Luisa stared coldly back at her. "I want a blanket and paraffin."

"I'm sorry," said the woman, her pink cheeks bunching up under
the force of her smile. "You can't have anything yet. Not until after
the pictures." She squeezed the inside of Luisa's elbow and began to
gently push her back along the row. "Why don't you just go on and sit
down," she said sweetly.

Luisa shrugged herself free. She felt her face flush, and a bitter anger
welled up inside her as she looked around at the others, who sat there
like sheep watching the flickering screen.

She turned back to the nurse. The urge to slap her face, to pull at
her bottled hair, to scratch the rosy flesh from her fattened cheeks, was
almost too strong to resist. But there were soldiers in the garden, and
Luisa knew that if she touched the woman, they would not hesitate to
descend upon her with their batons. So she sat down again and folded
her hands in her lap.

"Do not touch me again," she said quietly, almost to herself, and
stared off towards a bare space on the wall. Out of the corner of her
eye, though, she could still see the whistling mouse steering his boat.

Cordelia Maglietta made a dinner of grilled mushroom, green salad,
and lamb shank with risotto, followed by simmered pears served with
mascarpone cheese. It was better than Greaves had eaten since he'd last
been to Tenerello. Afterwards they went out to the garden, where the

arbour was lit with oil lamps, and sat in a cocoon of light and drank plum brandy and smoked Maglietta's sharp-smelling cheroots. On a raised stone platform a brazier sputtered, its smoke curling beneath the overhang of the trellis. The night air was cool but with the suggestion of spring in it, like a faint scent carried on the wind. In the cloudless sky the stars shone dimly, the glow of the nearby lanterns drawing off their brilliance even as they flickered in the soft breeze coming up from the valley.

Maglietta, sitting in a bentwood chair, stroked his abundant moustache and mused about his inability to grow grapes on the rocky farmland. "I'll tell you, Thomas, it is as if the ground here is cursed. It holds nothing. Every year I plant vines, and every year they wither. Shrivel up like an old hag's bony fingers. When I came here, I was full of dreams. I was going to have a vineyard, I was going to make wonderful wine and finally stop being a policeman."

"Will you try again?" Greaves asked.

Maglietta laughed. "Of course I will. Otherwise, what's the point of my being here? If I don't have the foolish hope that somehow things will change, then I will just wither away like the damn vines."

"Maybe you should try to grow something else."

"I could do that, but then it would still be like I was giving up. And I am too stubborn a man for that. Besides, sometimes failure is as good as success. It's the attempting that matters."

"You really believe that?"

Maglietta leaned forward in his chair and rested his elbows on the table and looked across at Greaves. "I believe it absolutely, Thomas. A man's intentions say more about him than his achievements. Take our friend today. What are his achievements?" Maglietta held out a hand and counted off on his fingers. "He killed a boy not much older than himself. And he was a good boy, too. I knew him, knew his family. So he did that. And he ruined a young girl's life. What is her future going to be like, knowing that she was the cause of her brother's death? A family he left devastated. Actually, two families. Because now there is a vendetta, and it will collect its victims—the next male in line. And how far will *it* go? To the cousins? The cousins of the cousins? Right now some poor fool is out there somewhere sleeping soundly in his bed, not a care in the world, but one day there is going to be a knock at the door and when he opens it, he'll be shot or stabbed or have his head bashed in, and he won't even know why. And then there is our young friend himself. His life is over. He is going to Poggio Reale, and that will be it for him. These, Thomas, are his achievements. And they are appalling, contemptible, shameful."

Maglietta sipped his plum brandy and drew deeply on his cheroot. Then, as the blue smoke he exhaled caught the breeze and swirled like a mist before him, he said: "But his intentions, now, that is a different story altogether. I say that his intentions were the most honourable. Don't you think? All that he did, all this misery he caused, it was driven by love, or at least what he thought was love. And even though it is my job to arrest him, my job to make sure that the rest of his life is continuous anguish—even after all of this, I can say quite honestly that I have admiration for him. Admiration and a great deal of sympathy."

Greaves watched Maglietta as he sat back and began to run his fingers again through his thick moustache. The *brigadiere* was pleased with himself.

"So are you saying, Francesco," Greaves said, "that you believe in redemption?"

Maglietta made a face. "Redemption?"

"Yes. You believe that a man can make amends for the wrongs he's done."

"Absolutely not." Maglietta shook his head. "It's impossible."

Now it was Greaves who sat forward and propped his elbows on the table. It was the way their conversations often went, a push and pull of opinion, eagerness drawing one forward and then, argument made, easing him back again.

"My grandfather," Greaves said, "always preached that sacrifice was the way to redemption. A man can atone for his sins through acts of selflessness. If you give of yourself, he used to say, if you honestly give of yourself—forgo your own comforts and your own desires and strive only to do good—then absolution will be your reward."

"And you believe this?"

Greaves considered it for a moment. "I don't know. What do you think?"

"I think that your grandfather was a wise man, Thomas. But I also think he hadn't a clue of what he was talking about. It's a fairy tale. A man cannot undo what he has done. That child locked up in the station cannot make un-dead the little girl's brother. Perhaps that family could forgive him for what he did. But to make amends, to achieve some sort of redemption—no, Thomas, I don't think so."

"So there's no point, then? There's no point in trying to make up for your mistakes?"

"I didn't say that," replied Maglietta. "There is always a point. Even if a man can never make amends for the things that he has done, it is important that he try. In fact, it is *everything* that he tries. Because what kind of man is he if he does not?"

There was the sound of giggling behind them, and they turned to see Cordelia with Maglietta's two daughters.

"They wanted to tell you good night," Cordelia said.

Each girl in turn came around the table to Greaves and let herself be kissed on each cheek. Then they went to their father. Maglietta tossed his cheroot away and swept them up onto his lap. He tickled their sides and they nuzzled their faces into his neck.

"Francesco, please," said Cordelia. "I'll never get them settled again."

"Of course you will," Maglietta said. He looked at both girls and said, with feigned severity: "You're not going to give your mother any trouble, now, are you?"

"No, Papa," they chirped in unison.

"And you are going to go straight to sleep without any complaint?"

"Yes, Papa," they chirped again.

"Good, now off you go with your mama."

After the girls had gone inside, the stillness of the night lengthened. They finished off another two glasses of plum brandy and played a few hands of cards, and then Maglietta got up from the table and went to the brazier. He stirred the embers with a stick, flattening them out so they would cool. A small flurry of sparks rose up but burnt out before they reached the trellis.

"The dead boy's family will know that you are here," he said.

"I should leave early, then," said Greaves. "Daybreak is probably best."

"I think so, yes." Maglietta turned away from the brazier. "Come. Cordelia has made up your bed for you."

TEN

"It's the dark as much as the cold," Varone said, "that would get to me."

He looked down at Renzo Abruzzi, curled up on the floor, his arms wrapped around his shins and his chin tucked into his knees. He could smell the sharp tang of the man's urine and imagined that his trousers must be stiff and raw against his flesh. It had been more than twelve hours now since they'd put him in the meat locker. The lunch crowd, mostly American officers from the AMGOT headquarters two streets over, had just begun to arrive when Paolo wrestled him out of the car and down the stairwell into the cellar of the café. He'd put up a good struggle—Paolo had the split lip to show for it. The fight, though, seemed to have gone out of him now.

"We used to keep sides of beef in here," Varone said. "Pork and lamb, too. Prosciutto we had shipped straight from Parma. You can see that we have other uses for it now." Varone turned to Paolo. "Get him out of there."

The cellar of the Caffè Diplomatico was littered with empty crates and boxes of restaurant supplies. It had a faintly earthy odour, and there was, as well, the stink of something gone rotten. The only light came from a single bulb that hung from a wire in the middle of the room.

Varone grabbed a chair and set it below the light bulb. "Sit him down."

Abruzzi blinked against the brightness as Paolo forced him into the chair. The slivery brown twine that bound his wrists had rubbed the skin raw and there was dried blood on the backs of his hands. Paolo pulled the gag out of his mouth and he began to cough and retch.

"Can I have a drink?" he asked hoarsely.

"Give him some water," Varone said.

Paolo went to one of the crates and pulled out a bottle of mineral water. He pried the cap off with his belt buckle then held the bottle out to Abruzzi, who took it in his bound hands and drank greedily. Water spilt from the corners of his mouth and down his shirt front. When he was finished, Paolo took the bottle away.

"Better?" Varone asked.

"Yes, thank you," said Abruzzi. Then he shrugged and asked: "Why are you doing this to me?"

"Why? You already know why, Renzo."

"No," Abruzzi said. "No, I don't."

"But you said so yourself. Remember? Because I am a businessman."

Varone began to walk a slow circle around the chair, so that Abruzzi had to crane his stiff neck to see him.

"But I thought we had an agreement."

"I don't recall agreeing to anything," said Varone. "I recall that you came to me with a proposition and that I listened, but now I've decided that I don't like it."

"I don't understand."

"I know you don't." Varone held out his hand and Paolo passed him the knife. "This is yours, isn't it?" he said to Abruzzi. "People know you by it, I'm told. You have a reputation. Is that right?"

Abruzzi nodded.

"Well, my young friend, I also have a reputation. A reputation it has taken me a very long time to build. And to maintain it, on occasion I have to do some very unpleasant things—things I have not always wanted to do, things that I have found distasteful, but, at the same time, things that have been entirely necessary. I'm sure you understand what I mean. I'm sure that you've had to do things yourself that you wished you could've avoided. Are you following me, Renzo?"

Abruzzi shook his head. "No. No, I don't know what you mean."

Ignorance, Varone thought: forever the first line of defence. It always amused him to see people revert to the position of stupidity, as if somehow this made them more sympathetic rather than less, never imagining that a further deceit would likely only help to seal their fate.

"Let me put it to you another way, then," he said. "Tell me how it would look to others if—after having taken such care to preserve my name—I were to let a man like you not only steal from me, but also dictate the terms of ... what should we call it? A truce? A partnership?"

"But I could work for you," Abruzzi protested. "Me and my men. We would all work for you."

"No, I don't think so. I'm afraid that wouldn't do either."

Abruzzi was frightened. It seemed that for the first time since Paolo had disarmed him and bundled him into the car that was waiting outside the gates of the Villa Comunale, he understood the gravity of his situation. Now, as Varone unfolded the knife and held it out for him to see, he began to tremble.

Varone touched the tip of the knife to his thumb. "Tomorrow morning, they are going to find your body on the Corso Umberto Primo, outside that shitty little *ristorante* you like so much. And people are going to recognize your face. They will know who you are and they will know who put you there. And that way, the next man who thinks he can steal from me will think twice."

In one swift movement, Paolo slipped in behind the chair and grabbed hold of Abruzzi under the chin, pulling his head back.

"Please—"

With two quick stabs, the words died in Abruzzi's throat. A spurt of blood arced across the floor. Paolo released his hold of him, and Abruzzi quickly put his hands to his neck. The blood pulsed between his fingers, leaking over his shirt front. He tried to stand up, but the chair slid out from beneath him and he landed heavily on the floor. He sank slowly onto his side.

Varone stepped past the overturned chair. He crouched down and tilted his head to the side and regarded the stunned expression on Abruzzi's face: it was the look of a man who realizes too late that he has understood nothing of his life.

He patted Abruzzi gently on the cheek. "Big fish eat small fish," he said. "Now, close your eyes, Renzo. Just close your eyes."

Abruzzi's breathing became shallow, his mouth filled with blood. He shuddered and his pupils dilated, then they swelled again until the blue iris turned fully black, and there was a soft sound like air escaping a deflating tire.

Varone stood up. He wiped a spot of blood from the palm of his hand. "Like I said," he told Paolo. "Put him out on the street where he'll be seen."

Greaves woke before the sun, frightened from sleep by the dream of Agira, only this time, when the screaming started, he imagined it was the patients of Ospedale del Santo Sepolcro who suffered the burning agony, and as he walked through the rubble, a cold black rain fell from the night sky, and all around him was the smell of burnt flesh. He tripped over limbs, feet, hands, bits of hair, bone; and the blood mixed with the rain and made a thick stew of the ground that pulled at his boots.

He threw back the blankets and put his feet on the cold floor. He could feel the sweat cool on his skin. He rubbed his arms and then stood up. The wind howled and beat against the shutters. He went to the window and looked out.

There was a strange radiance to the night. Across the mountain range were lightning flashes of a distant storm. It was like observing a battle from afar, the bursts of brilliance at once beautiful and terrifying. Watching it, Greaves was gripped by a cold fear. He sensed, for a moment, his world coming apart. As if there were a force at work over which he had no control. He had felt like this before, in the days after the assault on Agira, when he lay on the ward in the field hospital, unable to move, though the doctors could find nothing that might explain the paralysis.

Greaves was dressed and waiting when Maglietta knocked gently on the bedroom door. He came in carrying a tray with coffee and *cornetti*. The sun had not yet risen.

"We'll go as soon as you're ready," he told Greaves.

They drove through the early morning darkness, the beams of the headlamps picking out the low stone wall that guarded the cliffside. When they arrived at the Carabinieri station, the young policeman was at first hesitant about opening the door; the distant thunder of the early morning storm across the mountains had unsettled him.

Inside, Maglietta went to his desk. He double-checked the transfer orders and placed them in an envelope while Greaves walked over to the closet to inspect the prisoner. The boy, he noticed, had a swollen lip and there was dried blood in his left nostril. A bump below his eye had begun to turn purple, like a small grape beneath the skin.

Maglietta brought the documents to Greaves. "You should take him now," he said.

Greaves put the envelope into his satchel. He got out a pair of handcuffs as Maglietta helped the boy to his feet.

"Take the *tenente's* keys," Maglietta told the young policeman, "and go start his car for him. Keep an eye outside until we bring the prisoner." Then he went to the gun cabinet behind his desk and took out an ancient Cei-Rigotti carbine and slipped the bolt and checked the magazine.

"You'd better be careful with that," Greaves said.

Maglietta patted the stock of the gun. "I like that it's unreliable. This way, I have to think twice before I pull the trigger."

Greaves went to the doorway and looked out into the street. The sky had begun to lighten, but in the roadway everything was still cast in shadows. Soon, though, the sun would climb high enough to burn off the night's dampness that slicked the cobblestones. He saw the young policeman standing by the wall, watching the doorways of the other buildings. He had started the engine of the dark green sedan and left both the driver's door and the rear passenger's door open. Greaves went back inside to collect the prisoner.

He came out with the boy at his side and Maglietta behind, the butt of the carbine propped against his hip. After a few steps the boy stumbled and fell to his knees. As Greaves bent down to help him up again, he caught something out of the corner of his eye, like a shadow that had sprung to life. Maglietta shouted and Greaves turned in time to see the flash from the sawed-off muzzle of a shotgun. The *brigadiere* levelled his carbine and fired off six quick shots that sounded like six sharp handclaps. Then Greaves's head began to spin and he fell onto his backside on the cobblestones. He felt a searing pain on the left side of his face, and his ears hummed as if he had a head full of cicadas.

Maglietta was kneeling at his side. "It's all right," he said. He put a hand on Greaves's back to keep him from toppling over. He slipped another hand beneath his collar.

"What happened?" Greaves said. "Where's the boy?"

"Don't worry about the boy. Are you hurt anywhere else? Can you feel your fingers? Your toes?"

Greaves nodded. He looked past Maglietta. In the middle of the road, his body stretched out at an odd angle, was the boy, his head turned to the side so that he was facing Greaves. Everything below the cheekbone was gone, and white bits of brain speckled the pavement.

"Is he dead?"

"Yes," Maglietta said. "He's dead. And the other one too."

"The other one?" Greaves said, his own words sounding far away to him. "Who's the other one?"

"Who knows? Another brother, maybe, or a cousin—it doesn't matter now."

A wave of nausea washed over Greaves, and he vomited down his shirt front.

Maglietta yelled to the young policeman. "Come help me get him into the car." Then he looked Greaves in the face. "Listen to me. You are wounded, but it is not very bad. I am going to take you back to my house. Cordelia will fix you up."

"And then what?" Greaves said.

"And then we must all leave," said Maglietta.

ELEVEN

Cioffi could sense someone watching, but he carried on with what he was doing. He reorganized the cameos on the narrow shelf of the display case and then stepped back as if to admire his handiwork. When he did so, he also shifted the medical bag with his foot, surreptitiously tucking it behind the base of the cabinet. Then he turned around to check who was there.

"Ah, Luisa," he said, seeing his uncle's assistant standing in the doorway of the small gallery.

Luisa came into the room. She looked into the display case. "What are you doing, Aldo?"

Cioffi closed the glass-fronted door of the cabinet and locked it with the keys that Augusto had given him. "I am doing the same as you. I am taking the inventory."

"These exhibits have already been catalogued."

"Yes, but you know how particular my uncle can be."

"Are you saying Augusto asked you to do this?"

"Yes, that's right," said Cioffi. "Augusto asked me."

"You're lying."

"Don't be silly. Why would I—"

Luisa stepped around him and picked up the bag from where he'd tried to hide it. He made to take it from her, but she swatted his hand away. Then she reached into the bag and brought out a handful of cameos.

"What's this?" she said, holding them out to him.

"Please," Cioffi said. "Let me explain."

"I knew you couldn't be trusted."

"But you don't understand—"

"I understand fine. You are a thief. You always have been." She dropped the cameos back into the bag. "Your uncle will not help you this time. I won't let him."

As she started to walk past him, Cioffi grabbed hold of her arm. "Please," he said. "I beg you."

"Let go of me."

But rather than release her, Cioffi held her more tightly, digging his fingernails into her forearm. He had hoped to hurt her, but her face betrayed no hint of pain.

"They'll kill me," he said. "And then they will kill him."

"What are you talking about?" said Luisa. "Kill who?"

"They'll kill Augusto," Cioffi said, his voice high-pitched and anxious. "They will kill me and then they will kill Augusto."

"Let go of my arm," said Luisa through gritted teeth.

When he took his hand away, she struck out at him, a flurry of open palms that caught him about the head and face. He shrank from her, but she pursued him until his back was to the wall. She kept swinging, boxing his ears, her nails stinging his cheeks. Before he was even conscious of it, he was weeping. Tears streamed down his face. With upraised arms he tried to shield himself from her blows. Then his knees weakened and he felt himself sliding slowly to the floor. Finally, she stopped.

She loomed over him, and in a calm voice said: "Who, Aldo? Who are *they*?"

"Salvatore Varone and his people."

"Who is Salvatore Varone?"

"He is Camorra," Cioffi said through his sobs. "A boss."

"And you let yourself get involved with him?"

Cioffi nodded.

"My God. You're not just a fool, are you? You're a dangerous fool." She put her hand to her forehead and sighed. "What have you promised?"

"I'm to bring him things," Cioffi said. "Pieces from the collection that he can smuggle through the lines to contacts in the north."

"It's not enough that they loot the excavations, now you invite them into the museum as well. Perhaps I should let this Varone kill you."

For a moment it seemed as if she were considering the option, until he said: "And Augusto? What about him?"

She stared down at him, and Cioffi thought she might attack him again. But she did not. Instead, she went to where the medical bag lay. She picked it up and went to the display case. She unlocked the door and began to return the cameos to the shelf—all but one. This last cameo she held out to him.

"Give him that," she said. "I'm sure it will satisfy him for the moment. And don't you breathe a word of this to your uncle."

Cioffi took the cameo. He held it to his chest. "I won't say a thing," he told her. "But … but what will you do?"

"You let me worry about that," Luisa said.

Then she turned and left the gallery. And when she'd gone, Cioffi felt not relief but an even greater dread, as if somehow a terrible thing had been not so much avoided as simply put off for a time.

"To tell you the truth, I've always found the French more cultured than the Italians."

Major Woodard used an atomizer to spray the leaves of an aspidistra that had arrived the day before at Capodichino airfield. It came on a flight from London: a gift from his wife. Its arrival seemed to have lifted the major's spirits considerably, though Greaves sensed something forced about his distraction.

"You know, when I was FSO at Philippeville, I used to go quite often to visit one of the local *colons* on his cotton plantation in the countryside. He always had excellent port. And after dinner we would have ourselves a few glasses in the salon and listen to Gilbert and Sullivan recordings on a phonograph. He had the entire collection. Even *The Grand Duke*, which he claimed to have seen at the Savoy Theatre, though I doubt that very much. Still, it goes to my point: Gilbert and Sullivan on the edge of the desert—it's just civilized."

Greaves waited for the major to go on, but it seemed he had finished. He stood admiring his smuggled houseplant, swaying slightly as if to a remembered tune from one of the *colon*'s comic operas. Then he set the atomizer aside and came back to his desk.

He nodded towards Greaves's wound without looking directly at it. "A nasty bit of business, that. You're certain you don't want to stop by 21st GH and have someone proper look at it?"

Greaves touched the swatch of gauze taped to his neck. "The *brigadiere*'s wife saw to me. She was a nurse before she got married."

"Well, it's up to you, I suppose," said the major. He leaned back in his chair and pressed his fingertips together. "And how did you leave things in Tenerello?"

"The Carabinieri have cleared out," said Greaves. "It's too dangerous for them now."

"The *brigadiere*, too?"

"I took Francesco and his wife and daughters to Nola. They'll be staying with family there until things get sorted out."

"He'll have to answer for leaving his post."

"I'm sure he'd rather do it in Nola than Tenerello, sir," Greaves said.

"Then it's the Italians' problem now, not ours." Major Woodard leaned forward and began to shuffle absently through the paperwork on his desk. "And how about you, lieutenant? How are you holding up?"

"I'll be fine," Greaves said.

"I was thinking you might want some time off."

"Sir?"

"I mean, it's only natural, isn't it, after something like this. A close call like you had can rattle a man—throw him for a loop. Especially if he's someone who ..." The major searched for the right words. "Especially if he's someone who's faced stress before. Perhaps you should take a few days to recuperate. Get your legs back under you, so to speak."

"I am all right, sir," said Greaves. "Really, there's no need—"

"Nonsense," said Major Woodard. "I thought Sorrento might be a good idea. Sergeant Roylance should have settled himself by now. I'm sure he'll see that you're well looked after. And I'll have Sergeant Jones see to your liaison duty—he can manage that much on his wonky leg. I've checked, and you haven't anything on the docket at Castel Capuano. Bennington's fine with the wire-cutting investigations and Philbin can take care of any vetting that might crop up."

"That's very good of you, sir."

"Yes, well, we see to our own, lieutenant. We see to our own."

What happened in Tenerello seemed to have upset the major. He was nervous in Greaves's presence, like someone who finds himself in close proximity to the sick and fears the spread of contagion.

"If you really think it's best, sir."

Major Woodard nodded. "Yes, lieutenant. Yes, I do think it's best."

Colonel Romney and his men descended on the museum like a regiment of accountants. Attaché cases and file boxes in hand, they set themselves up in a conference room on the second floor. They arrived with a detachment of military police that took over the guard duties from the Carabinieri and sent Parente's workmen home for the day. Sentries were posted at all the doors.

"I'm sorry about this," the colonel said later in Parente's office. "It must all seem heavy-handed."

"It does," Parente told him. "And we have not yet finished the inventory."

"Yes, I know," said Romney. "Don't worry, though, my men are professionals. Most of them worked in galleries and museums stateside. Cataloguing is second nature to them."

"But I don't understand. I thought we had more time."

"You do," the colonel said as he picked up the Head of Isis from the window ledge. "You have all the time in the world. But I haven't. For you, this museum is your only concern. For me, it's just one of many. I still have the Capodimonte and the Civico Filangieri to worry about, and by all accounts they haven't fared near as well as you. I've got a list of missing pieces as long as my arm."

"Then why not let us finish our work?"

"Look, *professore*," said Colonel Romney. "The thing is this: The Fifth Army is about to break through at Monte Cassino. And after Monte Cassino it's a clear road straight through to Rome. My men need to be there when that happens because, let's face facts, there are greater treasures in Rome than there are in Naples." He returned the statuette to its place and wiped his dusty finger on his trouser leg. "We should have it all finished up in a day or two, and then we'll be out of your hair."

"I want to oversee your men," Parente said.

"Of course. You are more than welcome to observe our entire operation. I must ask you, though, not to interfere. You understand, of course, that the museum falls under the purview of the Monuments, Fine Arts and Archives Section."

"You mean it belongs to the Americans now," said Parente.

"For the time being, *professore*," Romney said, "yes, it does."

Luisa arrived just as the colonel was leaving. He tipped his cap to her and wished her a good day and then strode out of the office. Once he was gone, Parente felt himself sag; it was as if what little spirit remained in him had been quashed under the heel of the colonel's boot. He went to his desk and sat down.

"Augusto? Are you all right?"

"Where have you been, Luisa? All of this going on and I can't find you anywhere."

"I'm sorry. I was with Aldo. We were rechecking some of the exhibits."

"It doesn't matter anymore. They've taken it from me, Luisa. The Americans—they have taken my museum."

How many times had he secretly wished it would happen, wished that someone would come along and relieve him of the burden, so that he didn't have to worry anymore about the bureaucracy or the bombs or the thieves? But now that someone had done just that, Parente faced the unpleasant reality that, without the museum, he did not exist. Without the museum, he was just a useless old man in a city that was already overflowing with useless old men.

Luisa came and stood behind him. She put her hands on his

shoulders and gently massaged his tired muscles. "Perhaps it is better," she said. "For a little while, at least."

Her words left him hollow, as if in saying them she became part of the betrayal.

"Maybe you are right," he said. "Maybe it is for the best."

She kissed him gently on the top of his head. "And before you know it, they will be gone and everything will be back to the way it was."

"Do you think?"

"Yes, Augusto, I do."

Parente sighed. "Ah, Luisa. I wish I could believe that was true."

She spent the better part of the afternoon helping the colonel and his men get acquainted with the layout of the museum. She shepherded them about, like a guide steering a group of ill-mannered and wayward tourists. She had to continually remind them to stay together and not to touch anything. One of them had nearly knocked to the floor a blue glass drinking jug—a singular example, she'd explained to him, of the Pompeian glass-cameo technique.

Afterwards, when she returned to Augusto's office, she saw him, his neck bandaged and the edge of his left ear burnt and scabbed over. She felt compelled to touch him, and he did not move away when she reached out and traced her finger along the edge of the gauze where it emerged from beneath his collar.

"Does it hurt very much?" she asked.

"Not so much," Greaves said.

Augusto was standing by the window. "Thomas was just telling me what happened," he said. He shook his head. "So terrible, so terrible. I tell you, I don't know anymore what people are thinking. I don't know why they do such horrible things to one another."

"I should have known better," Greaves said. "I wasn't paying attention."

"What were you to know?" Augusto said. "No sane person can expect to know such a thing could happen. It is an insane action."

Luisa could see that he was agitated. He paced in shortened steps between the window and the nearby bookcase. He had left his cane by the sofa. The events of the day, it seemed, were proving too much for him.

She went to the field stove behind his desk. "Why don't I make you some coffee? It might help to calm you some."

"I don't need coffee," he snapped at her, and then was immediately apologetic. "I'm sorry, my darling. Perhaps you're right."

Luisa poured water from a jug into the *caffettiera* and lit the burner. Then she retrieved Augusto's cane from where he'd left it and brought it to him. "Why don't you sit down," she said. "You don't want to wear yourself out."

She led him back to the sofa and helped him to sit. He took in a deep breath and slowly let it out again. Then he said, in a measured, straightforward manner that suggested his agitation was behind him: "That boy was already dead, Thomas. He was dead before you even arrived there."

"I suppose you're right, *professore*," Greaves said. "I suppose there really wasn't much I could do about it. It was coming one way or another."

When Luisa looked over at him, she saw that he was watching her and she suddenly felt self-conscious. She turned away and began to prepare the cups. Over her shoulder she asked, "Was he very young?"

"Yes," said Greaves. "He was."

"And was he frightened?"

"I could feel him trembling when I held his arm."

"And did he see the man who shot him?"

"No. It came from behind."

"Well, at least there was that," she said.

There was a knock at the door. One of Colonel Romney's men came into the office. He needed some clarification on the contents of one of the smaller exhibits and wondered if the *professore* wouldn't mind coming with him.

"I'll go," Luisa said.

"No," Augusto said, struggling to his feet. "You stay here with Thomas. I will go."

"Are you certain?" she asked.

"Yes, Luisa, you stay." He began to hobble towards the door. "Besides, I want to make sure they aren't making a mess of things."

Luisa was glad of the chance to be alone with Greaves, even though, after Augusto had left, she could find nothing to say to him. They stood in silence until the *caffettiera* boiled. Then she set about pouring the coffee.

He came and stood beside her. "I've been given a short leave," he said. "Two days. I think the major is worried that I'm going to crack up."

"Why does he think that?"

He shrugged. "He has his reasons, I suppose."

"What will you do?"

"It's been arranged for me to go to Sorrento."

"It is beautiful there."

"You've been?"

"Yes, of course."

"Would you like to go again?"

"I'm sorry?"

"Would you like to come to Sorrento with me?"

He was standing so close to her that she could smell the talcum he wore under his shirt.

"Why are you asking me this?" she said.

"I don't want to be alone," he said, then added quickly: "You would have your own room. And I thought maybe you would show me the ruins at Pompeii. I haven't been yet, and the *professore* tells me that you know them as well as anyone."

"I cannot leave Augusto."

"There's nothing you can do here until the Americans are finished. I would think that this is probably the only time you could leave him."

She felt the urge to touch his wound again.

"Just think about it, will you? That's all I'm asking. If you decide not to, I'll understand."

"When will you go?"

"Tomorrow."

Luisa nodded. "I will come with you."

TWELVE

The American military police captain cut his spaghetti with a knife and pushed it onto his fork with a heel of bread. He lifted the fork slowly to his mouth, but still managed to spill sauce down his chin and spatter the napkin tucked into his shirt front. As he set about loading his fork again, Varone lit a cigarette.

"You are unhappy with our arrangement, maybe?" he said.

The captain shook his head. He spoke through a mouthful of pasta. "Arrangement's fine. I got no problem with that. But what you're asking now is a lot different than looking the other way when your trucks come into the port."

"I think not so much."

The American put his fork aside and wiped his mouth with the corner of his napkin. "I'm not your private errand boy, Sal. We do our business and that's all well and good. We both benefit and everybody walks away happy. But this is a whole different ball game you're talking about here."

Varone shrugged. "I have decided nothing. We are only talking."

"This kind of talk, I don't like. And I'll tell you right now, I'm not going near any security police. Neither should you. That kind of trouble you don't need."

"What about the other one?" Varone said.

"You can deal with that yourself," said the captain.

"You do not understand."

"Oh, I understand fine. You want someone else to do your dirty work for you. Well, it ain't gonna be me."

Varone reached across the table and stopped the American raising his fork to his mouth. "You *will* do this," he said.

"Or what? You gonna send that ape of yours after me, are you?"

Varone stared at him. The captain turned his attention back to his pasta. He had no table manners. That he was a messy eater had always bothered Varone. If he was careless with his food, he could be careless with other things too.

"How much?" the captain asked.

"Four hundred thousand lire," said Varone.

The captain shook his head. "Six hundred, no less. I'll have to detail men to do the job, and they're going to need to be paid too. And I figure, if it's my ass that's gonna be on the line here, then I say my ass is worth six."

Varone nodded and stood up from the table. "Paolo will find you when I have decided."

"That's fine," said the American, his mouth full again. "You just make sure he brings the money."

Luisa had collected him from the section office early in the morning. Parente had given her the museum's car for the trip. Greaves, with his duffle bag and a lunch packed for them in a wicker picnic basket he'd found in the pantry of the palazzo's kitchen, waited for her outside in the square. On their way out of the city she pointed out to him the rocky beach where she used to swim as a child, but after that she didn't say much and Greaves wondered if maybe she'd started to regret her decision to join him. A while later, as they passed through Castellammare and the winding seaside road opened onto a magnificent view of the coastline—the chalky cliffs of the Sorrentine peninsula stretching into the distance, and the deep blue waters of the bay—he said that he couldn't imagine anything bad happening in a place that was so beautiful.

"Bad things happen everywhere," she said. "Especially in beautiful places." And then she was quiet again.

When they reached the ruins, she parked the car alongside the empty platforms of the rail station. Over the roof of the station he could see the tarnished crucifix atop the bell tower of La Chiesa della Nostra Signora del Rosario. The steeple marked the new town of Pompeii, built on a bedrock of ancient volcanic ash a half mile to the east of the ruins.

While he collected the picnic basket out of the back seat, she raised the hood of the car and loosened the wires to the distributor cap. "Just to be safe," she said.

Then they crossed the road to the ruins.

American military police sentries patrolled the buried walls of the ancient city. In the arched gateway of the Porta Marina, a makeshift visitors' centre had been set up. It was also manned by MPs, who checked identity documents and warned visitors against attempting to remove any artifacts from the ruins, a crime punishable by court martial or military tribunal.

"Could you tell me where is Cosimo Moccia?" Luisa said to one of the MPs.

"Who?"

"Cosimo Moccia," she repeated. "He is the site director. He is in charge of the digs."

The MP held her papers out. "Why don't you move along, little lady," he said.

Greaves stepped forward. "She asked you a question."

"Yeah, buddy, I heard her. But there ain't no ginzoes in charge of this place."

Greaves showed his security police identification and said: "Maybe you could ask someone who knows."

"Is that supposed to impress me? Field Security ain't in charge of this place either. But if you're looking for the wop workers, they got a hut set up inside."

They passed through the gate and began to climb the narrow stone roadway. Near the crest of the short rise they found the small hut that the MP had mentioned. It was built of mismatched lengths of planking. It stood across from what looked to Greaves to be a bomb site.

Before he could ask what it was, Luisa had pulled open the door of the hut.

"Hey you," a voice called from farther up the road. "What are you doing there?"

A stocky middle-aged man wearing dusty trousers and a tattered cable-knit sweater came lumbering down the roadway towards them. His face glistened with sweat.

Luisa let go of the door and smiled. "Cosimo," she shouted.

The man opened his arms, and when he reached her, he picked her up and swirled her about. "My darling Luisa. I haven't seen you in so long. I thought you had forgotten about us out here."

Greaves noticed the dirt caked behind the fellow's ears. And his hands—which held firmly still to Luisa's waist—were equally begrimed, the nail of each finger a filthy half moon.

"Stop that," said Luisa. "You're embarrassing me."

"Embarrassing you?" he said, and let her go. "Since when have you ever been embarrassed?" He noticed Greaves then. "Ah, I see. And who is this, then?"

The man eyed him up and down, and Greaves wondered if he didn't detect a hint of jealousy in his manner. The smile had gone from his face, and it seemed he had squared himself a bit, as if perhaps to display his potency. He had a powerful body, and Greaves was reminded of the photographs of a young Parente.

"Don't worry," Luisa said. "He is a friend."

But there was something about the way she spoke that made Greaves suspect that his presence had suddenly made her self-conscious.

"Augusto trusts him," she said.

Cosimo Moccia watched him a moment longer, and then his smile returned and he held out his hand. "What do they call you?" he said.

"Thomas," Greaves replied.

"Well, Thomas, is it you that has been keeping this lovely woman away from me? Or is that Augusto's doing?"

"Please, Cosimo," Luisa said.

"I think you'll have to blame the *professore*," Greaves said.

"Why not?" Moccia said with a laugh. "I blame him for everything else." He turned again to Luisa. "Now, tell me, what is it that finally brings you to see me after—how long has it been? Two months? More, I think."

"Thomas has not seen the ruins."

"Then you must allow me to introduce you to Pompeii, my friend."

"I'd like that very much," said Greaves. "But do you mind if I ask what happened here?" He pointed to the collapsed building across from the hut.

"That," Moccia said. "That is what is left of the antiquarium, a repository for artifacts collected in the digs. Or at least, it was until our American friends made a visit with their B-24 bombers. Liberators, I believe they call them."

"There was an air raid?" Greaves said.

"Oh, there have been many air raids. But all was not lost. Their bombs did uncover a lovely villa outside the city walls." He put his arm around Greaves's shoulder. "But enough about that. Come, let me show you around."

The conference table in the second-floor reception room was strewn with ledgers, files, pieces taken from various display cases in various galleries, document boxes that had been brought up from the archives, and a scattering of photographs that Parente had not seen before: pictures of paintings and statues from the museum's collection.

"I realize that it may seem a bit unorganized, *professore,*" Colonel Romney said, "but it really isn't. In fact, we're just about finished."

Parente looked around the room at the colonel's men, hard at work taking notes and sifting through the mess they'd made. He couldn't believe that anything could get done in such chaos.

"We've gone through the inventory you prepared and checked it against what's on the floor," the colonel continued. "And then we compared that with the museum's original catalogue. We've come across a few inconsistencies."

"What do you mean, 'inconsistencies'?"

"Here, I'll show you." Colonel Romney led him to the far side of the table, where he flipped through the pages of one of the ledgers then rummaged through a stack of paperwork and found his notes. "It's nothing too serious, really, just a few smaller objects that appear in the catalogue but can't be accounted for. It could be nothing. Perhaps you moved them, lent them out, maybe, and forgot to make a record."

"That is unlikely," Parente said.

"It's something else, then." The colonel shifted the ledger so Parente could see. "As I was saying, it's nothing substantial, at least not in the grander scheme of things. Some coins and cameos, an Egyptian statuette."

"It's not possible," Parente said. "I know these pieces. I have seen them myself. They are here in the museum."

Colonel Romney shrugged. "So you say, *professore*, but my men have checked and double-checked and they can't find them. Trouble is, though, there's not a lot we can do to help you out. If these pieces were of more consequence, say, wall paintings or mosaics, or one of the sculptures, it would be different. Maybe you should think about having a word with some of your own people."

"Yes, of course, colonel," Parente said as he looked down at the open page of the inventory ledger. He recognized Aldo's handwriting. "Thank you. I will do that."

A cloud of dust hung in the air over the ancient arena, kicked up by the scuffling feet of the English soldiers as they chased the ragged leather ball across the makeshift pitch. They were from a detachment of Royal Engineers stationed at Torre del Greco, and they'd brought with them from their barracks a set of collapsible goalposts strung with camouflage netting. Once a week they descended upon the amphitheatre to play a soccer match that lasted the whole of an afternoon.

Luisa wondered aloud if it was such a good idea.

"They do far less damage than some of the others," Moccia said.

The others he referred to were the Americans, who, it turned out, were rather too fond of collecting souvenirs. Earlier, they'd come across two GIs on Via dell'Abbondanza who were whittling away a piece from a wall painting above the doorway of a shop. When Luisa made to say something to them, Moccia stopped her with a gentle hand and said: "It's better not to start anything. The MPs will be on their side."

"But it's a punishable offence," Luisa said. "They told us so."

"That was for show. Now, if it were you or I chipping away keepsakes, it would be a different story. The city is theirs for the time being."

He had seemed, she thought, resigned to the fact. And now, with the *inglesi* and their soccer game, he was full of boundless enthusiasm. "Next week," he said, "we are going to play them. It's been arranged. The site workers against the engineers."

Just then, one of the soldiers shouted up to where they stood on the terrace at the far end of the stadium. "Hey, Cosimo, mate. I hope you're taking notes."

"Who was it that won the last two World Cups?" he shouted back. "I can't remember."

The soldier laughed. "We'll see about that on Tuesday," he called out before chasing after the ball again.

Cosimo Moccia proved an entertaining guide, just as Luisa knew he would. She was glad they'd found him. And she could tell by the wide smile on his face that he was glad as well. He had taken quickly to Greaves, and had walked along much of the time holding him by the elbow and talking, in his rapid-fire manner, about the excavations, explaining to him the history of each building they stopped at. Neither did he miss an opportunity to be mischievous. When they came out of the House of the Moralist, he pointed out some Latinate graffiti scratched into the soft limestone wall. "You see what is written here, Thomas," he said. "*Myrtis bene felas.* Do you know what that means?" He didn't give Greaves a chance to answer. "It means: 'Myrtis gives good blow jobs.'" His laugh rumbled in his chest. "So you see, things have not changed very much. Men are still crude." Then he nodded towards Luisa. "And women still blush."

On the floor of the amphitheatre, the players were taking a break. They congregated around the temporary goalposts at the far end of the pitch and drank greedily from their canteens.

"Come," Moccia said. "We've seen enough here."

He led the way down to the tunnel that ran beneath the seats of the arena. In the dark interior of the amphitheatre the air was cool and dank. Outside, the sun had risen high in the clear blue sky and the heat was noticeable. Winter was behind them now, Luisa thought, and she found herself becoming uneasy about what spring was to bring. Her sense of the future was more uncertain than it had ever been, and she wondered how much that had to do with Greaves, and how much had to do with the fact that soon the war would be moving on to the north.

When they emerged again into the sunshine, they came upon an old man pushing a handcart. His wrinkled face was framed by a shock of white hair, and his smile showed a mouthful of rotten teeth. On his cart was a tin bucket, and in the bucket a block of melting ice. He had a bowl of barely ripened lemons and a small stack of cones made from twisted bits of old newspaper.

Greaves went to him. "How much? *Quanto?*"

"*Cinquanta lire,*" the old man said.

He asked for three and the old man took a scarred carving knife from his jacket pocket and began to scrape away at the ice. He put the shavings into the paper cones, then halved two of the lemons and squeezed their thin juice over the top of each.

"*Grazie,*" Greaves said, taking the cones from him.

"*Prego,*" replied the vendor. And then he laughed, a consumptive rattle that seemed to shake his entire body. He pointed towards Vesuvius and said, "*Presto la montagna erutterà.*"

"Is that right?" said Greaves. He passed one cone to Luisa and another to Moccia. "This fellows says that the mountain is going to erupt soon." He took a bite of his ice-lemon. "Do you think he knows something that we don't?"

Luisa put a hand on his forearm and then quickly withdrew it again. "Ignore him. He is just a crazy old man."

"Oh, I don't know," said Moccia as he scraped his teeth over the cone. "Sometimes we ignore the elderly at our peril. I'd have thought you would've known that. Augusto says as much to me every time I speak to him."

"You're still afraid of him, aren't you, Cosimo?"

"Out of my skin," said Moccia with a smile. "If I weren't, I would have run away from this place a long time ago."

They made their way once more along Via dell'Abbondanza, stopping briefly at the crumbled dwelling called La Casa del Moralista. "This is my favourite place in all of Pompeii," Moccia told Greaves. "It was the home of a wine merchant. But you see here." He pointed out several slogans written on the walls of the triclinium. "He was also an advocate for temperance. I love the idea that it was profits from selling wine that paid for the paint to write these mottoes. I always wonder if he appreciated the paradox of his beliefs. Or maybe, after all, it was simply a joke."

When they came again to the Forum, where the streets of the ancient city converged and the broken colonnades of the temples of Jupiter and Apollo looked like a harvest of dried bones left to bleach in the sun, Moccia bade them goodbye. He shook hands with Greaves and then hugged Luisa tightly. "Next time, don't stay away so long," he said to her. "I miss looking at your pretty face."

After they parted, Luisa led the way along a narrow road that took them outside the city walls. It followed a gentle slope towards a house on a hillside. She had decided on the Villa of the Mysteries the night before. She wanted to take Greaves somewhere that was close to her heart. It was the place to which Augusto had brought her years before, when she first came to work with him and when he still made regular trips to the ruins. He had taken her by the hand then and stood her before each panel of the magnificent fresco that had given the villa its name. He told her that he thought of her as the initiate.

Luisa did not take him inside at first. Instead, they sat in the garden which overlooked Pompeii and ate the lunch that he'd packed—wine and cheese and bread, and canned meat that he apologized for but that she savoured as if it were chateaubriand.

"He's quite a fellow, isn't he," Greaves said, removing the jelly from the beef before he put it on a heel of bread and popped it into his mouth. "I don't know if I've met anyone quite so cheerful since I arrived here. It's almost contagious."

"He wasn't always like that," Luisa said.

"Really?"

She shook her head. "His brother was killed during a bombardment. He was the site director at Herculaneum. It very nearly destroyed Cosimo. They were very close. I think now he tries to be happy so that he won't think about it."

"He must feel very down sometimes. Does he have other family?"

"He has a wife and a son. But they are in the north, with his sister in Milan. He sent them there before the Americans came. He did not want them to be caught in the fighting."

"Is he in touch with them?"

"He used to pay a woman to smuggle letters through, but she was caught several months ago. I think she is in Filangieri prison now."

"And has he had any word from his wife since?"

"Not that I know of," said Luisa. "But I am sure that she is fine."

"I hope so," said Greaves.

They finished eating and packed away the basket. Then she stood up. "Come with me. There is something I want you to see."

She took him into the villa, into the room with blood-red walls.

Within the fresco that dominated the triclinium chamber, the half-naked figure of Silenus played his lyre and beside him a woman suckled a goat. It was the narrative of a young bride's initiation into the cult of Dionysus. Silenus appeared again, looking this time like a corrupt old man as he offered his wine to a nearby satyr. After Silenus was Ariadne, bare-breasted in repose, then Dionysus himself, his head missing along with a large section of the original plaster. The young bride, too, made her appearance here: prostrated before a flagellating angel, her veil draped over the erect phallus of the seraph.

"What do you think?" she said.

"It all seems a bit frightening."

"Only because we do not understand it. There is nothing sinister in it." She went to the final panel of the frieze and pointed out the figure of a woman dressed in flowing robes and seated on a cushioned chair. "This is the matron of the house. She is a priestess of the cult. If the fresco had been discovered, she would have been punished."

"For her beliefs, you mean?" said Greaves.

"Yes. So you see, she is a brave woman."

Luisa watched him as he approached the image of the matron. He stood close and studied her figure. "It must be such a terrifying thing to do," he said. "Knowing that it could cost her everything." He turned round and looked at her. "That sort of fear can destroy a person."

"If you believe," Luisa said, "then fear becomes secondary. To know that you are doing the right thing should be enough comfort."

He looked again at the matron. "I suppose. But not everyone has that kind of strength."

"I disagree," Luisa said. "That strength is in everyone. They just have to be willing to find it."

She stepped forward and took hold of his arm. "We should go. It is still a long way to Sorrento."

THIRTEEN

The setting sun dazzled against the coming shadow of night and lit the chalky cliffs of the peninsula, while Naples, far across the bay, lay like a jewel caught in the failing light, a splash of brightness on the horizon, a white city. Below, at the water's edge, chaises longues obtruded from beneath blue-striped umbrellas, and farther along, on the flat rock beach, the last sunbathers collected their towels and folding chairs as the late boats from Capri spilled their passengers onto the quayside. Watching it all from his hotel room window, Greaves could imagine that the war did not exist.

An hour earlier, they had found Sergeant Roylance having drinks with his mistress on the terrace of a streetside café in Piazza Tasso. The boy who worked for Roylance in the former travel bureau that now served as the office for the Sorrento detachment had told them he would be sitting to the right of Saint Anthony the Lesser. "*Sempre all destra di Sant'Antonino,*" he'd said.

"The boy, Niello he's called," said Roylance when they finally arrived at the café, "he's a bit soft in the head, but he's a hard worker." Then he motioned towards the bandage on Greaves's neck. "I'd heard that you had a rough time of it in the countryside. I'll say this for the Italians: they are a dramatic lot. Incapable of finding the simple solution to things—too emotional by half."

Maddelena Giordano, Roylance's mistress, sat aloof. She was a player at the Teatro Tasso. "My Italian has improved," he'd said to Greaves, "but it's still not good enough for us to argue, which does make things easier."

Luisa had seemed transfixed by Maddelena's hair. Dyed so blond that it was nearly white, it stood in stark contrast to her thinly plucked charcoal eyebrows.

Roylance had arranged for their rooms in the Hotel Excelsior Vittoria. He kept a suite for himself on the top floor—one of the perks, he'd told them, of being the only intelligence officer in the town.

From his window, Greaves could see the faint outline of Vesuvius, hazy in the last moments of the day. It struck him as a rather solitary image: a single peak on the horizon.

In her own small room on the second floor, Luisa also stood at the window. Hers, though, looked out over a narrow street. Across the way was an adjoining hotel. Through the undraped windows opposite she could see an American officer, an older man with short silver hair, bathed in the yellowish glow of electric light. He stood before a mirror, straightening his tie. He fixed his hair with creme and put on a dark brown uniform jacket. He polished the brass on his epaulettes with his cuff. He disappeared, returning a moment later wearing a peaked cap that he adjusted so that it sat an angle. She could tell by his pursed lips that he was whistling. Then he disappeared again and the light went out.

She left the window and went to her own mirror and looked at herself. Maria's dress was too big in the bosom for her, so she had tied a white silk sash about the waist to gather in the extra material; it drew together uncomfortably at her hips. She had wanted to wear something subdued. The best she could manage was this mauve silk with white buttons down the front.

There had been a moment earlier, in the café, when Thomas caught her watching him. She was sitting across the table and hadn't realized until he glanced over at her that she had been staring. His smile embarrassed her. The English sergeant had noticed her brief loss of composure and mistook it, she thought, for something else. He said that he had always found Sorrento a romantic place. He told her that he had come to the town with his wife after they were married. He had said this in front of his mistress, who, if she'd understood, seemed not to care.

Luisa said to him: "We will have separate rooms."

"Of course," he told her. "I understand."

But Luisa didn't know how he could, when she did not understand herself.

The actors were brightly attired in reds and greens and whites that reflected almost painfully in the stage lights. It was a cartoon-like landscape: cookie-cutter tenement houses with laundry strung between balconies, thick-wheeled papier mâché drays pulled by costumed donkeys, a cardboard sun splashing its floodlit rays. Romanticized stage poverty—such gaiety for such a sad story: love lost, love doomed, love traded in back alleys, or bartered away, and always with mournful songs. "Santa Lucia." "'O' Sole Mio." Why was it, Greaves wondered, that these people seemed to sing of nothing but heartbreak? Why was it forever calamity? Perhaps, he decided, it was simply the way it was. Perhaps love was something that did not last. Perhaps they believed that love was only a fleeting sensation, like the pain of hunger or the satisfaction of a good meal.

Greaves had not known which of the women was Maddelena until she was pointed out to him. During the dancing of the tarantella,

Roylance leaned across and said to him: "There she is, my capricious Capri girl." Her platinum hair was hidden beneath a brunette wig and her face was garishly painted: kohl around her eyes, her cheeks rosy, her lips an exaggerated rosebud.

Afterwards, though, in the café, Greaves found her somewhat disappointing. Without her costume and makeup, without the dark wig, Maddelena looked worn down. It was as if she had aged years in the span of hours, as if she were the older, harried sister of the woman he had met that afternoon in the Piazza Tasso.

Around them, the café bustled with the after-theatre crowd. The air was filled with laughter and the sound of clinking glasses, but Maddelena was soon bored. She no longer had an audience and so grew restless and fidgeted as Roylance talked of his love of the theatre.

"Do you know," he said, "that Henrik Ibsen lived just round the corner from here? This is where he wrote *A Doll's House*. Can you imagine that? What a dreary play to be thought up in such a wonderful little town. He really must have been a miserable codger. Then again, he was Norwegian. I can't imagine they've got a lot to be happy about, what with all that snow and not seeing the sun for half the year."

Roylance took the bottle of wine and topped up everyone's glass. Then he toasted their being there. "I'll tell you this much: I feel sorry for you lot, stuck back there in Naples. The filth and corruption—it's bloody horrible. I'll gladly while away my days here, thank you very much. I'd be happy enough if I never left."

But Greaves thought that there was something forced about the sergeant's enthusiasm. In Naples he'd been cordial enough but always rather distant. His manner was very professional, and even the others, Bennington and Jones in particular, had joked about him, called him the company man. But now, after four weeks by himself in Sorrento, the solitude seemed to be getting the better of him. And to Greaves, his effusiveness for the place was like a compensation, as if he were tying to convince himself as much as he was trying to convince them.

Finally, Maddelena had had enough. She leaned over to him and said: "*Mi sono stancata. Possiamo andare a casa?*"

"But it's early yet, darling."

"*Lo so, ma mi sono stancata.*"

Roylance was clearly let down, but Maddelena would not be convinced. He got up from the table and helped her on with her wrap. "There is a wonderful little nightclub," he said to Greaves. "It's cut into the cliffside below the central square. I had thought to take you, but it seems Maddelena is too tired. I hope you don't mind."

"That's fine," Greaves said. "We've had a pretty full day ourselves. We might just head back to the hotel."

"Nonsense," Roylance said. "I won't have you calling it a night on my account. This is a lively place after dark. You should have a wander round. If nothing else, you should make a visit to the public gardens below Piazza San Antonino. If the stars are out and if the wind is down, you'll see two skies—one above and one below. But really, you must have a look for yourselves."

They did not stay long at the nightclub. When they arrived, it was crowded, so they ordered their drinks standing at the bar. An orchestra of American servicemen played swing music and the dance floor seethed, rising and falling like a disturbed pool of water, waves of dancers breaking over the white-clothed tables that ringed the floor. The air was close. The low stone ceiling was damp with condensation; it dripped. Luisa could smell the odour of her own sweat. When his lips brushed her ear, she wished that she had used more of Maria's talcum powder under her arms. Did she want to leave? he asked. Would she like to go somewhere else? She said yes.

So he took her to a *gelateria* in a cobbled laneway beside the Duomo. The lights were bright inside the shop; there was no blackout in Sorrento. Soldiers lined up with their women, Neapolitan girls mostly, though she recognized accents from farther south, from Amalfi and even Salerno. She felt uncomfortable among them, much as she had at the Gambrinus, and asked him if they could leave.

They walked the streets. Once, pushing through a crowd that had gathered outside a café, their hands touched. He held on to hers a moment, as if to make sure he did not lose her in the crush, then let go of it again once they were free of the crowd. He apologized afterwards.

They had not discussed going to the public gardens, but that was where they found themselves in the end. She had thought that the *inglese* was talking nonsense, but as they leaned against the iron railing that ran atop the cliff's edge, she saw that there were indeed two skies: one pristine, exact, the stars like pinpricks in a rich black cloth; the other wavering, slightly out of focus, like the work of an Impressionist painter. And yet it was difficult to judge where one began and the other ended, difficult to decipher whether it was the sea reflecting the sky or the sky reflecting the sea. It was almost, she thought to herself, like looking into eternity.

A cool breeze blew and he took off his jacket and put it around her shoulders. His hands lingered a moment, then he stepped away from her. He looked out over the water.

"You've never asked me what I did before I came to Naples," he said.

"Perhaps I don't want to know," she said.

"Is that true?"

There was something in his voice that made her uncertain. She hesitated, then said: "Were you in battle?"

"I was, yes."

"Was it very horrible?"

He shook his head. "No, not at first. To tell the truth, in the beginning it was quite exhilarating, almost like the games we played when we were boys."

"I don't believe you."

"It sounds ridiculous, I know. But there was something rather intoxicating about the whole situation."

"You liked it, then?"

"I think so, yes. At least, for a time I did. We landed in Sicily at the beginning of July, near Ragusa, then made our way north. The Germans had pulled out, moved into the mountains. We had a few skirmishes, but nothing of real consequence. In most of the villages we were given a hero's welcome. People came out into the streets. They gave us food and wine. That's what made it all so appealing, I suppose. But it wasn't real. I mean, those first couple of weeks, that wasn't really what war was like. It was more like a performance of war, like tonight at the theatre was a performance. There were hints of what it could be like, but we really hadn't had a taste of it, not yet. Of course, we didn't know that then. We thought we were kings of the battlefield."

"But you found out that you weren't," Luisa said.

"Yes. We found out." He was quiet a moment. "I was what's called a Forward Observation Officer. It was my job to direct the fire onto the enemy positions. Once I had established a target, I would radio to the artillery batteries in the rear—the big guns, 105-millimetre howitzers mainly—then I would make readjustments, that sort of thing. We prepared to make an assault on a place called Agira, a town in the mountains north of Masseria. We had to come at it across a wide plain. The unit I was with had the job of attacking the left flank. We knew it would be different from the other towns. The Germans were dug in there, and we were scared. I was scared. We moved out after dark. The night was so black—no stars, no moon. We couldn't find our markers, we got lost. When the initial barrage started on the right flank, we weren't where we were supposed to be, and I panicked. I found my wireless operator. He was just a kid, but he knew better than I did. He tried to stop me, tried to tell me that we were out of position, but I wouldn't listen to him. Intelligence reports had said that there were supposed to be tank emplacements off to our east, so I called in the coordinates to the Fire Direction Centre. But there weren't any tanks there."

His voice trailed off. He took a deep breath and then slowly let it out again. "It was a schoolhouse—a schoolhouse with women and children inside. They knew that there would be fighting and they had gone there to hide. They thought they would be safe, and they should have been. It was on the edge of town, away from the German emplacements. Had I not misread the map, had I listened to my wireless operator ... "

Luisa tried to read the expression on his face, but in the darkness she could see only his silhouette as he stared out at the stars reflected on the water.

"I was a wreck afterwards. I think I wanted to kill myself."

"Why didn't you?" she said softly.

"I don't know." He took hold of the railing and rocked back on his heels. "They all told me that I wasn't to blame—my commanding officer, the men in the squad, the doctors at the field hospital where they took me after my corporal found me with my gun. They said sometimes these things happen. But I knew it wasn't true. I dream about it almost every night. I hear them screaming as the building burns, and it's like I'm killing them all over again. It's like that every time I close my eyes, and I know that it will never stop. I know that they will always be there."

Luisa was confused by her emotions. "Why are you telling me this?"

He looked at her now. "Because I want you to know who I am. I want you to know what I've done."

The sun did not shine on that side of the hotel, but Luisa knew the hour by the sounds coming from below her window: street sweepers brushing the cobbles clean, the whisk of their straw brooms against the worn stone. She reached a hand across to the empty side of the bed, gathered the loose sheets in her fingers. He'd left her room while it was still dark. She had asked him to go, and he told her that he understood. He dressed without turning the light on, and then stood a moment at the foot of the bed before moving towards the door. He did not say anything to her before he went. There was nothing left to be said.

After they made love, she had gone to the toilet and washed herself. When she came out, he was sitting on the edge of the bed, smoking a cigarette. He gave her one and she sat down next to him. She was uncomfortable in her nakedness, and uncomfortable with his, too. For a time they didn't speak, and she thought that, even after all this, she did not understand him.

Then she told him about Aldo, about his stealing, and about Salvatore Varone. He told her that he thought he'd heard the name before.

"What can I do?" he asked her.

"I don't think there is anything to be done. Perhaps it is all just a bad dream and it will go away."

"You know that won't happen. Bad dreams don't just go away like that."

"I know."

Now she pulled back the blankets and got out of the bed. Her back was sore and her legs stiff. She found her robe and pulled it on, and then she went to the window and drew back the curtains.

The sun was low still and the street outside was cast in shadow. Across the way, the American officer was standing again before his mirror, though now he was dressed only in loose-fitting, drab underpants and a sleeveless vest, and he leaned in towards his reflection and studied the morning image of himself. He drew his fingers across the sagging flesh under his chin, pulled it taut, then let it go again. Luisa thought he looked rather disappointed with the prospect of himself, and she felt suddenly very sorry for him.

FOURTEEN

Salvatore Varone sat under the shade of an umbrella and sipped a cappuccino, while beside him Paolo consulted his battered notebook. A shipment of auto parts bound for a motor pool in Posillipo had been temporarily diverted to the abbey in Montecalvario.

"Who is dealing with the negotiations?" Varone asked.

Paolo told him that he'd found a man who had been a director at the Banco di Napoli who had agreed to speak with the head of the military government's civilian liaison department. "It should not be a problem. Though his cut will be high."

"What did he take last time?"

"Twenty-five percent."

"He'll want more."

"Yes," Paolo said. "I think as much as forty."

"Tell the banker to offer thirty. That should get us thirty-five."

"Working with the Americans is getting expensive," Paolo said.

"It will only get worse. They know we haven't much left to bargain with. Soon enough we'll be giving them half of everything we take in."

"And there's nothing we can do about it?"

"For the time being, no."

A waiter approached the table and begged their pardon.

"What is it?" Varone said.

"There is a man at the bar who wishes to speak to you."

"Who is he?"

"He claims to be a Dottore Aldo Cioffi, but he does not look like a *dottore* to me, *signore*."

"That's fine. Send him out."

The waiter bowed and went back inside the café.

"I didn't think he would come," said Paolo.

"I was beginning to have doubts myself," Varone said.

A moment later, Cioffi emerged. As he came towards them, Varone could see the sheen of sweat on his face. His complexion was drawn and there was a noticeable hitch in his step.

"I see you've already had a couple of glasses of courage, *dottore*," said Varone. "Why don't you have a seat."

Cioffi plunged a hand into his coat pocket and Paolo was quickly out of his chair. He grabbed hold of the *dottore's* arm and wrenched it behind his back. Cioffi yelped in pain.

"You should be careful," Varone said as Paolo prised open the *dottore's* fingers. "My nephew doesn't like sudden movements. They make him nervous."

"I am sorry, *signore*," Cioffi said, wincing. "I have something for you, that is all."

Varone raised a hand. "It's all right, Paolo. Show me what he's brought." He took the small gem and turned it over in his hand.

"It is very valuable," Cioffi said, massaging his elbow. "Agate and sardonyx. It is a cameo originally from the private collection of Cosimo de' Medici. You see?" He leaned forward and pointed to the figure incised in the stone. "It is the god Dionysus. He is riding on the back of a satyr. I think your wife will like it very much."

"Yes," said Varone. "I'm sure that she will. Perhaps it can be made into a pendant, or a brooch. I know a jeweller in the Spaccanapoli who is quite good at setting pieces." He gave the cameo back to Paolo, who slipped it into his trouser pocket. "How about I give you five hundred lire for it?"

"Five hundred lire?" Cioffi said. He pulled out a chair and sat down. "But Signore Abruzzi gave me two thousand for a piece that was nowhere near so valuable."

"Well," Varone said, "I suppose I can't be outdone by a dead man, now, can I?" He waited to see the *dottore's* reaction. "I assume you heard about poor Renzo?"

Cioffi nodded solemnly. "Yes. It is very unfortunate."

"For him, perhaps. But not, I think, for you." He sat back in his chair and crossed his arms. "So, two thousand, then?"

Cioffi cleared his throat. He shifted uncomfortably. "I thought, maybe, four thousand."

"Four? That seems quite a bit."

"Yes, I know, *signore*. But I find myself in a situation. I need to find a new place to live."

"A new place, eh? And where are you living now?"

"I am with a friend, in an apartment on Piazza Carolina."

"Really? Which one?"

"Number 14. But I must leave. My friend and I … we have had a disagreement. A falling-out of sorts."

"That's too bad," said Varone. "Have you any idea where you will go?"

"Not yet. I am looking still."

Varone nodded thoughtfully. Then he reached into his pocket and took out his billfold. He counted off four thousand lire and handed it to Cioffi. "There's two thousand for what you brought me. We'll call the other two thousand an advance—for what you will bring me next. And as for you finding a new place to live, there is an apartment house on Via San Sebastiano, next to Chiesa Santa Marta. I know the *portiere*. You go talk to him, tell him that I sent you. He will see that you are looked after."

"You are too kind, *signore*," Cioffi said, and reached out and took his hand. "Too kind."

"Please," said Varone. "We are associates now. It's the least I can do."

Once the *dottore* had gone, Varone turned to Paolo. "Number 14, Piazza Carolina. Make a note of that."

Paolo scribbled in his book.

Major Woodard continued to inspect the sagging leaves of his aspidistra.

"To tell you the truth, lieutenant, I thought you would be excited at the news." He turned back to Greaves. "You're being given your own command. It's an opportunity to redeem yourself."

"Redeem myself, sir?"

"Well, yes. Let's be honest, shall we? You came to us under a cloud. Now that cloud's been lifted. You'll be an FSO, like me. And I imagine that there's the likelihood of a promotion in the offing. And it isn't a stretch to say that Campobasso will be an improvement on Naples. Not to mention that you'll be with your own again—surely that must appeal to you. Besides, the term of your secondment has already far exceeded what could be considered conventional."

Greaves was at a loss for words. He had been caught completely unawares. When the major had called him into the office, he assumed it was to do with the botched marriage vetting that Corporal Philbin had conducted the day before, when Greaves was still on his way back from Sorrento. A young woman who was engaged to a captain in the Royal Fusiliers had been given a clearance to wed, only for it to be discovered later in the afternoon that she had twice been arrested on charges of prostitution, which caused the permission of marriage to be revoked. The betrothed officer had returned to the section office and brandished his pistol.

"Are you all right, lieutenant?" said Major Woodard. "You're looking rather ill."

"May I ask, sir, where the order originated?"

"It came direct from General Crerar's office. It seems you know someone who has some pull."

"Yes, sir. That would be my father."

"Then you might want to write and thank him."

"If I could, sir," said Greaves, "I would rather decline the transfer."

The major frowned. "Decline the transfer? You can't decline the transfer, lieutenant. I'm afraid that's not how these things work."

"But there's still work I have to do here in Naples."

"I'm sure that it's nothing that the others can't see to." Major Woodard turned again to the aspidistra. He pulled a yellowed leaf from the plant and let it fall to the floor.

"When am I to leave, sir?" said Greaves.

"You are to report to Campobasso no later than the twenty-fourth."

"That's less than a week."

"Yes," said the major. "It's amazing how quickly the army can work when it puts its mind to it."

Parente watched Luisa as she walked ahead of him across the gallery. Sun streamed in through the second-floor windows and lit the wide, pale marble floor. The statues on their pedestals looked like living shadows, the bronze patina deep, rich, almost ebony. Parente had hired street boys to help take away the sandbags. He paid each of them one hundred lire. In one afternoon they had removed all of the heavy burlap bags to an inner courtyard, where they were stacked and covered over with tarpaulins to keep them dry, though there hadn't been rain in weeks.

The Americans had gone and left a mess behind them. Parente had cleaned it up himself, spent an entire night returning various pieces to their proper display cases.

Luisa stopped and looked back at him. "What's wrong?" she said.

Her hair had begun to grow out; it was no longer so severe. It curled slightly around her ears and framed her face. She seemed softer to him, except for her eyes. There was something cautious about the way she looked at him. All that she had to say to him about the trip to Sorrento was that they had gone to the theatre and there were drinks afterwards. When he asked her about Pompeii, she said only that there were too many soldiers. There was more that she wouldn't tell, of that he was certain; she was being careful with him. And he thought maybe it was better that she have some secrets.

"Augusto," she said, "what is it?"

"It's Aldo."

"Aldo? What about him?"

"You were right. He's been stealing from the collections."

She made to say something, but hesitated. Then she asked: "Are you certain?"

"Of course I'm certain. I saw the evidence for myself. He falsified the ledgers. Colonel Romney showed them to me."

Luisa sighed. She shook her head. "What will you do?"

He looked off towards the figures of Harmodius and Aristogeiton, the Tirannicidi, their smooth marble bodies now unfettered.

"When Thomas comes next," he said, "I will tell him. And then I will ask him to arrest Aldo."

"Arrest him?" Luisa said, and he noted the alarm in her voice. "Are you sure that's best?"

"I won't defend him anymore. I have defended him his whole life, and look what's happened—he's made a fool of me. But worse than that, I've made a fool of myself. I trusted him even when I knew that I shouldn't, even when I knew, deep in my heart, that he would betray me. We all have to answer for the things that we do, Luisa. Now is Aldo's time."

Cioffi was sitting in the *salotto*, stuffing old pamphlets into his shoes to cover the holes worn through the soles, when he heard the knock at the door. Lello had left an hour earlier to meet with some of his old colleagues, who were trying to organize a new workers' weekly. Before he went, he reminded Cioffi that he had to be gone by the day after next.

There was another knock.

Cioffi got up from his chair and went into the hallway. It was quiet now on the other side of the door, but he knew that, whoever it was, he was still there. Then the doorknob turned and he realized that Lello had forgotten to throw the bolt when he left.

The door slowly opened and Cioffi held his breath.

"Tenente Greaves," he said with relief when he saw the young man's face peek through. "I thought you were someone else."

He went to the door and looked into the corridor before he pushed it closed again. The *tenente* walked past him and down the hallway. Cioffi followed him into the *salotto*, where he collected his shoes and sat down to put them on. The *tenente* walked over to the balcony and flicked open the louvres of the shuttered door. He stood there for what seemed a long time, looking out through the slats.

"This is a surprise," Cioffi said. "I hope nothing is wrong."

The *tenente* moved away from the window. He came and stood by the table. The pamphlets that Cioffi had been using to mend his shoes lay spread across its top. He picked one up. The banner read: ASSOCIAZIONE COMUNISTA NAPOLETANA—I LAVORATORI UNITI! He put the pamphlet down again.

"Those do not belong to me," Cioffi said. "My friend Lello—"

"Do you know, *dottore*," the *tenente* said, "what the penalty is for trafficking in stolen artefacts?"

Cioffi only hoped that the flash of panic sparked by the *tenente's* question hadn't registered on his face. He smiled. "I do not know what you are talking about."

Greaves raised a hand to stop Cioffi speaking. "I spoke with Luisa. She's told me everything." He looked about the room. There was little that Lello hadn't had to trade away or use as fuel; just an overstuffed armchair and the small end table remained of the suite of furniture. "I want to meet the man you're working with," he said. "Can you take me to him?"

"You want to meet with Salvatore Varone?"

"If he's the one, then yes."

"What will you do?"

"If I can, *dottore*, I will keep you out of Poggio Reale."

As Augusto pulled the car to the curbside, the narrow beam of the blacked-out headlamps momentarily illuminated Signora Ciccione's chair sitting next to the entrance to the courtyard.

Augusto kept the engine running. "I will wait until you get inside."

Luisa wished he wouldn't. She wished he would just drive away and leave her in the dark and to whatever it was that might await her there.

She felt sick sitting next to him. She'd said nothing of her conversation with Aldo from a few days earlier, and it tore at her heart. It was as if she too were making a fool of him. She leaned across and kissed him gently on the cheek.

"Be careful," she said, and got out of the car.

She walked quickly through the gateway and towards the entrance of the building. Partway there, a noise startled her. She stopped and looked into the shadows.

"Who's there?" she said.

"It's me. Thomas."

"Is everything all right?" Parente called from the idling car.

She looked back through the gateway and called to him. "Yes, Augusto. It was only a cat. I'm all right."

She walked on towards the door of the building and opened it, then turned and waved to him. When the car pulled away, she walked back into the courtyard.

"Thomas?" she whispered.

"Here," he said, and stepped out from a darkened corner.

"What are you doing? You frightened me."

"I had to speak to you."

"And I have to speak to you as well. It's Augusto. He knows about Aldo. He's going to ask you to arrest him."

"Don't worry about that," Greaves said. He came close to her.

"What do you mean, don't worry? Did you hear what I said?"

"Listen to me, please. I haven't got a lot of time."

There was something in his voice that frightened her. "What's wrong?"

"I'm to be transferred out of Naples in a few days. I'll be leaving."

His words left her cold. "You're going away?"

"Yes. But I want to help you before I go."

"Help me? How can you help me if you are not going to be here?"

He reached out and put his hand to her cheek. His palm was warm, dry, and she could smell the tobacco smoke on his fingers. Then she laid her hand over his so that she could hold it tighter to her face.

"I'm going to see Salvatore Varone tomorrow," he said. "I'm going to see that everything is taken care of."

She shook her head but couldn't speak.

"It'll be all right," he said. "I'll make it all right."

"Come upstairs with me," she said, but he told her that he couldn't.

"There's too much I still have to do," he said. "I'll get word to you."

"How?"

He took his hand away and brought hers to his lips. He softly kissed her fingers. "Don't worry," he said. "I will."

Then he turned and walked out of the courtyard.

The electric torch sat on the low table between them, its beam pointed towards the ceiling. The rest of the *salotto* was plunged into shadows. A recent proclamation from the military government had reinstated the nightly blackouts. Things were going badly for the Germans in the north, and it was thought that they might step up their strikes on the city in response, even though the longer flights from bases in Bergamo and Modena put their bombers at greater risk. There was a growing fear among the people that the sense of hope which had started to sweep through Naples—a belief that their long suffering would soon end—would be snuffed out by a last-gasp raid that would kill them in their sleep.

Cioffi expected as much. For him, at least, that was how things went. He took a chunk of bread from the loaf Lello had put out, and a piece of hard cheese. There was fruit as well—plums in syrup, and brandied cherries. And wine: a bottle of sweet Lacrima Christi. Everything had been donated by those loyal to the cause: the baker, the cheese maker, the wine merchant, all of them good socialists. The small feast, Lello said, was in celebration of their long friendship. He wanted Cioffi to know that he wasn't angry with him anymore, that he forgave him his shortcomings.

"You will always be like a brother to me," Lello had said to him, "but I can't be around you anymore. Not if I am going to do the things that I need to do, not if I am going to help to change things. The time has come for Napoli to start taking care of itself, and I don't mean Neapolitan crooks taking over from the American and British crooks. I am talking about the people of this city looking out for one another. We are coming out of a dark time, where it has been every man taking care of himself alone—individual survival. But we have a chance now to be better than that. The fascists are gone, and soon the soldiers will be gone too. And then it will be our time, and—who knows?—what begins here may spread north, and one day through all of Italy."

Cioffi liked hearing his friend give speeches. It reminded him of the years before the war, when Lello was passionate, when he would stand on his chair in the Gambrinus and shout down the blackshirts and call on all of the drinkers to march with him into the street, all the way to the steps of the Prefettura, where he would scrawl I FRATELLI UNITI on the pink stone walls. He missed that Lello.

"I'm glad things have worked out for you, Aldo."

Cioffi savoured the sharpness of the cheese. That afternoon he had visited the apartment house on Via San Sebastiano. A flat with three rooms would be his the day after next. He had only to wait for the *portiere* to put out the family that was currently living in it. He smiled now at his friend.

Lello lifted the bottle of wine and refilled both of their glasses. "To new beginnings," he said.

Cioffi held up his glass. And they toasted like they used to do.

FIFTEEN

They sat on the terrace of a small café on Piazza Gagliardi, sipping cappuccinos and sharing a plate of *zeppole*. Luisa did not have Parente's sweet tooth, but in honour of the Feast of San Giuseppe she ate the pastry. It was important, Augusto had said to her, that things get back to normal. Doughnuts and a new suit of clothes to mark the saint's day was a start. Augusto had on the waistcoat that had been made for him from the Red Cross blanket, and Luisa wore a short, tapered jacket cut from the same material, with a neat row of pearly buttons down the front.

Back to normal? she thought. She didn't think she knew what that meant. Could anything be called normal anymore? Perhaps, to look at them, one might think that there was nothing out of the ordinary: two people enjoying a spring morning. But what, she wondered, of the two people themselves? What about them was commonplace? Augusto, fading away, not sure anymore of who he was; the museum, which had been his breath and soul, had become a palace of deceit. And what of herself? She who had, for eight years, pledged herself to him, stood loyally by his side, guarded him from those who sought to impose themselves upon him—she had been his confidante, his protector, and, in her grief, his ersatz daughter. And yet, in the blink of an eye, it seemed she was willing to throw it all away. She had protected

Aldo—why? She'd tried to convince herself that in protecting Aldo she was really protecting Augusto, but that wasn't true. The truth of it was, she saw advantage. She knew, in some dark corner of her brain, that protecting Aldo would bring benefit—even if, at the time, she had no inkling of what that benefit might be.

She looked over at Augusto, watched as he wiped a crumb from his bottom lip. He had no idea what she'd done. If he found out, would he understand? Would he forgive her?

He looked back at her now. "Are you thinking of him?"

"Who?" she said.

"Thomas. Your face looked sad and I thought that perhaps you were thinking of him."

Luisa smiled. "I'm not sad. And I'm not thinking of him. I was thinking of us, you and me, and what will happen after this is all done."

Parente reached out and took her hand. "And what have you decided?"

"I have decided that we will be fine," Luisa said.

Already, it had become easier to lie to him.

Cioffi waited beside the Monument of the Martyrs as the funeral procession made its way through the square towards the church on Via Poerio. He was sober and twitchy, and he didn't like it.

He watched mourners crowd round the rough-hewn plank coffin that was borne aloft by four pallbearers, old men who struggled under its weight. Through the open end of the box he could see the corpse's feet, turned at an awkward angle and swaddled in dingy grey rags. Dried flowers were piled high on top of the coffin and brittle stems fell to the ground as the pallbearers stumbled along. These were gathered up by the phalanx of black-clad women who followed, weeping, clutching rosaries and handkerchiefs and faded pictures of the young man dressed in a dark suit, his hair combed smartly to the side. Cioffi muttered a prayer under his breath.

Then, through the cortège, he saw the *tenente*. He waited until the last of the mourners had gone before he crossed the road.

"Where are we going?"

"There is a small café," Cioffi said, "in Piazza Amedeo."

"Are we expected?"

"He will be there," said Cioffi.

"I don't want you around when I speak with him. Just point him out to me and then go."

"But *tenente*—"

"Don't argue with me, *dottore*. That's the way it's going to be. Do you understand?"

"Yes," said Cioffi.

"Good. And later tonight, at six o'clock, I want you to come back here. I'll be with the others at evening mess, but I'll make sure that the service entrance in back is left open. You'll come in through there and go up to my room on the second floor. It's at the far end of the corridor. Go there and wait for me. I'll have something for you. Do you promise that you will be there?"

Cioffi nodded. "I promise."

"All right, then. Let's go and meet your friend."

Varone noticed how the man did not move his hands when he spoke. He kept them flat on the tabletop in front of him.

"As far as I can tell, no one really seems all that bothered. I've spoken to a fellow at the port and the chief clerk at 21st General Hospital, and they seem to be of the mind that it's the way things are."

The security policeman spoke in a rush, as if he worried that if he didn't get his words out, better judgment might swallow them up again. He still seemed somewhat uncomfortable with the decision he'd made.

Varone studied his face. He was young—younger, Varone assumed, than he actually looked. Mid-twenties, perhaps, no more. There was the impression that his features had been worn away, so that he seemed a person who was less than he'd once been. He was clearly a man who suffered horrible dreams.

"Tell me, Tenente Greaves," Varone said, "this man at the port, who was he?"

"I'm sure you'll forgive me if I choose not to mention his name. Suffice it to say, he was a man in a position to know of what he spoke."

"Of course," Varone said with a shrug. He wondered if it was the Irishman, and decided that it must have been; he couldn't imagine Mangan letting any of the other port officers field such inquiries.

He sipped his espresso. "Now perhaps you will forgive me, *tenente*, if I ask you what any of this has to do with me?"

Greaves cleared his throat. "I need medical supplies. Antibiotics and saline and penicillin and whatever else you might be able to get your hands on. And I need it as quickly as possible."

Varone nodded thoughtfully and scraped a fleck of dirt from under his fingernail. Ten minutes earlier, when the *dottore* had shown up at the café with the young security policeman, he hadn't known what to expect. The appetites of such men were often unpredictable. To look at him, with his tired eyes and sunken cheeks, Varone would have guessed that he had a taste for morphine. The talk of 21st General Hospital had him thinking the same. And the last thing that Varone wanted was to be tied to a *drogato*. But he had this one all wrong.

By the sound of it, he had something of the Samaritan in him. And Samaritans were sometimes more bother than they were worth.

"That is a significant request," he said. "For something like this—if it could be done—it would be a large debt."

"I expect that it would."

"How would you pay for this?"

"Before I answer, you should know that there is a stipulation."

Varone smiled. "You seem quite certain that we can do business."

"I'm confident, yes."

Again, Varone thought, he had misjudged him. Anxious as he might appear, it did not seem that he was having any doubts after all.

"All right, then, *tenente*. What are your stipulations?"

Greaves leaned forward with his elbows propped on the table. "You are to forget about the museum. And you are to forget about Aldo Cioffi."

"The *dottore*?"

"Yes. Forget about him and all the rest. Your deal now is with me."

"You are asking me to forgo a sizable profit. The museum is like a treasure trove. I could live off it and nothing else."

"We both know that's not true," Greaves said. "Sooner or later the authorities would step in. Not even the Carabinieri would let you get away with that for too long."

"You might have a point. But in the meantime, I could do quite well for myself."

"What I have to offer you could prove much more valuable."

Varone stroked his chin. "Really? And what is that?"

Greaves lifted a hand from the table and laid it flat against his chest. "Me," he said.

"You?"

"I'm sure you can appreciate how beneficial I could be to a person in your line of work. Think about it: no more front-line checkpoints to worry about, no restrictions at Capodichino airfield or at the port. Clearance to go anywhere in the city. Your very own field security policeman—all the doors of Naples would be open to you."

Varone finished his espresso and gently replaced the small cup on its saucer. He pursed his lips and nodded. "I think, maybe, something can be arranged."

When Greaves opened the door to his room, he found the *dottore* waiting for him. He'd half expected—had Cioffi bothered to show up at all—that he would already have left. It was nearly eight o'clock by the time Greaves was able to slip away from the others. The major had arranged a little send-off for him, and after mess had passed around cigars and opened a bottle of French brandy. Sergeant Jones broke out a deck of cards, and dealt hands of penny-a-point fives while they drank and smoked and told stories about their time together in the city. He had finally managed to slip away after bowing out of a round early.

Now he crossed the room, opened the balcony doors, and stepped outside. He lit a cigarette. Cioffi hovered behind him in the doorway.

"Come out, *dottore*," Greaves said. "The others are busy downstairs in the library. No one will see you."

Cioffi stepped out onto the balcony but stayed back from the railing. Greaves offered him a cigarette.

"No, thank you, *tenente*." He spoke in little more than a whisper.

The sun had dipped below the buildings on the far side of the square and everything was cast in shadows. That was how Greaves thought of Naples: a place that was murky and indistinct, where things looked one way but were actually the other. The truth of the matter was in constant flux in Naples. The city could be depended upon to be undependable.

"*Dottore*," he said, "I want you to do something for me." He reached into his jacket pocket and withdrew an envelope. On the front of it he had written: *Major Andrew J. Woodard, FSO, 803 Field Security Section*. "I want you to go to Luisa tonight and give this to her. There is a note for her inside. Tell her to read it. It will explain everything."

Cioffi took the envelope and slipped it into his inside pocket. "I'll make sure that she gets it."

"And tell her that she should stay home tomorrow. She shouldn't go to the museum and she shouldn't go to the hospital. Make sure you tell her that too."

Cioffi nodded. "And what about you, *tenente*?"

"Me? Don't worry about me. I can look after myself. You, on the other hand, *dottore*—you're going to need to watch out for yourself. You got mixed up with some pretty serious characters, and I can't imagine that they're going to be too happy with you."

He went inside and found his satchel. From the side compartment he took out a thin roll of military scrip. He brought it back and gave it to Cioffi. "It's all I could get from the counter-intelligence fund. It's what we use to pay the informants. You take it and use it to get yourself away from Naples for a while."

There was a noise from below the balcony. Sergeants Bennington and Jones, along with the major, had come out into the courtyard, cigars and snifters in hand. Cioffi stepped quickly through the balcony door.

"There you are, lieutenant," Major Woodard shouted up to him. "We thought you'd run off. Come back down and have another drink, will you?"

"Of course, sir," said Greaves. "I'll be right there."

Back inside the room, he said to Cioffi: "You'd better get going." He put a hand on his shoulder and ushered him towards the corridor. "I'll take you down the back stairs."

SIXTEEN

Maria held a damp cloth to her forehead.

"If you're not well, I can stay with you."

"No," Luisa said. "You go. I'll be fine."

"Well, at least you haven't got a fever. We can be thankful for that."

She felt awful about worrying Maria. The prospect of illness frightened her cousin, who knew how quickly even the simplest of sicknesses could become much worse—the common cold pneumonia in waiting, a slight rash the first suggestion of dreaded typhus.

"Are you absolutely sure?"

"Yes," Luisa said, "I'm sure. Just telephone Augusto when you get to the club so that he doesn't fret."

"All right, then."

She watched Maria as she pinned her hair and tied on her pale blue kerchief. She looked more beautiful, Luisa thought, in her dark brown uniform—a simple A-line dress with an emblem identifying the American officers' club sewn over the left breast—than she had in her finest gowns. Her face was delicately powdered. The only other makeup was a light tracing of kohl around her eyes. The colour in her cheeks was her own.

"I don't like leaving you like this."

"Please," said Luisa. "Now go, or you will be late."

Once she'd left, Luisa went to the window. In the small courtyard six floors below, two boys gathered together the rubbish that had been dropped there from the windows facing onto the yard, while another searched through the growing pile, separating out anything that might be reused or sold on to a *bancarellaro*.

Luisa stood there until she saw Maria appear. The boys stopped what they were doing and watched her as she passed. One of them whistled at her, and Maria blew him a kiss.

Luisa closed the shutters. She stood in the middle of the dim *salotto*. She hated lying to Maria, but it was the only thing she could think of to keep her from becoming suspicious.

Late the night before, there had been a knock on the door. When she answered it, she found Aldo standing there. "What do you want?" she'd demanded.

"I've a message from the *tenente*."

"From Thomas?"

"Yes," he'd said. "You are not to go to the museum tomorrow. You're not to go to the *ospedale* either. And he wanted me to give you this." He handed her the envelope.

"What is it?"

"I don't know. I did not read it."

She wasn't sure if she believed him. "Is he coming here?" she asked.

"I don't think so," Aldo said. He waited in the doorway.

"Was there something else?" she said.

"No. Only I wanted …" He hesitated. "I wanted to tell you that I am sorry."

She stared at him for a moment, then said: "I don't ever want to see you again. Ever." Then she closed the door on him.

She took the envelope now from her pocket. She opened it and took out the two sheets of paper from inside. On the first was his short, handwritten note to her: *Luisa, I know how to make things right—right for you and Augusto and Aldo, too. And perhaps even for myself. I will come to you if I can, but if you have not heard from me by tomorrow at noon, then take the letter I've enclosed to Major Woodard at the section office. He'll know what to do.—Thomas.*

The letter she was to give to the major was a list of charges. The suspect named: Salvatore Varone. Included was the address of an apartment house on Via Cimarosa, as well as that of the Caffè Diplomatico on Piazza Amedeo.

Luisa put the letter and the note back into the envelope. She felt as if she were a prisoner in her own home, and already she wished she'd let Maria stay with her. The apartment was such a lonely place with her gone.

She went to the sideboard crowded with photographs. Looking up at her out of their gilt frames were the faces of her dead parents, her dead brother. And Luisa thought how she would give anything to have them back again.

Paolo drove the truck to the abbey to collect the supplies, while Varone and three others followed in the battered Lancia Ardea, in case anything went wrong. Varone was prepared for a double-cross; perhaps the young *tenente* was already working with someone else. There were so many crews operating in the city—deserter gangs, corrupt military police, other *camorristi*—it was foolish to trust anyone. So they were prepared if the truck was hijacked: in the Lancia they had a Sten gun and two carbines loaded and ready.

But the trip passed without incident. It was early still and the roads were empty of traffic. When they reached the Ospedale del Santo Sepolcro, they drove in back to the delivery dock. The *tenente* was there waiting. He helped Paolo to guide the truck into the bay.

Varone got out of the car and told the others to leave their guns behind. The sun was warm on his face, and he thought how lovely the day was promising to be. When they were finished here, he decided that he would go back home and collect his daughters and take them for a walk through Villa Floridiana, and then maybe they would go down to the harbour and look at the boats.

He passed through a side door into the loading bay and climbed the steps up to the dock. It was cooler here, and filled with the smell of damp stonework and motor exhaust. He walked over to the *tenente*, who said: "I won't ask you where you got the truck."

Varone smiled. "It is better that you don't."

They stood quietly aside and watched as Paolo and the others unloaded the crates from the bed of the truck. They stacked them at the side of the dock.

"You see," Varone said. "It is everything that you asked for."

A door opened behind them and a voice said: "Excuse me, Tenente Greaves. May I speak with you, please?" The white-coated doctor glanced nervously at Varone.

"Of course, Dottore Serao."

Varone watched the two men as they spoke, the doctor talking in urgently hushed tones and every so often casting a wary eye in his direction, and the *tenente* putting a coaxing hand on the doctor's shoulder as if to reassure him. Finally the doctor sighed, and Varone heard him say: "You cannot make deals with these people."

Varone approached the man. "Dottore Serao? That is your name, is it?"

"Yes, that's right." The *dottore* looked him straight in the eye, unconcerned about who he might be, and Varone admired him for this. Serao was a man certain of himself.

"I wonder, *dottore*," Varone said, "how is your memory?"

"Very short," Serao replied.

Varone nodded. "Good. Very good."

The *dottore* turned and went back inside the building.

After the last of the crates was unloaded, Paolo closed the tailgate of the truck, climbed back into the cab, and started the engine. He drove out of the bay, leaving a blue fog of exhaust hanging in his wake.

"What now?"

"I have a car outside," said Varone. "We should go somewhere. We have a lot to talk about."

Parente drew back the curtains and let in the sunshine. He lifted the latch on the window and pushed it wide. Papers on his desk shifted in the light breeze. The office needed a good airing out. He had lived too long in the stuffiness of it.

He went to the field stove and made himself a cup of coffee. Then he went to his desk. He sat down and opened a side drawer. Inside, there was a half-finished bottle of honey grappa. He took it out and poured some into his cup. Coffee in hand, he sat back in his chair.

The workers who had shown up that morning he'd sent home after Luisa's cousin telephoned to say that she wouldn't be coming in. She had assured him that there was nothing to worry about, that Luisa was just worn out and needed some rest. Parente decided that he could do with some rest too. The chaos of the preceding weeks had taken its toll on him. And there was Aldo to think about as well. He had seen nothing of him in days now, but before he came back to his office, he'd told the *carabiniere* at the front entrance to watch for his nephew. If he arrived, Parente wanted to be informed at once.

Now he leaned back and closed his eyes. The pull of sleep was strong, and he thought about a nap.

When the first tremor came, it was insignificant, barely noticeable. Still, it brought him upright in his chair. The second tremor was more pronounced: a quaking that juddered the cup against the saucer and splashed coffee onto his lap. He looked towards the bookshelves: a volume had fallen over onto its side, and one of the figurines, the Farnese Bull, set too close to the edge, toppled to the floor. Next came the roar of thunder, as if a storm had broken just outside the window. The floor continued to tremble.

Parente leapt to his feet. He ignored the stabbing pain in his hip and hurried across the room. The quaking intensified as he grabbed hold of the window jamb, the rumble outside low and constant. He pushed himself away from the window and hurried out the office door. In the corridor, the statues rocked on their plinths. As he crossed the main gallery, he could feel a tightness in his chest, but he kept moving. He scaled the central staircase to the mezzanine level, and from there went up the next flight of steps and into the high-ceilinged Hall of the Sundial. He hurried through the long room, passing the statue of Atlas—the world bearing down on his shoulders—threw open the tall shuttered doors, and went out onto the balcony that overlooked the square.

Only then did the burning in his chest become too much to ignore. He was overtaken by a fit of coughing and bent forward, hands on his knees. It was like a hand had reached in and grabbed hold of his heart and was squeezing it dry. Beads of sweat broke out on his brow—he couldn't catch his breath. He tried to inhale more slowly, to steady himself. He grew faint, and for a moment he was sure that his heart was going to shrivel up and die. But then the coughing subsided, and so too did the tingling that he felt in his fingertips. Soon the old pain returned, the persistent sciatica, that daily reminder that he was still alive. Slowly he straightened and looked out across the city.

The words of Pliny the Younger in his letter to the historian Tacitus sprang to Parente's mind: the cloud of ash rising out of the now-gaping maw of the mountain did indeed resemble a pine tree—a pine tree with a very long trunk, its branches spreading out to fill the sky, the small boughs of which trailed earthward, breaking off at their tips into what looked like the mist of distant, menacing rains. Slowly the tree climbed, growing ever larger, while at the same time seeming as if it were not moving at all, seeming as if it were some awful blight fixed upon the landscape. Parente knew well enough the illusion; he had poured plaster into the voids, made the casts, chipped away the stone-hard ash to reveal the death-throe disbelief of those who had been mesmerized by the stillness of just such a cloud.

Come now, he thought to himself. Come now and bury us all.

The abbot scurried along the corridor ahead of him. He stopped before a low wooden door, took a ring of keys from beneath his robe, and began to fumble through them. When he found the one he was looking for, he turned back to Varone.

"I've done what I can to make him comfortable," he said.

"You shouldn't have bothered, padre."

The abbot hesitated. "What will you do? I can't have trouble for the abbey."

"You should have thought about that before."

He waited until the old monk had scuttled off again before he opened the door. The room was small and dim; a narrow window set high in the wall let in a grimy, ashen light. In one corner stood a simple iron bedstead, the mattress neatly made up with a thin woollen blanket. In the other corner were a plain wooden table and the straight-backed chair where the young *tenente* sat.

Varone went to him and took hold of his chin. He tipped his head back and looked at the bruises on his face. His left eye was swollen shut and his bottom lip was split near the corner of his mouth; blood caked one nostril and there was a deep gash in his chin. He had known that beating him wouldn't do any good, but he at least had to try.

"Has there been a raid? The noise earlier—the shaking."

"Not a raid," said Varone. "Worse." He let go of his chin. "The mountain."

"It's erupted."

"Yes. It has erupted. Vesuvio has awoken and is ready to take its revenge on us."

"Maybe Virgil's egg *has* cracked, then."

"What's that?"

"Nothing," said the *tenente*.

Varone took a packet of cigarettes from his pocket and offered one to the *tenente*. He leaned forward and struck a match. The flame lit the fear in the young man's eyes. Varone watched him smoke: he winced when he brought the cigarette to his lips and inhaled. Even the smallest movement of his mouth caused him pain.

"Have you changed your mind?" Varone said.

"I haven't."

Varone went and sat down on the edge of the bed. "I don't understand you. I was ready to give you everything that you asked me for. What am I supposed to do now?"

"You can do whatever you choose," Greaves said.

"Is that the way you see it, *tenente*? You think there is a choice in the matter, do you?"

"Perhaps you should think of the consequences."

Varone smiled. "That's right—you've written a letter. Tell me again who this letter of yours will go to?"

"The commanding officer of 803 Field Security Section, British Army Intelligence Corps."

"That sounds very impressive. And I suppose you think this concerns me—you think it frightens me."

"I know it does," Greaves said. "When that letter reaches his desk, you go from being a criminal nuisance to a security threat. And when that happens, whatever friends you have aren't going to be able to help you."

"You think they will put me in prison, do you?"

"It's not a question of thinking—they will."

"So, I will go to Poggio Reale, maybe even to Procida. Of course, you might be right. They might lock me up. But have you asked yourself, *tenente*, what happens when the armies leave? Do you think they will keep people like me inside when that happens? Or do you think maybe they will throw the doors to the jails wide open? Now you won't be around for that, will you. But what about your friends? They aren't going anywhere, are they?"

Greaves shifted on his chair.

"No," Varone said, "you hadn't thought of that, had you?"

The *tenente* looked down at the cigarette burning between his fingers. "I don't imagine you'll do anything."

"You don't know me very well, do you, *tenente*?"

"I don't need to."

"And why is that?"

"Because you gave me your word."

"And that's worth something, is it?"

"I think so."

"It didn't have to be this way."

Greaves looked at him. "Yes, it did. It always had to be this way."

"From the beginning?"

"From the beginning."

Varone shook his head. "Then you are a martyr," he said. He glanced up at the sliver of a window; the leaded pane was cracked in the middle. "Maybe they will build you a statue." He got up from the bed and walked back towards the door. "I suppose that, in an odd way, I can admire you for what you're doing. But really, would it have been so bad to do business with me? Are your scruples so strong?"

"It has nothing to do with you," Greaves said. "It never did."

"I see. Then it's penance for something else." Varone opened the door. "Someone will come soon."

Paolo was waiting for him out in the corridor.

"This has become too messy," Varone said to him. "Nothing good can come of it now."

"What should we do?"

"There are too many loose ends. They need to be tied up."

"And what about Ospedale del Santo Sepolcro?" Paolo asked. "Do you want me to send the boys back with the truck?"

"No. Leave it be. He's earned that much." He looked back at the door. "When you do it, Paolo, be quick about it. And then go and find our American friend and tell him that it's time for him to do us a favour."

Aldo Cioffi lay curled up on the floor. There was a wrinkle in the thin mat he used for a bed. It was late, well past midnight, and Lello had just come home. He had been out with his comrades, celebrating the eruption: a sure sign that the revolution was at hand. From the sound of his fumbling in the hallway, he was quite drunk. Cioffi wondered if he had been at the Gambrinus.

He feigned sleep when Lello came to the doorway of the *salotto* and looked in at him before moving on down the hallway to the toilet. Cioffi heard whispered voices and wondered if Lello had brought company back with him. Then he realized that the voices weren't coming from within the apartment but from outside, in the corridor. After a moment they stopped. Cioffi sat up so as to listen more closely, but the only sound now was the noise of Lello making water.

Then the apartment door splintered open and the flat filled with yelling. There was the thumping of heavy boots scrabbling down the hallway towards the toilet. There was more shouting. Cioffi felt a cold terror and looked about the darkened *salotto* for somewhere to hide himself. He quickly gathered his bedroll and slipped out the shuttered doors onto the balcony.

There was a scuffle inside the apartment. The raised voices were American. He could hear Lello pleading with them. The light went on in the *salotto*. Cioffi could see the shadow of his friend through the half-open shutters. Lello was pushed and then punched in the stomach. He sank to the floor.

A gruff voice said: "Your name's Cioffi, isn't it? *Il tuo nome è Aldo Cioffi.*"

Lello protested, "*No non è il mio nome. Non sono lui. Sono Lello Conforti.*"

"What's he jabbering about?"

Through the slats, Cioffi could see the American who'd just spoken. He was tall, lean—he wore a band on his arm. They were military policemen, and they were looking for him. Perhaps the *tenente* had turned him in after all.

"This ginzo says we got the wrong guy. What do you think?"

The tall American stepped close to Lello, who was on his knees now, his hands pressed together before him. "I figured you'd say something like that. Well, let me tell you something, fella, you got yourself into some pretty hot water. Seems you upset some pretty important people."

"*Per favore*," Lello begged. "*Non sono lui.*"

"We haven't got time for this," said the other MP.

"Now hold on a second. We got time."

"Not for this we don't."

"If you say so," said the tall MP. He drew his pistol and pointed it at Lello's face.

It was the same whip-crack sound that Cioffi had heard that day outside the university. And then complete silence. Lello's body lay on the floor. It had fallen without a sound.

"Jesus Christ. What a fucken mess."

The tall MP shook his head. "I was hoping we coulda had a little fun with him first."

"We got better things to do."

"Sure, sure. But still." The tall MP holstered his pistol and squatted down. He cocked his head, then reached out and pushed Lello's hair away from his shattered face. "What'd this guy do, anyway?"

"Who knows? Somebody welched on a deal with one of the Camorra heavies. That's what the captain said, anyhow. Could've been this guy, I guess, though he don't look like much."

"Should we clean the place up, you think?"

"Leave it. Nobody's gonna give a shit about him."

"Yeah, you're right. Let's get outta here."

SEVENTEEN

With the windows covered, the apartment sank further into darkness. Luisa and Maria had gathered linens from the cupboards and beds and put them into place with upholstery tacks they'd pried from the sofa and chair in the *salotto*, but nothing, it seemed, could keep out the ash. It spread like a fine, slippery dust across the floors and settled on every flat surface. It tainted the air and made it difficult to breathe.

Finally, they went into the kitchen. They wet strips of cloth and wedged them beneath the door and around the frame. They lit candles and got out bread and cheese, and then, even though it was still morning, they opened a bottle of wine that Maria had brought home from the American officers' club.

"Are you frightened?"

"No," Luisa said. "Are you?"

"A little, yes."

When the eruption had started the previous afternoon, she had been frightened. She had gone down into the street. But her fear was soon replaced by a powerful sense of guilt. She thought of Augusto alone at the museum. For a time she considered going to him, but then she went back upstairs to the apartment.

"Luisa," Maria said.

"Yes."

"I have something I want to tell you."

Luisa suspected what her cousin had to say, but she let her speak.

"I've met someone."

"Is that right?" said Luisa.

"You know him. Captain Roth."

"I know him?"

"Yes. From the interviews—he was the man with the clipboard. He runs the club."

"I see," said Luisa.

"No, it's not like that. He's not like that. He is good, like your Thomas."

To hear Maria say his name made him sound somehow unreal to Luisa. And suddenly she felt as if he were no more than a figment of her imagination, a brief fantasy. She thought now of his letter, tucked away in the trunk at the foot of her bed. That was where it would stay. Luisa knew that he wasn't coming back. She'd known when Aldo had come knocking on the door. She'd known when she had read his note. He wouldn't have written it had he thought otherwise—the letter for the major he'd given her as insurance. It was a guarantee of her safety, but what he'd never understood was that her safety was not something he could ensure—nobody could. A piece of paper in the hands of a British officer, regardless of what was written on it, was just that—a piece of paper. It wouldn't stop anyone from getting to her or to Augusto. The only reason she'd kept it at all was that she knew, except for a cheap music box, it would be the only piece of him left to her.

"How do you know," she said, "that Thomas is so good?"

"By the way your face looks whenever you mention his name," said Maria.

Luisa smiled. "We shouldn't always trust our faces."

She sipped her wine. Then she broke off a piece of bread and put it in her mouth: it tasted of ash.

"Will you go to the museum today?" Maria asked.

"Perhaps later," said Luisa. "I am going to go to the hospital first."

"May I come with you?"

"To the hospital?"

"Yes. Do you think it would be all right?"

Luisa reached out and took her cousin's hand. "Of course it would be all right," she said.

Cioffi had sat with Lello's body through the night, until the early morning hours when the ash began to blow in through the open window. He watched as it slowly covered everything: the floor, the chair, the table—his friend's distorted face.

He covered Lello with a blanket and then wrapped himself in whatever he could find: an old shirt covering his head, a dishcloth tied around his face, covering mouth and nose. He left the apartment house on Piazza Carolina and began to walk. He passed the Gambrinus and headed in the direction of Via Roma. The streets were next to empty. Every so often the headlamps of a passing car or truck would loom up in the sooty haze. He met no one on the pavement; it was as if the city had been forsaken.

He made his way towards the museum. He had to warn Augusto. He had to tell him everything. When he had done that, he would go north. If he could get to Rome, he could lose himself there.

The ash, like a foul grey snow, overflowed the pavement and gathered in small drifts in doorways and in the mouths of alleys. It filled the air: a choking, sulphuric fog. He had to stop often just to clear his throat. It was becoming difficult to breathe. He felt like he was slowly smothering.

In the square in front of the museum, he had to stop again. He removed the cloth from around his face and cleared the claylike crust of ash that had collected in the corners of his mouth. His eyes had begun to sting, as well.

As he was doing this, a car pulled up to the curb at the bottom of the museum steps. The engine idled roughly. Then the doors opened and Salvatore Varone and his man stepped out.

Cioffi watched them climb the steps to the unguarded front entrance, and he knew that there was nothing now that he could do for Augusto. He waited until they disappeared inside, then he turned and walked back towards Via Roma.

The old man's tears made Varone uncomfortable; they embarrassed him. Normally, people's weeping did not affect him: it was commonplace in his business. Crying mothers, crying fathers—crying husbands and wives, crying children. There were those who cried out of fear and those who cried out of anguish. But there was something different about this old man's grief—something more to it than a mother's, a father's, a husband's, or a child's. It was as if he was mourning more than simply one man, more than simply one life.

And yet, his grief was silent. He sat behind his wide desk in an office lit with oil lanterns and wept without making a sound.

The room, suffused in a dim yellowish radiance, had the air of the candlelit nave of a small country church. And the thin layer of ash that lay over everything—the bookshelves, the statuettes, the open ledgers spread across the top of the cabinets—seemed to have settled on the old man too. He was like a greying spectre of himself.

Varone looked over at Paolo now, who stood near the tall window that had been covered over with a patchwork of tapestries. Slivers of tainted sunlight leaked through gaps in the fabric. Paolo glanced back at him and shrugged.

Finally, Varone said: "So, he was a friend of yours, then?"

"Yes, he was a friend."

"I'm sorry."

The old man looked over towards the shrouded window and nodded at Paolo. "Is he the one who did it?"

"Yes," said Varone.

"Then tell him to leave. I won't speak to you if he stays."

Varone told Paolo to wait for him in the corridor, then he watched as the curator dried his eyes with the backs of his hands. He took out a handkerchief and blew his nose. Then he got up from his chair and went to the small table with the field stove on it. The old man took out a packet of matches and lit the stove. He adjusted the flame, put a battered *caffettiera* on to boil. Soon the smell of brewing coffee filled the office.

"Thomas was a good man," he said finally.

"So I gathered," said Varone.

For a time, the old man was quiet. He waited for his coffee to boil and then poured a cup and came back to his desk and sat down. He watched Varone as he brought the cup to his lips. Then he said: "What do we do now?"

"We do nothing," said Varone.

"What do you mean?"

Varone went to the table and found a cup. He took the *caffettiera* from the stove and poured a coffee for himself.

"It's over," he said. "I gave him my word."

"And it's good? Your word?"

"It may be the only thing about me that is."

Varone took a sip of the bitter coffee and let it settle on his tongue before he swallowed it down.

The old man got out of the chair again and came round the desk. Varone could see that he'd once been a sturdy figure. He had broad shoulders and a thick chest. His hands still looked powerful, and Varone thought that there would have been a time when he'd have been a worrisome prospect. But all of his force had left him. He started across the room towards the window but stopped partway. He appeared momentarily lost as if he'd forgotten why it was that he had left his desk. Then he looked at Varone and, with a slightly bemused expression on his face, said, "He told me once that every man, though he knows he is going to die, can never know that he is dead. And that is why, in his mind, every man is immortal."

Varone frowned. "Only a fool would think such a thing."

"Perhaps, then," the old man said, "we are all fools."

Varone put his cup down on the table.

"Perhaps we are," he said.

AUTHOR'S NOTE

While the events and characters in this novel are wholly fictitious, the author owes a debt of thanks to a number of historical works, chief among them: Norman Lewis's wartime diary *Naples '44*, a staggering portrait of the city in the days and months after liberation and of the surreal situation into which the British Field Security Police were thrust; and Aubrey Menen's *Four Days in Naples*, which gives a harrowing account of the *scugnizzi* uprising in the few fateful days before the Allies arrived in the city, and which also presents a touching portrait of Amadeo Maiuri, the real curator of the Museo Archeologico Nazionale, and upon whom Augusto Parente was in no way based.

The author would also like to express his thanks to the Canada Council for the Arts and the Ontario Arts Council for their assistance in the writing of this book.

ACKNOWLEDGMENTS

I am enormously grateful to a number of people who offered guidance and support during the writing of this book. Among them, Andrew Jefferson, who accompanied me to Naples and Sorrento, and who, map in hand, wandered with me through the ancient streets of Pompeii; thanks, also, to Georgina Kelly and Jon Lusher for the road trip to Derbyshire in search of the wartime Intelligence School at Matlock Spa. I am thankful also to Christine Pountney, Michael Winter, Chris Sommerfelt, and Ray Robertson, who offered advice and encouragement along the way. I would like to thank my two wonderful editors, Barbara Berson, who saw promise in me and whose generosity, persistence, and unflagging optimism kept me going, and Nicole Winstanley, whose enthusiasm and confidence saw this book to its fruition. I am also grateful to my agent, Anne McDermid, for her patience and sage counsel. As always, I wish to express my love and gratitude to my family: to my brothers and sisters, Scott, Shannon, Stephanie, Mark, and Christine, and to my parents, Josephine and Bradley, and to my aunts Marg and Marge and my uncle George. And lastly, for her love and conviction, and her tireless belief in me, I thank Alcmene Stathoukos; you make it all worthwhile.

The Fallen

A Penguin Readers Guide

PENGUIN
CANADA

ABOUT THE BOOK

It is the winter of 1944, and the Allies have liberated the city of Naples from the Germans. In the resulting disorder, a fascinatingly varied collection of characters struggles to find its way through the postwar chaos. Some are the soldiers assigned to govern the shattered city; others are members of the flourishing organized crime gangs; and some are civilians, hungry, disillusioned, and labouring to make ends meet in a city with scanty resources. Complicating attempts to clean up the city is the corruption that is rampant in every sector of society.

Among those responsible for establishing order is Lieutenant Thomas Greaves. A fresh-faced Canadian, Thomas is part of the British Field Security Police charged with keeping the city secure. It's a dangerous and, at times, seemingly futile task, but Thomas hopes his work in Naples will allow him to make amends for a terrible mistake he made on the Sicilian battlefield.

Greaves isn't the only one attempting to deal with memories of death and destruction. Beautiful and aloof, Luisa Gennaro, also struggles with the fact that her entire family, save one cousin, died during the war. Luisa is an employee of Naples' Archaeological Museum; it is there that she meets Thomas, who has been asked to watch the curator, Augusto Parente, a former high-ranking Fascist. Initially, Luisa is judgmental of Thomas and all that his uniform symbolizes, but eventually she sees past his professional role and starts to open up to him. As Thomas discovers that Augusto is indifferent to politics and is mostly concerned with protecting the treasures in his collection, a friendship grows between the two men as well.

Although Thomas's relationships with Luisa and Augusto bring him much needed comfort, they also draw him into Naples' nefarious underworld. Augusto's nephew, Aldo Cioffi, is a petty criminal who, out of desperation, becomes indebted to some of the city's worst gangsters. To repay his debts, Aldo wants to get a job cataloguing the archaeological collection at his uncle's museum. Augusto, who no longer trusts his nephew, agrees only after Thomas speaks on Aldo's behalf. Unbeknownst to Thomas, his support of Aldo makes possible the theft of a number of the museum's prized artifacts.

Aldo's thieving thrusts Thomas into direct contact with Salvatore Varone, one of Napoli's most ruthless criminals. Thomas, however, sees this as an opportunity to make amends for his disastrous error in judgment on the battlefield. By saving Aldo, he believes he can save Luisa and Augusto, too. But his benevolent plan goes awry, and we are left to wonder if the danger he exposes himself to is a kind of penance for his past.

Gritty, evocative, and powerful, *The Fallen* is an unflinching exploration of the terrible consequences of war and its aftermath. While Stephen Finucan makes it clear that the murky line separating right from wrong in wartime is even more confused in liberated Naples, he doesn't offer any easy solutions to the morally complex questions he poses. *The Fallen* compellingly creates the chaos of this time and allows readers to come to their own conclusions.

AN INTERVIEW WITH STEPHEN FINUCAN

Q: Why did you choose to set this novel in the months after Naples' liberation rather than during a time of active, legitimized combat? What opportunities did this power vacuum offer in terms of character development and narrative?

I always had it in mind that I would write about the aftermath of war rather than actual combat because my interest was in the lingering effects of war, how it impacts the citizenry, the innocents—for lack of a better term. I was interested in the "collateral damage" of war. I suppose, really, it was the culture of euphemism that arose in the wake of Iraq and Afghanistan that spurred my decision. It became difficult to abide the clouding of what was actually happening to actual people. With Naples I had a historical setting that leant itself to address, even if subtly, some of the questions that these present day situations posed. As for the opportunities offered by the power vacuum that existed in Naples at the time, well, they were almost limitless, really. Though the truth of it is that anything I might have created within the narrative frame afforded by the setting pales in comparison to the reality of what happened there—my wildest imaginings were trumped by actuality. ■

Q: The opening image of the dying donkey is vivid and detailed. What made you decide to begin with the highly symbolic image of a suffering animal?

The decision to open with this scene came very late. In most of the early drafts the opening was, in fact, the scene with Thomas Greaves waiting out the air raid in the square in front of Field Security Headquarters. The scene with Aldo Cioffi and the donkey followed. My reasoning for this had always been that, of the two characters, Thomas is the more pivotal, and because of this the reader should see him first. The problem, of course, was that the symbolic power of the dying donkey was weakened by this, not to mention that of the two scenes, Aldo's is much more visceral and dynamic, whereas Thomas's is more ruminative. It wasn't until the second-last draft that I made the switch, and then only after talking to my editor about it. Once it was done, however, it seemed obvious because it gave the book this wonderful grounding: the donkey was Naples, and in the end Naples as a character was more pivotal than Thomas or Aldo. ▪

Q: In general, when members of the mafia are depicted in literature or film they are seen as the epitome of corruption. But in your book, the mafia figures aren't that much different from other people who are a part of an incredibly flawed system and, as a result, do appalling things to each other. Did you want the characters involved in organized crime to be equal participants in creating this dangerous environment? For you, how are they different from Aldo Cioffi or other corrupt officials?

It wasn't a question of wanting members of organized crime to be equal participants in creating the environment; that was simply the reality of the situation. The Camorra was, and still is, a very powerful influence in Naples. For a time, Mussolini held it in check, but it sprang to life again in the power vacuum that was the armistice. In many instances, as well, organized crime worked hand-in-hand with members of the Allied Military Government; Vito Genovese did indeed work as a civilian liaison officer with AMGOT. As for the depiction of these people in the novel, the thing to remember is that there is something very ordinary about criminals: they are not without depth and complexity, but neither are they without many of the same everyday worries as those who are not criminals. I tried to keep this mind as I created the characters because, for me, this is what makes them real. Varone, for instance, who is a cold-blooded killer, loves his daughters very much and likes to take them for walks in the park. In many ways, and as trite as it may sound, they—Varone and Abruzzi—are honourable fellows. Not, though, in that foolishly Hollywood gangster way, but in the sense that they behave in a manner that is to be expected. They are criminals and murderers, and they rob and kill. The corrupt members of the military government, on the other hand, are the ones to be despised: they were expected to help the citizens of Naples, and they took advantage. ■

Q: Why did you choose to make Thomas a Canadian lieutenant? Did his nationality affect the way you approached him as a character?

There was never any question that Thomas Greaves would be Canadian. From the outset, when the novel was still just an idea brewing in my head, he was Canadian, and not only that, but a Canadian who would be stuck, in a way, between Brits and Americans. He was always, for me, very representative of our country. And this did affect the way I approached him. His character is quite Canadian in that he is very much a mediator, very much a man who tries to do the decent thing; there is a great deal of conscience about him. Of course, it is presumptuous of me to imply that these are strictly Canadian traits, but he was my character so I presumed away. ■

Q: Augusto Parente seems to offer the most hope to the other characters in the book (especially Luisa and Thomas, who see him both as a father and a child), and yet it is Augusto who, in the end, wants the erupting Vesuvius to "come now and bury us all." What made you decide to have Augusto utter these powerful words of resignation?

Parente utters these words because he appreciates, like Varone—who has similar feelings about Vesuvius—the reality of the world in which he lives. In some respects, for Parente, Naples is like the world before the flood, and he sees the eruption as the deluge that will cleanse the land. ■

Q: One reviewer said *The Fallen* had the feeling of a play. There is certainly a sense of confinement throughout the novel, and much of the action happens in a limited number of locations.

Did you ever think of the book as play-like? Are you inspired by any specific playwrights?

I did not set out to write a play-like book, though I do acknowledge that there is a cinematic quality to my writing. I like to set the scene fairly quickly—I've never been one for drawing out descriptions of people or places, I don't think. If anything, I feel my descriptive passages could be described as succinct. And while I do love the theatre, specifically the work of David Hare, I wouldn't say that this has any relation to the style of the novel. If there is an influence on my style, I would have to say it comes from my equally strong love of film. In fact, when I am creating a scene, I quite often imagine it cinematically first. ■

Q. Your other published books are collections of short stories. What challenges existed for you in writing a novel?

The challenges were many. First and foremost, I discovered, like many have before me, that a novel is not simply a long short story. They are two very different things, indeed. I would not presume to say, though, that after having written both stories and now a novel that I have figured out the trick to either. You see, the one real thing I have learned is that they are equally difficult to write, as they should be, because if it isn't difficult, then it isn't worth it—at least that's what I keep telling myself. ■

Q. You mention in your Acknowledgments that you travelled to the area around Naples while writing the book. How did this enhance your understanding of the historic texts you also mention as inspirations?

It was amazing. Wandering through the streets that I had read about not only brought Norman Lewis's and Aubrey Menem's books to life for me, it brought the city to life as well. I went to the Bar Vittoria, the little tavern frequented by Lewis and the other field security officers, and stood at the counter he described and could imagine Thomas Greaves standing there with Aldo Cioffi, looking out at Castel dell'Ovo. I walked through Piazza del Plebiscito, drank coffee at the Caffe Gambrinus, strolled the Lungomare where I bought a lemon ice. It really was a antastic experience. I had my good friend Andrew Jefferson with me, nd I'm glad I did because his presence helped to keep me grounded, I ,ink. On my own, I'm sure I would have fashioned a fairly idealistic view he city, but Andrew is quite a pragmatic fellow, and with him one gets ry genuine impression of things. ■

Q: • Why did you choose to write the book in the third person?
• What kind of freedom did this point of view offer? Was it constricting in any way?

The earliest draft of the book was actually written in the first person, d it clearly did not work. It was very limiting. I had too many charac- that needed to be heard, and it just wasn't possible to do this rough the eyes of one person. It all felt very, very forced. So the switch to third person was quite liberating. It gave me the space to explore the other characters—gave *them* the space, really, to come alive. ■

Q: • What are you working on now?

I am hesitant to answer this question only because I don't want to jinx myself, not that I'm terribly superstitious or anything. It is simply that *The Fallen* took a long time to write. In many ways it was my education in how to write a novel. Before I started, I was rather blasé about the whole process—like I said earlier, I considered it as little more than a long short story. I have since learned that the novel deserves much more respect than that. Having said that, I am very close to beginning the next novel, though what it will be about is, for now, between me and my keyboard. I will say, though, that I have been writing short stories again, which feels good because I've been away from them for far too long. ■

DISCUSSION QUESTIONS

1. Stephen Finucan's title *The Fallen* can be read on many different levels. Why do you think he chose this title, and did it influence how you initially approached the book?

2. At the beginning of the book we are introduced to Aldo Cioffi by way of a dying donkey and then to Thomas Greaves, who is

sitting at the foot of a statue of a lion that is writhing in pain. Ostensibly, these men are very different, but Finucan seems to suggest they are similar in some important ways. What do we learn about Thomas through Aldo and about Aldo through Thomas?

3. Early on in the book Finucan states that the safekeeping of Naples "was a hopeless mission," and yet there are a few rare glimpses of hope throughout the story. How does the author seem to offer hope?

4. Why does Thomas burn the letter his father sends?

5. In discussion with Thomas, an American MP says, "I don't blame nobody for nothing. Not anymore. Not after the things I seen." What do you think Finucan is saying about war and its repercussions?

6. How does Pompeii serve as an interesting foil to Finucan's Naples?

7. Luisa's palpable resentment of Thomas and all that his uniform symbolizes eventually becomes less fervent. What brings about this change in her?

8. In the context of the novel, did Salvatore Varone, Renzo Abruzzi, and other characters involved in organized crime seem as ruthless as you imagined they would? At one point, referring to humanity in general, Luisa states that "cruelty is our most banal attribute." Everyone seems to be implicated in this statement, not just those usually considered overtly immoral. Is Finucan calling into question society's accepted distinction between right and wrong? What makes Salvatore and Renzo worse than corrupt military/church officials or warmongers?

9. At the end, is Thomas's choice to get into bed with Varone his second suicide attempt? Varone calls Thomas a martyr and wonders if his actions are penance for something else. Do you think Varone is correct?

10. What did you make of the final dialogue between Salvatore and Augusto? How did you understand Augusto's statement "Perhaps, then ... we are all fools?"

To access Penguin Group (Canada) Readers Guides online, visit the Penguin Group (Canada) website at **www.penguin.ca**